Praise for *MISFITS*

"*Misfits* is a startling collection of short stories—heartfelt, compassionate, full of sentiment yet unsentimental. Mark Harris draws on his experience as a crime reporter, professor, filmmaker and novelist to weave a dazzling portrait of modern life that I can only compare to the works of Raymond Carter and Anton Chekhov. Personal, political, full of pathos, insightful, *Misfits* delves deeply into the American psyche. Read and prepare to think differently about where we live and the "misfits" who populate contemporary America."

- Paul Wolansky, Film Professor
  Co-writer of *The Guide* and *Dovbush: Lord of Black Mountain*

"Now Mark Harris brings his genius for documentary film to the page, verbalizing inside stories where the camera can never go. *Misfits* portrays hidden dramas of becoming—its shame, its fury. The chaotic emotions and taboo impulses of early life often lie buried. But these brief narratives can stir us to life. The molten energy of *Misfits* reminds us that we've all, at one time or another, inhabited a core identity—and the longing to belong."

- Elizabeth N. Goodenough, University of Michigan

"*Misfits* is a discovery of brilliant, concise writing that one does not see often. Harris has built a collection of stories that shatters the heart yet engages the mind in casting a view of situations and characters to which the reader can easily relate. Straightforward, without pretention—this book is classic storytelling."

- Mike Lee, author of *The Northern Line*

"An outstanding new collection with a cast of wild and eclectic, yet relatable, characters; the verisimilitude palpable. Harris presents fun, fresh stories on par with other contemporary California greats like T.C. Boyle. You'll never see a flowering cactus or a canceled flight the same way again."

- R. Conrad Speer, author of *Saint Lazarus Day and Other Stories*

MISFITS

(STORIES)

MARK JONATHAN HARRIS

atmosphere press

For Susan, who never lost faith

Table of Contents

Land Mines

Dana stands at a table of scarves in the men's department of Bloomingdales, feeling the softness of the cashmere, wondering if the price is too high for an apology. Does admitting you're sorry always have to cost more than you can afford? The pale gray Burberry check scarf is handsome, a perfect match for Jeremy's tan overcoat. Its expense makes it an even greater act of contrition. She glances around the store as she strokes the delicate Scottish wool. The nearest salesgirl is walking toward the dressing rooms with another customer. Dana's heart pounds, her stomach flutters, adrenaline courses through her. It's been years since she did this, but she quickly folds the scarf and stuffs it inside her large purse.

* * *

She started stealing at twelve, about three months after they moved to Los Angeles so her father could teach painting at Cal State Northridge. The San Fernando Valley wasn't a place she would have chosen to live. Then, her father and Robin never asked her. The ugly public school—a bunch of low buildings surrounded by cement and a steel fence—wasn't her choice either. Only shoplifting was.

At first, she took only what was small enough to fit inside her pocket—bubble gum, candy, lipstick, a pressed flower key ring. She did most of her shoplifting at the Rite Aid a few blocks from her new school. To avoid suspicion, she always bought something else. Buy a Coke, steal a compact. Pay for the chips, but not the M&Ms.

The first time her heart was racing so fast she felt she would faint right there at the register. When she finally caught her breath—a block past the drug store—and bit into the stolen Almond Joy, her stomach recoiled. She quickly ditched the candy in the street. Yet two days later she was at it again.

What she didn't eat she kept in a shoebox in her closet. Sometimes she'd take the box out at night and lay her treasures on her bed. Pathetic, most of them, cheesy, made in China junk she'd never think of buying. They gave her pleasure nonetheless. Like postcards or souvenirs of places she'd visited. She remembered where and when she'd stolen each of them. Mementoes of her secret life, one that set her apart from all the other fifth-grade rejects.

The teachers at Topeka Drive Elementary were younger and peppier than in her last school in Chicago, but the children were no friendlier. All that made school bearable was that she could walk there by herself. While her teachers droned on about math problems that bored her, or vocabulary words she never used, she planned which stores to steal from. The anticipation, the uncertainty, the risk of getting caught, was more exciting than any video game. The sweaty palms, the knot of fear in her stomach as she entered a store, the mix of relief and exhilaration when she emerged safely, thrilled her.

After a few months of petty drugstore theft, she lengthened her route home to include the mall, moving upscale to brand names. Glittery Monet earrings, a pink-and-turquoise Tumi change purse, Ralph Lauren sunglasses. She never entered a store with a particular object in mind. She would just wander around and see what caught her eye. The items had to be small, something she could fit in the pockets of her father's navy peacoat—a coat he wore all the time in New York before her mother ditched him for a more successful artist. She'd rescued it from a pile of clothes Robin was donating to Goodwill when they moved from Chicago. Perhaps the coat was a mistake, called unwanted attention to her. The cuffs were frayed and the wide shoulders spilled over her slender frame. Other kids mocked her for it. "Where did you steal that? From some homeless bag lady?" Still, the jacket was warm and comforting on cool mornings and the pockets deep enough for all kinds of booty.

She knew stealing was wrong, but she couldn't stop herself. Shoplifting was like rollerblading through a minefield. All her senses were heightened. She saw more, heard more; even her gum tasted sharper. Although she feared that at any moment there might be an explosion, the danger made her feel alive.

One rainy day, walking out of Nordstrom with a purloined Liz Claiborne scarf, she felt a hand on her shoulder. She turned to face a twenty-something blonde with too much lipstick and too smug a look. "Can I see your sales slip, please?"

She felt a heaviness, like wet cement, slowly fill her body. She'd finally hit a mine. She wondered if this was how soldiers felt when one exploded.

* * *

"A classic choice." The voice behind her at Bloomingdales is male.

Startled, Dana whirls to face a slender Black salesclerk she failed to notice before. "But way too expensive," she says, her heart pounding against her ribs. She tightens the grip on her purse to contain her panic and steps away from the table.

"You can't go wrong with Burberry."

"I could. You can't imagine how much." She laughs shakily at her narrow escape. "But thanks, I'll remember that." She laughs again, too loudly, as she rushes away from the puzzled clerk. She has to be unhinged to let another scarf tempt her into shoplifting. Is she trying to be caught again?

* * *

They made her wait in the office of Nordstrom's security chief, a short, mustached man in a pale-blue shirt who looked as bored as the uniformed guard at her school. She sat in an uncomfortable plastic chair beneath a bank of television monitors bolted to the wall above her. The security chief sat across from her at his bare desk, cleaning his fingernails with a paper clip.

He asked only which parent he should telephone. After that, silence.

He remained at his desk, eyes flicking back and forth between his nails and the monitors above her, ignoring her on purpose, she supposed. Let the kid squirm a while, worry what will happen next. She had no clue what that would be. They didn't throw kids in jail for shoplifting, did they?

Her father took only a half hour to get there, less time than when he forgot to pick her up from her guitar lesson the week before. He was in his studio when they called and he arrived in jeans and a paint-spattered T-shirt underneath his windbreaker. He glanced at her in bewilderment as he entered the office, as if unsure she really was his daughter.

The security chief sat them both down across from his desk. "Your daughter's very young to be stealing," he said, handing her father the gold paisley silk scarf she'd swiped.

Harold ignored the evidence, reached for his wallet instead, and pulled out a credit card. "I'm happy to pay for it," he offered.

"That's not the point." The security chief pulled the scarf back. "Shoplifting's a serious offense."

"I realize that. I understand how serious this is . . ." Harold launched into a long and conciliatory apology, explaining that they had just moved to Northridge in August, that it was a difficult adjustment for the whole family, that Dana had never been in trouble like this before. They often shopped at this store, always paid their bills on time. He repeated his willingness to pay for the scarf.

The longer he talked, the deeper Dana plunged her hands into the pockets of his peacoat. Did all parents of shoplifters grovel like this? She wanted to scream at him to stop.

Perhaps his pleading embarrassed the security chief as well, because after a few minutes he agreed that there was no need to report this. "Just keep your daughter out of our store," he warned. "Because the next time we catch her, my first call is to the police."

They were both silent in the car. "I don't get it." Harold finally spoke. "You don't even wear scarves."

"I thought it was pretty."

"A lot of things are pretty, Dana, but stealing? What the hell were you thinking?"

The scarf was the kind her real mother wore. She'd thought of giving it to her if she ever visited L.A.

Harold kept staring at the road, waiting for an explanation. She had no answer that would please him.

"I know it's hard starting all over again," he finally said when they pulled into the driveway of the ugly ranch house they were renting. "But if you don't talk to us, Dana, we can't help. We want to understand . . ." He let the question dangle.

"I messed up, okay?" she muttered because she wanted to end the conversation.

Robin didn't want to talk about it either. She went into the bedroom with her father and shut the door. When they emerged an hour later, her stepmother had arranged an appointment for her with a shrink.

* * *

Dana's pulse throbs in her temples as she ducks into a gastropub. She sits in a booth and orders an Old Fashioned to collect herself. Although she rarely drinks more than wine, and certainly not at three in the afternoon, she needs to calm her agitation. It was truly mad to steal the scarf. She thinks of the shame and humiliation she just avoided; she imagines Jeremy's mortification if he had to retrieve her from the police station. Would he grovel like her father? Would he even come to get her? She'd hoped that moving in with him might bring them closer; it only magnified her faults. After fifteen months living together, the qualities that had attracted him—her breezy, free spirit and disregard for convention—had become grave defects of character. His discovery yesterday of a stack of parking tickets in the glove compartment of her Honda reminded him again of all her flaws.

"Jesus! Don't you put money in the meters?"

"Sometimes the time runs out."

He added up the fines. "There are two hundred bucks of tickets here."

"I know. I've been meaning to take care of them."

"You mean you haven't paid them yet?" Her negligence launched a tirade of indignation. A computer programmer who never missed a deadline, he couldn't understand how she could just ignore the tickets.

"You've made your point," she said after a minute. Yet he wouldn't or couldn't stop. The tickets were part of a larger pattern that somehow she failed to grasp: the unwashed pots left overnight in the sink; the clutter on her desk and dresser; the laundry piling up in her closet. And couldn't she even make the bed in the morning? He was still railing about her failings when she pulled into the parking garage of their North Hollywood apartment building. What the hell was wrong with her?

"Say something for Christ sakes," he shouted.

* * *

"So, dear, tell me about yourself." The psychiatrist was short and squat, with graying hair and little makeup. Dr. Rosenthal leaned back in her leather chair and peered intently at her.

Dana shifted uneasily in her chair.

The doctor waited.

Dana's eyes wandered around the cluttered office. She took in the children's drawings on the wall, the wicker basket stuffed with toys, the wild-haired Barbies and helmeted G.I. Joes, the Victorian dollhouse with the tiny, uniformed maid standing at its front door, the large sand tray on a side table. Her gaze kept drifting back to the small but conspicuous stain on Dr. Rosenthal's cream silk blouse.

"You have a spot on your blouse," she said.

The doctor looked down at the offending blotch. "I'm sure the dry cleaners can get it out."

The stain looked like salad dressing or maybe grease, something fattening the shrink shouldn't have had for lunch. "What if they can't?"

Dr. Rosenthal looked at her a moment. "Are you asking about the blouse or about yourself?"

She felt her cheeks go hot.

"This isn't the dry cleaners, Dana. You're not here to be cleaned up or repaired or for me to remove whatever spots or defects you or your parents might think you have. My job is to help you understand your feelings so you can make the best choices for yourself. Do you understand?"

She stared at the stain again. She was sure the blouse was ruined. She glanced at her silly Cinderella watch with its cheap fabric strap to see how much longer she had to sit there. Though her stepmother could force her to see a shrink, she couldn't make her speak.

Jeremy provoked the same stubborn wordlessness as Robin. Her silence drove them both to despair. "You're depressed, listless. In a terrible rut," Jeremy said when they entered the apartment. "You need to see someone—a therapist, a psychiatrist, somebody who can shake you out of it. It's obvious I can't."

She was so hapless, so deficient, that only a professional with advanced degrees could fix her.

* * *

"School okay today?" her father asked as he drove her to her third appointment with the shrink.

The truth, she knew, wasn't what he was asking for. Did he really want to hear how she spent the day trying to be invisible? It was a strategy she'd adopted in her last school in Chicago, one of four cities in which she'd lived because her father kept moving from one teaching job to another. Never speak in class unless the teacher calls on you. Avoid talking to the other girls. Eat alone rather than sit next to a weirdo or a loser. Better to be ignored than shunned, although it was always hard to tell why other kids weren't speaking to you.

To fend off more questions, Dana popped a piece of bubble gum in her mouth and turned on the radio.

"Would you please just pick a station and stick to it?" Harold stopped her hand as she switched from station to station.

She was happy to see his irritation surface. She didn't trust any of his and Robin's fake solicitude. They both had been acting as if they'd just read some book on how to be a good parent and were faithfully following its advice. Do not nag your child. Do not ask uncomfortable questions. Be patient, respectful. Give your child the space she needs. Or maybe they were just waiting for Dr. Rosenthal's miracle cure to kick in.

She clicked the radio off. "You ever go to a shrink?" she asked.

He hesitated a moment before answering. "As a matter of fact I did."

"When?" She eased up on the gum.

"In college."

"You never told me before."

"I only went a few times."

"You get cured that fast?"

"I was having trouble sleeping at night, so I went to the health center for some sleeping pills. They wouldn't give me any unless I saw a therapist."

"Oh . . ." Her father's insomnia was disappointing. She had hoped for a fault or an affliction that they shared, a reason her mother had left both of them. She started to form another bubble with her tongue.

"Why do you ask about the shrink?" he said cautiously.

The bubble broke and she cleaned the gum off her face. "Just wondering."

"Well, I dropped out of school shortly afterwards and had no trouble sleeping after that."

"Yeah, but you can't drop out of grade school, can you?" she said and turned to the side window.

"If school's the problem, Dana . . ."

"Then what? We'll move again."

"I wish . . ." he started, then changed his mind.

"Yeah, if wishes were horses," she repeated the nursery rhyme her birth mother had often recited and flipped the radio on to end their conversation.

Harold remained silent until they pulled into the driveway of Dr. Rosenthal's office, which was attached to her hillside home. She quickly opened the door and started up the stone steps to the doctor's office.

"Have a good session," he called after her, as if he were dropping her off at her guitar lesson.

* * *

Dana orders a second Old Fashioned. Although the first slowed her heart rate, her mind is still racing. She isn't sure what she expects from the alcohol. Will there be revelation or amnesia at the bottom of the glass?

If she's so screwed up, so defective, why did Jeremy invite her to move in with him? And why is she always the one who must apologize? What about his flaws? The defects in *his* character? His self-righteousness, his constant faultfinding and disapproval. She wonders what Dr. R. would say about him. Would the psychiatrist be surprised if she showed up on her doorstep again? What would she say about the stolen scarf inside her purse?

* * *

Each appointment, Dana expected her to bring up the shoplifting, but she never did. She suspected that the therapist was sneakier than she looked. She wanted you to believe she was a kindly Jewish grandmother who never heard a problem that couldn't be cured with chicken soup, while all the time she was just luring you to confess.

"I received the test results from your school today," Dr. R. announced at their fourth session. "You are a very bright girl, Dana, yet you're not doing very well in school."

"School's boring."

"They often are."

Dr. R. waited. She had the patience of a rock. At the rates her parents were paying, Dana imagined the shrink could wait happily for years.

"I don't give a shit about school."

"What do you give a shit about, dear?"

Dana laughed. It was funny to hear Dr. R. swear.

"Well?" The shrink smiled.

Dana looked around the office at the toys and objects Dr. R. had collected over the years. On the end table by the couch was a pretty carved wooden bird, from Mexico she guessed. She wondered if it was valuable.

"What about your parents? Do you care what they think?" Dr. R. was uncharacteristically pushy.

She shrugged. "My father and Robin are already disappointed in me."

"And how do you know that?"

"I see the way they look." Her stomach tightened. "They want a different daughter."

"Different?"

"Yeah . . ." The tightness rose to her chest.

"And what do they want you to be?" the shrink prodded.

"What I'm not," Dana snapped. "Prettier . . . chattier . . .

thinner. I don't know. Different . . ."

"That makes you angry."

"Duh," Dana mocked her.

"And now I'm making you angry."

"This is stupid."

"Feelings are never stupid, Dana. They give us information about ourselves and about the world. But when we don't pay attention to them, we can become dumb. Even a girl as bright as you are."

"So I am dumb then." Her whole chest began to ache.

"About your feelings, yes."

"Well, my parents must be too, because they're paying you a lot of money for nothing."

"Go on," the doctor encouraged. "It's good to see your anger."

"Fuck you!" The force of it surprised Dana almost as much as the words. She sank back into the couch, wanting to vanish. She wouldn't let that happen again.

"And your birth mother, does she feel that way too?" Dr. R. persisted.

"I haven't seen her since New York. She just sends birthday cards."

"That must make you angry too."

Dana stared at the wooden bird on the table to avoid the shrink's gaze. She wondered what Dr. R. would do if she smashed the carving.

"It's not going to bring her back," Dana said.

"Neither will holding back your feelings."

The pressure in Dana's chest swelled like a balloon about to burst. The roaring in her ears drowned out everything the shrink was saying. She had tripped on another land mine and there was only one way to keep it from exploding. The moment the doctor opened the door to release her, Dana palmed the wooden bird on the table. As soon as she slipped it into her pocket, she was able to breathe again.

Her relief lasted only through dinner.

After dropping her at home, her father had returned to his studio to work. He often retreated there when he and Robin were fighting. Dana rarely heard them argue. When they were angry at each other, they just stayed away. Now she was alone with a sullen Robin.

She ate quickly, placed her dishes in the washer, and fled to her bedroom. She closed the door and took out her box of trophies from the closet. Spreading them across her bed, she saw how pitiful they were. She wondered now why she had stolen any of them. Only Dr. R.'s beautiful carving was worth keeping. The multicolored bird with its huge red eyes was the most striking object she'd ever stolen. The thought that Dr. R. would be bereft at its loss had made her strangely happy. But imagining Dr. R. now, rummaging through her cluttered office for the carving, Dana felt a queasiness in her stomach. The thought that the bird's loss might pain the doctor made her ashamed. It was one thing to steal from Nordstrom, another to swipe something valuable from someone who would miss it. A sour taste of the leftover lasagna Robin had warmed for dinner rose in her throat. She swallowed hard to keep from heaving.

Suddenly, the door swung open and Robin stood at the entrance to her bedroom holding her backpack. Her stepmother's stunned look at the loot scattered across the bed revealed her dismay. Dana instinctively shoved the wooden bird under her pillow. "You're supposed to knock!" she yelled and rushed toward the door.

Robin backed away before Dana slammed it.

"I'm sorry," Robin apologized from the hallway. "I didn't mean to startle you. I thought you'd want your books."

Dana quickly propped a chair against the door to make sure Robin wouldn't re-enter.

"You don't have to do that, Dana. I promise I'll knock next time. Really, I'm sorry . . ."

Dana flung herself on the bed. Robin could make all the promises she wanted, but Dana had seen the horror on her face. There was nothing she could do to erase it or change her stepmother's despairing view of her; she was as hopeless as her father's tattered peacoat, which Robin was so eager to toss out.

* * *

The nose-ringed, punk-haired waitress asks Dana if she wants another cocktail, as if she's a sorry lush who drinks by herself in the afternoon. She doesn't want another Old Fashioned; she doesn't want to return to the apartment either. The alcohol or the memory of her stepmother makes her stomach squish. Or maybe it's the Burberry in her purse that's roiling her gut, forcing her to her feet. She grabs her purse and rushes to the restroom. Standing over the toilet, she can only retch.

She splashes cold water on her face at the sink and takes deep breaths to calm herself. It sickens her that she's stolen the scarf. The gift would hardly make up for all Jeremy finds lacking in her. If caught, her arrest would only have confirmed his worst beliefs about her. A familiar heaviness comes over her, an ache and weariness that makes her want to sleep.

* * *

The moment she started up the steps to Dr. R.'s, she felt the pressure mounting in her chest again. Her stomach clenched and her palms were sweaty. But Dr. R. said nothing about the stolen bird.

What was she waiting for? She had to have noticed it was gone. Yet here she was asking about Chicago? Did Dana have friends there? Did she like her old school?

Dana barely heard her. The shrink swam in and out of focus.

"Are you all right, dear?" Dr. R. reached out to feel her forehead. Dana instinctively recoiled.

"You look so pale. Do you have a fever?"

"I . . . I stole your bird . . ." Dana blurted it out without expecting to.

"I thought you might have," Dr. R. said calmly. "It's a beautiful carving, isn't it?"

Tears stung Dana's eyes. "You're not angry?"

The doctor shook her head. "Did taking it make you feel better?"

"For a little while . . ."

"That's one of the troubles with stealing. The pleasure doesn't last very long. Then you have to steal again."

Dana had discovered that herself.

"There are other ways to tell people you're angry with them," the doctor continued.

"I'll bring it back."

"I'd appreciate that. I'm very fond of that bird. My husband bought it for me in Oaxaca."

Tears spilled down Dana's cheeks.

Dr. R. passed her the Kleenex box. "Maybe you were angry at me for what I said last week and wanted to hurt me, but look at how much you're hurting yourself. You don't have to punish yourself like this for feeling angry."

Dana's tears kept coming. "They all want someone different . . . My dad, my stepmom . . . My real mother left because she hated having me . . ."

The doctor leaned forward and handed her another tissue from the box. "I don't know your mother, Dana, but I do know this, and I know it from all my experience as a doctor: you're not the reason your mother left you. When a parent gives up her child, it's never the child's fault."

Dr. R. leaned back in her chair and let Dana weep.

* * *

Dana pays the check and leaves the restaurant. The late afternoon light is already fading as it had years before when she slowly descended the stone steps from Dr. R.'s office to her father's waiting car.

Harold looked closely at her as she fastened her seat belt. "How was it today?" he asked.

She thought she'd left all her tears at Dr. R.'s. To halt them, she flipped on the radio as they pulled away.

Her father reached over and turned it off. "I'm sorry things have been so hard for you."

She didn't answer, just dabbed at her eyes with the frayed sleeves of his ragged peacoat. She turned the radio back on and saw him staring at the high-tech watch on her wrist with its bright red plastic band. "That's a new watch, isn't it?"

She avoided his eyes.

"Where did you get it?" he persisted.

"At Nordstrom," she confessed.

"Oh, Dana . . ." He reached over and gently touched her shoulder. "I wish you didn't do this."

"I know," she mumbled.

"Then why?"

She wanted him to pull to the curb, lean over, and hug her; the same wish she had the afternoon they caught her at Nordstrom. Instead of cringing with embarrassment, she'd wanted him to look past her petty thefts, put his arm around her, and say he loved her. But now, as then, he kept his eyes on the road and driving. If wishes were horses . . .

"I just don't understand," he said.

"I like stealing," she finally answered. "It's one thing I'm really good at."

* * *

Remembering her father's devastated look, she knows that wasn't true. If she'd been a better shoplifter, she would never have been caught. It's amazing that she escaped arrest today. No, stealing is just her clumsy way of expressing everything she can't cry about. She saw Dr. R. once more to return her wooden carving and then told her parents she didn't need to see the shrink again. She no longer had a desire to shoplift.

But now, years later, she's stealing again. This time she doesn't need Dr. R. to help her understand her feelings. She just needs the courage to acknowledge what she hasn't wanted to face.

On her way to her car, she passes a Goodwill store. What synchronicity to stumble on it. A thrift store was where she gave away her father's peacoat after her final session with Dr. R. The Goodwill store is open and she walks inside. It's a perfect place to dump the Burberry. Leaving Jeremy will be harder. But exiting the store, she already feels lighter.

Mute

Why do we have children? Is it a biological imperative to propagate? An egotistical desire to preserve our lineage? Or an attempt to fill some lack in our own lives?

These questions barely occurred to me before Samuel was born. Although Elaine always wanted to be a mother, I wasn't eager to be a parent. I worried how a baby might affect the stability of our five-year-old marriage. Still, when Elaine became pregnant—either on purpose or the failure of the pill—I couldn't bring myself to dissuade her from bearing the child she so clearly desired. Watching her give birth, I knew we'd made the right decision. It's hard to describe the wonder and euphoria of that moment. Here's a living being you've created, a miraculous infant that's part of you. And you're there the moment he emerges, all ruddy and glistening, with all his limbs intact. And suddenly he's crying, as astonished as you are to be there.

I'm a film producer, a midwife so to speak, and have guided the creation of several movies. I've been present at their conception, lived through their gestation (longer than most pregnancies) and witnessed their birth at glitzy, kleig light premieres. The movies I've made have usually been successful, but none has been more thrilling than the one I captured on my iPhone of Samuel emerging from his mother's womb.

I remember how carefully I drove Elaine and Samuel home

from the hospital, slowing to a crawl at every speed bump, as if my passengers were porcelain. I had a son now as well as a wife to care for and protect. I wanted to be the father and husband they deserved.

Although we'd been warned of the difficulty of those early months, Samuel proved to be an easy baby. He breast fed immediately and within two months was sleeping through the night. Having a nanny helped of course, but Elaine was a relaxed mother, in no rush to return to her interior decorating work, delighted to stay home with our beautiful, happy son. (And I'm not exaggerating when I cite his beauty. Long-lashed hazel eyes, delicate features; a child Raphael might have painted.) Samuel would lie in his baby seat watching the sun stream through the garden window of our sun porch, kicking his tiny feet and cooing with pleasure as he tried to grasp the dust motes floating through the air. I would rush home from work to see him while he was still awake. Like the sunlight he played with, his happiness filled the room, spilled over all of us.

As cheerful as he was, Samuel was slow to crawl, slow to walk. These delays concerned me more than Elaine, but our pediatrician saw no reason to worry. Every child develops at his own rate, she assured us. Samuel might be lagging behind other children, but he was still well within normal range. At sixteen months he finally started walking, and even though his gait was as wobbly as a drunk's, my anxieties eased. Elaine felt ready to work again and left Samuel for longer periods with Altagracia, our Salvadoran nanny.

The first serious unease I remember having about Samuel came when Elaine dragged us to a Little Monster-themed birthday party for a two-year-old in her baby group. The party was held at an L.A. home near ours that overlooked the ocean in Pacific Palisades. Affluent young mothers like Elaine, who'd quickly regained their figures after childbirth, gathered with their Boden-clad offspring amidst balloons, streamers, puppets and other Little Monster decorations—a theme the children raucously embraced. Except for Samuel. While the other toddlers raced around noisily, he clung tightly to Elaine. I confess to feeling more comfortable in a darkened room watching actors on a screen than I do at social gatherings; still, I gently tried to push Samuel forward to engage with the other children. My prodding only made him suck his shirt and cling fearfully to his mother. Then he dropped to the grass and started crying uncontrollably. When Elaine couldn't console him, we quickly left.

"I've never seen him cry like that," I said as we drove home.

"Too much noise and commotion. I think it frightened him." Although he now slept peacefully in his baby seat.

"Maybe he should spend more time with other kids."

She laughed. "Or maybe he's like you. Maybe he didn't want to come to the party either. He just expressed it differently."

Bathing Samuel that evening, I thought I might have over-reacted. His soft skin glowing from the steam, his dark hair slicked down over his forehead, he bore no resemblance to the distraught child who'd alarmed me at the party. Frolicking blithely in the water, he'd wriggle a rubber fish to the end of the tub and release it. Then he'd pick another fish and repeat the action, babbling with pleasure. When he'd moved all the toys to the opposite end, he began returning them, one by one, as if he could play at this forever. I finally lifted him from the water and swaddled him in a towel. He shivered as I dried him and I wrapped my arms around him, pulling his slender body into my embrace.

When Samuel was born, I promised myself that I wouldn't repeat the mistakes of my immigrant Polish parents, a mismatched couple, bitter about each other and the impoverished life they led. "The only thing you've ever produced of value is your son," I overheard my mother excoriating my father one night. Yet nothing I ever achieved was enough to make up for the emptiness and disappointment in her life. How could it? I knew her deep and querulous unhappiness had scarred me and I was determined not to inflict the same damage on

Samuel. Rocking him to sleep, I vowed again to be a more patient, loving parent than my demanding mother and distant, inaccessible father.

Despite my vows, I found it difficult to engage with Samuel. His absorption with his model cars and trucks was so intense that when I returned home from work, he rarely looked up to greet me. Over time I found myself staying later at the office. Many nights I would return after Samuel was asleep, or just in time to read him a bedtime story, the one activity he seemed to enjoy with me. The *Curious George* books were his favorite. He would sit attentively in my lap and turn the pages as I read. "George promised to be good. But it is easy for little monkeys to forget." If I altered the words, or improvised, Samuel would flip the page back so I'd read it correctly. However much he understood, at two he wasn't talking. Some of his guttural sounds might mean monkey; that was the closest word to any I could decipher.

"Doesn't it bother you that he's not talking yet?" I asked Elaine.

"Of course I want him to speak, but many boys don't talk until later. You told me you weren't a talkative child either."

"No one in my family was. My parents could go for days without speaking to each other."

"Well, happily, we're not your parents. When Samuel's ready, the words will come. It's his timetable, not ours."

I know patience is a virtue, but my rashness, my willingness to act decisively, is also a reason for my success, and I was becoming increasingly concerned about Samuel. The pediatrician only saw him for ten minutes at a time. She didn't see how he flapped his arms and fluttered his fingers when upset or observe his sobbing meltdowns. Was Elaine conveying all this to her? Fearing that her ease and assurance with Samuel was keeping her from communicating my fears, I decided to go with her to our pediatrician.

The day before Samuel's next appointment, the director

of a movie I was producing phoned to say he could no longer work with the lead actress. The actress called a half hour later to announce she was quitting. Though I also have difficulty dealing with insecure actors and temperamental directors, there was no one else to resolve the crisis. I caught a plane that night to Boise and drove to the location where they were shooting to try to mend their relationship. In conflicts like this, all you can do is sympathize with each party, assure them that the other is impossible, and promise this is the last time they'll have to work together. Then you offer them more money. I doubt my lies convinced them, but the money proved persuasive. Crisis averted, I called Elaine as I drove to the airport, to find out what the pediatrician told her.

"She suggested we get him tested."

"For what?"

"For developmental delays." She sounded subdued, uncertain.

"So there is a problem?"

"She didn't say that. It could be nothing. She just wanted to make sure."

"About what? What are they testing him for?"

"Autism." She said it so softly I wasn't sure I heard.

"Autism?" I repeated. The word sucked all the air from the car. "What does that mean?"

"It . . . I don't know . . ." Her voice broke.

"Well, we need to find out. Make an appointment as soon as you can."

* * *

It took another three months before the UCLA psychologist the pediatrician recommended could evaluate Samuel. I don't remember why I couldn't go with Elaine and Samuel to UCLA. Perhaps I didn't want to hear confirmed what I was already beginning to believe. Once the pediatrician broached the possibility of autism, I spent nights anxiously surfing the web to find out what I could about the disorder. Each search seemed to contradict what I'd learned the night before. Was autism a disability? Or a difference? An epidemic? Or an epidemic of discovery? The incidence was increasing; no, we were just primed to see it more. It was a treatable disorder; no, it was just another variety of human experience, "brightness gone awry," as one prominent researcher described it. Depending where you looked, the cause was either genetic or environmental or dietary. Too much pollution, too much gluten, too many autistics marrying each other. Too many opinions and too little hard evidence for any view. When Samuel was diagnosed in 2015, the only certainty, according to the CDC, was that every twenty minutes another child was identified "on the spectrum."

It didn't take the psychologist long to pronounce the diagnosis I feared. Samuel had "classic" autism. The three telltale signs are deficits in communication, deficits in social interaction, and repetitive behavior. Samuel matched the profile perfectly: he didn't talk; he responded to objects rather than people, endlessly plunged his rubber fish in and out of the water in the tub; and he obsessively rearranged the cars he played with by color and by size. I once thought he might be a mathematician (my skill with spreadsheets) or an architect (his mother's sense of design.) I now worried that he'd never speak, never hold a job, never marry, never leave our home.

Names have power. They bring certainty, clarity. The right title for a movie can make a difference between success and failure. Identifying a problem, defining its nature, is the first step to resolving it. For me, Samuel's diagnosis was a clear call to action. We'd finally confirmed the problem. The question now was how to fix it.

Elaine couldn't begin to think of that yet. From what I'd read, it's fathers, not mothers, who are often in denial. But it was Elaine who'd clung to the belief that Samuel was just a late developer. The psychologist's verdict devastated her.

Autism shattered the image of her beautiful, adorable son and her competence as a mother.

Maybe you never really know someone until they're tested by adversity. I fell in love with Elaine because of her poise and beauty and ease with other people that I lacked. I assumed from those qualities that she also possessed strength and resilience. Yet the diagnosis paralyzed her. Why hadn't she recognized the signs earlier? Had her failure to perceive Samuel's symptoms made his autism harder to address? She was overcome by remorse and guilt and grief. I had little patience for her mourning and regrets. Although I didn't say it at the time, I, too, blamed her for not recognizing autism earlier, even though the fault was mine as well. I should have acted on my fears sooner. Now I was determined to make up for my earlier inaction.

I phoned the psychologist for a frank prognosis. Autism comes in all varieties and degrees of severity. Maybe ten percent of those on the spectrum are savants with unusual artistic, musical, or mathematical talents, like Dustin Hoffman in *Rain Man*, but another quarter never learn to speak. What could we expect for Samuel?

The psychologist equivocated. Although a lifelong condition, there were many effective therapies that could ameliorate the disorder. I interrupted the stock speech I assumed he gave every parent. What about *my* son? What about *his* future?

"If you've seen one child with autism, you've seen one child with autism." He repeated the bromide that allowed him to evade the question. If I'd been in his office, I might have grabbed him by the throat and forced him to answer. Instead, I yelled into the phone, "That's no fucking answer!"

"I understand your frustration," he said coolly, clearly having heard it many times before. "There are several good treatment programs these days. My secretary can provide you a list."

I hung up as soon as he transferred me. I couldn't trust Samuel's future to callous equivocators like him.

* * *

"Nobody knows anything," is what William Goldman famously wrote about Hollywood. All my experience confirms his quip. Movie making is a volatile combination of art and commerce and narcissism. Public taste is fickle. There are too many variables, too many unknowns, to predict anything with certainty. I'm good at what I do, but I've also had my share of failures.

I didn't expect the same from medicine. Autism is an extensively researched, neurobiological disorder more common than pediatric cancer, diabetes, and AIDs combined. Yet nobody knows anything about how to cure it. Doctors and therapists who treat it will tell you otherwise; they'll speak passionately about the remarkable results they've achieved and why their method is better than others. You can't believe any of them. They don't know what will work for your child any more than Hollywood executives know what audiences will pay to see.

We started therapy immediately. We chose Applied Behavioral Analysis, because studies had substantiated its claim to be the most effective treatment for autism. Elaine stopped working to learn the behavioral treatment methods from the ABA therapists who came to our house every weekday. Lois, the main therapist, was blonde, petite, just a few years out of college, with a cheerleader's energy and spurious enthusiasm. Gloria, her supervisor, was older, plainer, heavier, and more reserved, as if she'd spent too much time with children with autism or suffered too many disappointments. Both made me question the effusive testimonials to ABA that I'd read.

It was hard to gauge Samuel's reaction. Although mute and withdrawn, he didn't throw tantrums or protest their presence the way he sometimes did when I appeared. He complied with their instructions and, after several weeks, was able to slip on his shoes and drop the triangles and squares in the right holes in the sorting box. Elaine remained cautiously optimistic.

Then Samuel began taking off his diaper and smearing

his feces on the walls. I would come into his bedroom in the morning and find him sitting in his crib, his face and hands dripping with shit, making soft humming noises to himself. Was this normal curiosity? Or a protest against his therapy? The current ABA philosophy was to ignore rather than call attention to the undesired behavior. So we bathed Samuel, changed the sheets and scrubbed the walls, and pretended we didn't care as we made his diaper harder to remove. None of it discouraged him.

Gloria thought that Samuel's interest in his bodily waste suggested he might be ready for toilet training. On her advice, Lois and Elaine started the training. To teach Samuel that he was going to the toilet to eliminate, he was taken to the bathroom every thirty minutes and showered with praise each time he sat on the potty. At first he sat fully clothed, then with just a diaper, and finally with no diaper at all. This painstaking, incremental process took weeks and tried even the therapist's well-paid patience. Some with autism, Lois finally admitted to Elaine, never learned to use the toilet.

Elaine and I debated whether to stop the toilet training. Maybe we would have tolerated it if it proved effective. But Samuel got worse, not better. He flapped his arms more, had more frequent meltdowns. In fact, teaching him to pull his pants down only made it more difficult to stop him from pulling his diaper off in his crib. He finally ended our uncertainty by throwing a head-banging tantrum in the bathroom one morning that it was impossible for even his therapists to ignore. Elaine fired them on the spot. To our relief, their dismissal ended Samuel's playing with his feces. He'd been communicating to us after all.

* * *

I will spare you the succession of therapies and therapists we tried in the next year. There was DIR/Floortime, a speech therapist, an occupational therapist, a nutritionist—$1500 a week of experts. I would've spent any amount to keep Samuel from receding into the shadows—we were fortunate to afford it—but those thirty hours a week of therapy brought little tangible progress.

It's true that Samuel pointed and gestured a little more; he uttered strangled sounds of what we optimistically took to be words—"cars," "book." Interpreting his babble was like guessing the meaning of a foreign language. He still wasn't toilet trained, still engaged in arm flapping and finger-dancing that the therapists called stimming. When I came home at night, he rarely met my gaze, or else looked through me as if I weren't there. I would bend and kiss his forehead and he would jerk his head back or push me away as if an unruly dog had leaped on him. Determined to ignore the rejection, I would often remain on the sun porch as the shadows deepened, hoping that my presence would somehow communicate my support to my solitary, impenetrable son. Sometimes he would look up at me from his cars and, for an instant, meet my eyes and I was certain we were connecting. Then immediately he'd become agitated and start to twirl his fingers in front of his eyes like a high-speed fan. Oh, Samuel, what were you thinking in these moments? Why did you need to retreat from me and soothe yourself with the fluttering of your fingers? "Samuel, Samuel," I would plead, or gently try to interrupt his finger flapping, but that would only increase his agitation and send him fleeing from the room. Seeing him bolt from the sun porch, I felt as helpless, as deficient, as I had as a child watching my mother weep as she gazed out the dirty windows of our apartment at the bleak tenements around us.

At moments I would catch Elaine in tears as well, although she would quickly try to hide them. Samuel's diagnosis destroyed her confidence as a mother. Now she questioned everything she did. Her uncertainty made it difficult to admit my own discouragement. After all, she was the person who bore the brunt of Samuel's care. Thirty hours a week of therapy. Hours more stuck in freeway traffic driving from one therapist to another. Then more time at home making gluten free bread and practicing what the "experts" taught her. If she gave up on Samuel, what hope would there be for him? So I kept up a false front of encouragement and cheer.

I would wake in the middle of the night and find her at the computer in her study, searching the net as doggedly as I had in the months before Samuel's diagnosis, looking for some miracle cure that we had somehow overlooked. I'd put my arms around her and urge her to come back to bed. "Don't worry about me," she'd say. "I'll be there in a little while." Or else she'd close the computer and meekly follow me back to bed like a child chastised for doing something she's not permitted.

"It doesn't help to beat yourself up like this. You're doing everything you can," I tried to reassure her.

"I know. It's just so confusing . . ."

And too painful to talk about. We'd lie there in the dark in silence, unwilling to confess our fears and recriminations, no longer able to seek comfort in each other's arms.

Finally, I suggested Elaine see a doctor about getting pills for her insomnia. The doctor was willing to provide a temporary supply on the condition that Elaine saw a psychiatrist. So we added another therapist to our team of experts. The psychiatrist diagnosed depression and recommended medication and weekly talk sessions. Elaine's depression, he explained, was a result of unexpressed anger—anger at autism, at Samuel, and at me. In his view, which Elaine gradually embraced, the apple didn't fall far from the tree: I was distant, unexpressive, almost as inaccessible as Samuel. I rejected the diagnosis of a doctor who'd never met me. I also balked at his suggestion to try medications for Samuel.

I researched the issue thoroughly and was convinced that the side effects of drugs were worse than their benefits, especially for a three-year-old child. As unsettling as Samuel's meltdowns were, they didn't happen every day. His stimming didn't hurt other people or himself. There was no reason to subject his already haywired neurological system to further chemical and biological stress. Under the sway of the new "expert" in our lives, Elaine argued otherwise. The drugs she was taking helped her depression. Why couldn't they help Samuel too?

Our arguments grew angrier and more divisive. What suddenly made her the authority on the issue? She hadn't even recognized the early signs of autism. "What makes you so certain you're right?" she shot back. "You don't even recognize your own remoteness in Samuel. You're the one he runs away from most."

We both said harsh things that would have been better left unsaid. It was as if Samuel's silence had given us license to utter thoughts we would never have voiced before. I began imagining Elaine leaving and taking Samuel with her. The relief I felt at the idea frightened me. Still, I distrusted the pill-pushing shrink who was advising her and resented his glib disapproval of me. Although I had no answer to Samuel's problems either, I was unwilling to accept the prescription of a man who'd never met my son or me.

I went back to the internet. Ordered more books and movies. The literature was full of stories of children considered severely retarded, some institutionalized, who were later discovered to be highly intelligent and, with the aid of alphabet boards or computers, learned to communicate, even write books of poetry. Could Samuel be one of those children and we the benighted ones, unable to recognize his true abilities? Other parents had found the miracle cure. Why hadn't we discovered it yet? If every child with autism was unique, as the psychologist who diagnosed Samuel told me, then there had to be a therapy, however unorthodox, that would work for him.

One Saturday morning I glimpsed what that could be.

On weekends, when the weather was warm enough, I

would often put on Samuel's helmet and strap him to the bike seat in front of me and we would cycle from Pacific Palisades to Venice. We both liked the wind in our faces, the feeling of gliding through space, the effortlessness between us. We had no goal, no task, no need for speech. There was just the sun and the ocean and the taste of salt air. I could pretend that we were like every other father and child pedaling along the bike path.

I couldn't do that at the toy store where we ended up, in desperation, one rainy Saturday when I couldn't think of any-where else to go. Driven by the weather, a few other parents chose the same destination. Only they had a way to communicate with their children. It pained me to see the simple exchanges between them. "Show me which toy you want," I asked Sam-uel, to no response. Unsure if he understood, I picked a small tow truck I knew he didn't have. "Would you like to take this home?" Maybe the other children in the store distracted him, or maybe having to choose a toy overwhelmed him. He raised his hand to his face and started to flap his fingers. I gently lowered his hand and led him to the far end of the store. In a section of stuffed animals, I spied a small monkey and pulled it from the shelf. "How about this? How about a monkey like George?" He held the monkey for a moment and then threw it to the floor. "That's not okay," I said, bending to retrieve it. Before I could pick it up, he kicked the monkey away. Then he kicked me too and sank to the floor and yowled, a high-pitched animal cry that reverberated through the store. All the parents, children, salesclerks turned to look at us. I yanked him to his feet. "I don't understand," I hissed. "What do you want?"

"Ma . . . ma . . .mon-kee," he stammered, flapping his arms in agitation. "R . . . Ruh . . . real monk-kee," he said louder. "Want . . . real mon-key." It was the longest, clearest string of words I'd ever heard him speak. Exhilarated, I lifted him in my arms and swung him in the air. "Of course you do. Of course you want a real monkey."

"Say it again," I said excitedly, seating him on the counter and taking out my iPhone to record it.

"Mon-kee," he repeated, tears streaming down his face. "Mon-kee," he said again and again, as if discovering a word no one had ever uttered before.

It was the first video I had taken of him in months that I wanted to share.

* * *

That night I started researching the idea of a pet monkey. The more I learned, the more I convinced myself that a live monkey could break down the walls that imprisoned Samuel. There were many reports of the positive effects of animals on children with autism. Dogs were found to be calming and stabilizing for children on the spectrum, as they were for soldiers suffering from PTSD. Swimming with dolphins in Florida, as well as horseback riding, also seemed to help. *The Horse Boy* documented one American family's journey by jeep and horseback to Mongolia that had a remarkable impact on their child. Couldn't a monkey have a similar effect? One organization had successfully trained capuchin monkeys to assist quadriplegics with spinal cord injuries. If monkeys could help with one impairment, why couldn't they treat another? And you didn't have to go to Mongolia or Florida to find one. With a few phone calls, I found a breeder in Malibu who sold them.

Elaine thought the idea mad. How could adding a monkey to our already stressed household make life easier for Samuel? Despite the video I'd captured, she remained unconvinced. A monkey was what Samuel wanted, I insisted. Because his desire for one was so strong, in a moment of distress, for the first time in his life, he had burst out with a fully articulated sentence. The toy store proved he was capable of speaking. We just had to build on it.

The incident proved nothing to her, especially since Samuel hadn't uttered anything comparable since. As despondent as she was about our son, she saw my plan to buy a monkey as reckless, another example of my inability to face the severity of Samuel's condition. We had to think rationally, not magically.

"If it works, it's not magic," I said. "I'm willing to try anything that might help."

Sometimes you have to take chances in life, leap without looking. Otherwise you never know what's possible. Elaine gambled on me, despite her parents' disapproval, when I was still struggling to establish myself as a producer. Why was she unwilling to trust me now? I've experienced enough failure in my life that it doesn't frighten me. The riskiest movie I ever made was my greatest success. If my instincts were right then, why shouldn't I rely on them again for Samuel, who mattered more than any movie? This wasn't chelation, where children died, or anti-psychotic drugs which turned them into obese, quivering zombies. It was a fucking monkey. If it didn't work out, I could always give it to the zoo.

I drove out to Malibu to see for myself. The ramshackle ranch house high up in the hills gave no indication of anything unusual. No "Beware Animal" signs, no steel cages, just a surfboard on the weathered deck overlooking the ocean. A heavyset young woman in jeans and an oversized denim work shirt opened the door. She had long, dirty blonde hair that fell over her shoulders.

"You're here about Henri," she said pleasantly.

"Henri?"

A tiny face, no bigger than my hand, peeked out of her shirt between her breasts and stared at me with jewel-brown eyes.

"Say hello, Henri."

The monkey tilted his black-capped head to look me over, smacked his lips a few times as if pondering the question, then emerged from his hiding place, clambered up her chest and perched on her shoulder, wrapping his long black tail around her neck.

"I'm Willow," she introduced herself. "My dad had to run some errands, but he told me you'd be coming."

Willow, whose name belied her shape, was twenty-four years old, a currently unemployed graduate of UCLA, and Henri's surrogate mother. She had taken care of the six-month-old capuchin monkey, nursing him with an eye-dropper for several months after he was separated from his mother a few days after his birth. She had named him for a French exchange student she'd fallen in love with at college who'd failed to get a work visa in the U.S. and had to return to France. She told me all this in the first fifteen minutes of our conversation while Henri climbed in and out of her shirt, as reluctant to leave the comfort of her ample breasts as she was to part with him. Still, when I asked, she held out the blue-diapered monkey for me to take. Henri hesitated at first, then pushed out his caramel-colored belly to be stroked. He flicked his long pink tongue in pleasure as I petted his soft downy fur, then leaped to my shoulder and, like Samuel when I lifted him on my back, draped one leg on each side of my ears.

"Wow, that was fast," Willow laughed. "If he could talk, I bet he'd tell you his life story as quickly as I did."

"He's just following your lead," I said, surprised at how much she'd been willing to confide.

"Animals know instinctively who they can trust. I'm sure you'll make a good home for him."

"It's a gift for my son, what he wants more than anything else in the world . . . He's autistic." It was a word I almost never used in describing Samuel, but I wanted her to understand the reason I was there.

"I bet they'll get along wonderfully," she said. "Monkeys don't need language to communicate. It's amazing how much they can say without words."

Relieved by her response, I snapped several pictures of Henri on my phone. I waited until Samuel was asleep that night then nervously showed them to Elaine.

Elaine's lip quivered as she scrolled through the photographs. "You've bought it already, haven't you?"

"I've put down a deposit," I confessed. "I want to bring the monkey home first to see how Samuel will react."

She flung the iPhone at me, narrowly missing my head. The phone shattered against the wall behind me.

We both looked at each other, stunned by the depth of our estrangement.

"I can't do this anymore," she said.

"I'm not asking you to do it by yourself . . ."

She raised her hands in front of her to keep me away. "You think you can be a better parent? That you can fix what no one else can?"

"You've given up on him."

"Not Samuel, you." She turned and fled the room.

That night she moved into the guest room. The next morning I overheard her telephoning a lawyer.

*　*　*

Obsession narrows your focus so all you can see is the goal you're pursuing. I experienced this blindness a few other times before—a screenplay I wanted to purchase, an actor I wanted to cast. Nothing else matters in that moment. I didn't want to lose Elaine, but I feared if I didn't act immediately, someone else would buy Henri. And finding him renewed my hope for Samuel. Watching our son stare blankly out into the garden, rubbing his rag doll monkey against his cheek, I would remember the wondrous moment at the toy store. If his desire for a monkey was intense enough to compel him to speak, wouldn't having a real one generate more words? Whatever Elaine thought now, if my instinct proved right—and I was certain it would—I was confident she'd change her mind. Henri could save both Samuel and our marriage.

First, though, I had to see how Samuel would respond.

I arranged for Willow to bring Henri to the house at a time when Elaine wouldn't be there. I was afraid her hostility to the idea would color Samuel's reaction. All I asked of Willow was that she rename the monkey George.

George was clinging to her back when she entered the house, hiding behind her vine-like hair. His black face and dark eyes peered cautiously between her blonde locks, then darted out of sight again. Samuel stared in open-mouthed astonishment. George parted Willow's hair again for another look, then quickly retreated.

"Come on, George, let me introduce you to Samuel. I know you're going to be good friends." She reached behind her and gently took the monkey by his leash and brought him into full view.

As shy as the monkey, Samuel hid behind me.

"Come and say hello," Willow encouraged. She knelt to make it easier for Samuel. "Don't be afraid. He won't hurt you."

Maybe George had the same instinctive fears, for he buried his face between Willow's breasts. She laughed and pulled him away.

George's eyes flicked back and forth as he surveyed his new surroundings; then he broke from Willow's grasp and leaped onto the banister of the staircase. Perched there, he began gibbering.

Startled, Samuel clung tightly to my knee.

"It's all right, Samuel," I tried to reassure him, fearing I'd made a dreadful mistake.

Watching from the kitchen doorway, Altagracia stepped forward to intervene, then changed her mind as Willow rose and grabbed the monkey's leash.

Samuel let go of me and pointed to the monkey with the excitement of a zoologist discovering a new species. "Diapers, diapers," he exclaimed, bouncing up and down. It was the first time I'd heard him say the word.

In his blue paper diapers, George mimicked his movements.

"Yes, two little boys in diapers," Willow agreed. "You two are very much alike."

I lifted Samuel in my arms and held him tightly as Willow brought the monkey over for him to touch. I felt an enormous relief as George extended his slender, delicate fingers toward Samuel.

"Mon-kee, mon-kee," he repeated in his high, piping voice.

George squeaked and whistled happily in reply.

"I can see Samuel takes after you," Willow said. "That's why Hen . . . George liked him immediately. I think they'll be great friends."

Arms crossed against her chest, Altragracia stared at us in disbelief, then abruptly turned back to the kitchen.

Samuel cried when Willow took George back to Malibu.

When Elaine returned, I recounted what had occurred and pleaded with her to at least give the experiment a chance. My brief test with George reinforced my conviction that a monkey was the right speech therapy for Samuel. I reminded her how she'd helped me rebound after my first film bombed at the box office, before we were even married. If she was brave enough to believe in me then, why not now? I appealed to her hopes for our son, whatever love she still felt for me, whatever chance there was of repairing the rift between us. If the experiment failed, if it harmed Samuel in any way, we'd end it.

Reluctantly, and with many qualifications, she finally agreed to a trial. She'd take Samuel to her parents in New York while I prepared the house for George. On her return, we'd bring the monkey home for a week, and then re-evaluate.

When I explained my plan to Altagracia, she gave notice on the spot. "*Loco, loco,*" she kept muttering. Although I knew she cared for Samuel, even an increase in pay couldn't persuade her to change her mind. With no immediate alternative, I offered Willow a salary she couldn't refuse, and she agreed to take care of Samuel and George while we looked for a replacement for Altagracia. Under Willow's guidance, I bought a seven-foot cage and installed it on the sun porch. We added a small trampoline, gymnastic rings, and a climbing structure and cleared the room of everything but Samuel's toys. Finally, everything was ready.

I don't know what upset Elaine more when she and Samuel returned—Altagracia's departure, the monkey cage on the sun porch, or Willow and George's appearance the next morning. Whether it was antipathy or fear, she was unwilling to even pet the monkey. Samuel reacted, though, with all the enthusiasm that I'd hoped. He bounded into our converted monkey room, squealing with delight. Whatever her doubts, Elaine had to smile at his reaction.

I knew a week was little time to prove George's value, and I didn't expect a miracle; yet within days of his arrival Samuel seemed a different child. At the first light of dawn, he would race to the monkey room to greet George, who would leap from ring to ring at his appearance, screeching to get out of his cage. We didn't let George out until Willow arrived to take care of "my diaper boys," as she called them. Once she opened the cage door, Samuel would watch intently as she put on a fresh diaper for George. Then he'd throw himself on his back and wait for her to do the same for him. We closed the sliding glass doors to the sun porch, and Elaine and I would watch from outside as the two scampered around the room under Willow's direction.

Every day brought progress—more focus, more engagement, even sounds that could be speech: nana (for banana), Gorge (for George), Lo for Willow, a slow dribble of words that I hoped would finally grow into a large enough pool to burst the dam that constrained him. Seeing him sit crosslegged on the floor by George's cage, fluttering his fingers at the monkey who excitedly imitated his gestures, I wondered what they were telling each other in their private sign language. What joke were they sharing when Samuel laughed at George's gibbering? What sympathy was he offering George when the monkey peeped and whined? Was Samuel saying he knew what it was like to be imprisoned in a cage? To lack words to express what he thought and felt?

Though Elaine still wouldn't touch the monkey, I could see her softening towards him. After all, she wanted the best for Samuel too, and his attachment to George was clear. Willow was another story. Elaine seemed to regard her as an even more alien presence than George. She'd treated Altagracia like a member of the family, and welcomed the many therapists who came to the house, but she was chilly toward Willow from the start. The fact that Samuel bonded with her as quickly as he did increased her resentment. How could a monkey trainer be a fit therapist for our son?

I hesitated to bring the subject up, waiting for more proof to convince her of what I found undeniable. We were both careful with each other, respectful but distant, living in the same house, though sleeping in separate bedrooms. We knew we had to reach a decision when the trial week ended; still, we refrained from discussing it while we gathered evidence for our final arguments.

The fourth day Willow was at the house, I came home early, hoping to see more progress. Elaine had left Samuel briefly with Willow to go to the market. When she returned, I saw her stiffen at the monkey smell which by now had seeped under the doors of the sun room and permeated the whole house. Like a patient forced to down some bitter medicine, she braced herself against the odor as she set down the grocery bags.

"How's Samuel?" she asked.

"Come and look." I led her to the sun porch.

We watched through the sliding French doors as Samuel lay on the floor raptly watching a diapered George delicately peel the skin from a banana. When the monkey finished his favorite food, he began scampering around the room, jumping from the trampoline to the ropes rigged from one corner to the other. Samuel chased after him, unaware of our presence.

"You see how happy he is," I said.

I thought I saw tears in her eyes.

"You can see that, can't you?" I insisted, unsure what she was feeling.

Running past the door, Samuel noticed Elaine. His face lit up and he started spinning in excitement, the way he always did when his feelings overwhelmed him. I gestured to Willow to capture George so we could enter.

"I'd rather Samuel come out here," Elaine said.

"But he wants you to be with George."

Her mouth twitched in distaste.

"Willow will put him back in his cage if you want," I offered.

"Please bring him out here," she repeated.

Samuel stopped his spinning and pressed his face to a glass panel of the door, ending our debate. I slid the door open and Elaine gathered Samuel in her arms. He let her hug him a moment then wriggled away and grabbed her hand, pulling her into the monkey room. Reluctantly, Elaine followed.

"He doesn't like to leave him," Willow explained as she returned the monkey to his cage.

Elaine's pursed lips couldn't hold back her antagonism. George must have sensed it as well. He arched his back and bared his teeth in protest.

Samuel dropped Elaine's hand in concern.

"It's okay, Sammy," Willow said calmly. "George is just a little nervous."

"He's not used to you," she said to Elaine. "It's best you don't come too close to the cage."

Elaine ignored her. How dare this intruder tell her to back away?

Inside his cage, a frenzied George jumped from one perch to another, scratching his arms and legs. He grabbed the bars and rattled them to get out.

Samuel moved to the cage to comfort him. The monkey reached out to him through the bars.

Elaine instinctively pulled Samuel away.

George let loose a shriek so shrill that it was hard to believe it had emanated from such a tiny creature.

Startled, Samuel fell backward and wailed in distress as acute as George's. Willow picked him up and held him to her breast. "It's okay. It's okay," she repeated, rubbing his back to soothe him.

George retreated to the back of his cage and pulled a blanket over his head.

"Look at him," I said to Elaine. "He wouldn't hurt Samuel. He's just as upset as he is."

Elaine looked around in confusion, watching helplessly as her son turned to someone else for consolation.

"This is crazy . . . crazy . . . You've got to stop it."

"No, you're wrong. George has been great for him."

"Because he can say a few words? Do you think that cures his autism?"

We glared at each other as if on opposite sides of an impenetrable glass.

She took a deep breath and her face tightened. "I've talked to a lawyer. I want custody." She turned and withdrew to the kitchen, slamming the door behind her.

It took a moment for me to collect myself.

Willow's expression suggested that she had been expecting Elaine's blowup for a long time. "Sometimes he reacts to people that way," she said. "Something about the vibe they give off."

She sat on the floor, stroking George. Samuel curled up next to her, sniffing back a few last tears as he watched her groom the monkey. George shivered with pleasure as her fingernails massaged his furry back.

"Animals have this uncanny sense about people," she said, as if George's reaction explained everything that needed to be said about Elaine. Bending over the monkey in her low-cut peasant blouse, she exposed the daffodil tattooed on her right breast.

I turned to Samuel to avoid staring at it.

"He took to you and Sammy right from the start," she said. "Once animals accept you, they're friends for life. They're very loyal that way. They don't judge you the way people do." She continued to stroke the monkey with her long, silver-painted fingernails.

I felt a rush of feelings toward her—gratitude for her acceptance, appreciation for her generosity, and something else that alarmed me. Seeing her sensually stroking George, I realized that her weight had prevented me from seeing how attractive she was. She brushed her long hair back from her face and looked at me with an amused expression as if waiting for me to recognize something about myself that she already knew. For a moment, maybe longer, I let myself imagine what could happen next. But she was here for Samuel, not me. I couldn't risk doing anything that might jeopardize that. The estranged husband and the twenty-four-year-old babysitter. Not a movie I would make. Not one destined for a happy ending.

She looked up at me with a curious smile that I couldn't quite read. Disappointment perhaps, or maybe it was disparagement. George suddenly plunged his tiny fingers deep into her blouse. "Stop that monkey business. Those aren't for you." She pulled his hands away, grinning.

"I think you better take him now." She rose and held George out to me. He immediately leaped onto my chest, clinging to my shirt with his tiny fingers. "I don't worry about leaving him anymore. He's completely at home here now."

I felt George's diaper leaking down my chest, a warning perhaps of wreckage still to come.

* * *

The crisis I'd created was one I'd never faced before, not something I could talk my way out of, nor money resolve. Elaine wasn't about to leave Samuel in my care, yet how could I deprive him of the monkey he adored? Sending George away would be as traumatic as Elaine abandoning Samuel. The only way I saw to defuse the situation was to fire Willow. A temporary fix, I knew, but maybe I could replace her with someone Elaine liked and still keep George.

Willow cried the next morning when I told her I no longer needed her.

"You knew this was only temporary," I said, "to make the transition easier for George. You said yourself, he's completely adapted now."

"What about Sammy? Who's going to take care of him?"

"His mother and I will."

"She going to change George's diapers too?" she asked, as if the idea were ridiculous.

I ignored the question. "I appreciate everything you've done for us," I said. "I can't thank you enough. You raised a wonderful monkey. You can see how he's changed Samuel."

"He's a beautiful child. I'll miss him too."

It pained me to see her weep again as she said goodbye to the animal she'd mothered through infancy. Did George understand that she was leaving him to a man uncertain what the future held? I think he did, for it was only with great effort that Willow pried him from her back, clutching strands of her hair he clung to till the last. He whimpered when she returned him to his cage and he stared at her through the bars with eyes as bereft as Samuel's when Willow picked him up and kissed him goodbye. Then, tears streaming down her face, she fled the sun porch.

Elaine watched all this from the other room. Seeing Samuel cry, she rushed in and held him in her arms as he sobbed. "It's okay, Samuel. I'm still here. I'm not leaving you." She tried to soothe him.

"And neither is George," I added.

George squeaked and whistled in response, as if he, too, understood what I was saying, or maybe that was just what I wanted to believe.

* * *

Willow's departure eased the tension a little between Elaine and me. Separately, we decided to table the subject of divorce and custody—not that those issues had been settled, but neither of us was ready to confront them again. Though frightened by George's volatility—and still reluctant to touch him—Elaine recognized his importance to Samuel. She also understood that I wouldn't let her take Samuel without a fight, and a custody battle would involve lawyers and psychologists, take months to resolve, and inevitably hurt Samuel. So she agreed to continue the trial a little longer. Thinking back, I don't know what she imagined would persuade me to send George away; and I don't know what I expected to change for her to accept George. Whatever we hoped or feared, we kept to ourselves and stumbled on while we searched for a suitable replacement for Willow. From the first prospect the employment agency sent us, I saw what an impossible task it would be. "You want me to change the monkey's diapers too?" the British nanny asked aghast.

"I'd be even happier if you could toilet train him," I said.

"I don't think I'm the person you're looking for," she said, crisply folding her references and returning them to her purse.

Elaine looked at me as if I was mad to expect anyone else to solve the problem I'd created.

I had no choice but to work from home until we found another nanny to help Elaine. It was now up to Samuel, George, and me, the three proverbial monkeys—mute, dumb, and blind—to make our case. If the three of us could band together, perhaps we could overcome our individual deficits.

Willow's departure left both Samuel and George listless, apathetic. No more lip-smacking chatter from George for Samuel to imitate. No more babel from Samuel for George to mimic. They were both as silent as an aquarium. When Elaine or I readied Samuel for bed at night, he didn't resist. Yet hours later, he would wake up thrashing in his sleep. We would rush to his bedroom to comfort him and find his rag monkey soaked in tears. Gathering him in my arms, I'd settle in the same rocking chair where Elaine had nursed him and try to lull him to sleep. Eventually his sobbing would subside; then, like a burst of torrential rain, he would begin crying uncontrollably again.

How do you assuage someone's pain if he can't communicate the reason for his torment? Was he grieving for Willow? Or his estranged parents? Or because he couldn't put any of his feelings into words? All either of us could do was hold him in our arms and rock him to sleep. Sitting in the dark, cradling the son we'd created, I remembered how happy we were when we brought him home from the hospital. Seeing Elaine now watching us from the doorway, her face stricken with worry, I, too, could find no words for the sorrow that enveloped us.

When a movie flops, you can only curse the director, the studio, the actors for so long before you have to confront your own part in the disaster. After all, you bought the script, hired the director, approved the actors. For a long time I blamed Elaine, her shrink, the therapists for Samuel's silence. But the miraculous "monkey cure" was my idea, not theirs. Other capuchin owners who blogged on the internet cautioned that bringing a wild animal into your home wasn't for the faint-hearted. Even the most docile and well-trained were unpredictable. So why had I been so obstinate? Was I unwilling to face my own contribution to Samuel's autism? Could my genes, my sperm, or my damaged childhood be the source of his disability?

"Samuel, Samuel," I whispered to him in the dark. "What have I done to you in my blindness? How can I make up for it?"

Before Samuel was born, I worried that I'd be too busy, too preoccupied with my career, to give him the time and attention he needed. Once I saw him, though, my fears vanished. He was my chance to make up for everything I'd missed as a child. I could be the doting father that I never had; Elaine and I could be the loving parents I'd wished for. I imagined simple pleasures like throwing a ball back and forth in the backyard, or flying a kite at the beach; when he grew older we could hike together in the rainforests or scuba dive in Hawaii, or take family trips to London and Paris or exotic places we'd never visited. He would be far more comfortable and agile in the world than I was, the man I'd wished to be. I found it difficult to admit how Samuel's autism had dashed my dreams; that my disappointment kept me from loving him. Now I was as ashamed as I was of my father.

After several sleep-starved nights, I persuaded Elaine to let me move Samuel's bed into the monkey room, hoping that George might assuage whatever nightmares were waking him. Samuel watched in silence as I lugged his bed down the stairs and onto the sun porch. George circled his cage excitedly as I dragged the bed into the room, which started Samuel whirling as well, each mirroring the other's movements like dancers in a frenzied pas de deux. "Hey, calm down, calm down, both of you," I ordered to no avail, so I grabbed Samuel's hands and started dancing with him. "Ring around the rosy, a pocket full of posies." I sang the old nursery rhyme, realizing I'd never done this with him before. George whistled from his cage, cheering us on as we twirled around the room, my voice rising louder and louder like an overaged rockstar attempting a drunken comeback. "Ashes, ashes, we all fall *up!*" I tossed Samuel, laughing, in the air. After days of mourning, we all had come to life again. This hopelessness, this despair we were all feeling, could pass. We might get through this after all.

That night Samuel slept without waking. I'd moved to the couch in the living room to hear him if he woke during the night. There was no need. I rose several times to check on him as I had when we first brought him home from the hospital. Each time he was sleeping soundly. A second night passed without incident. Then a third. But daytime was filled with meltdowns and tantrums. George grew more and more rebellious. Inserting his prehensile tail, as unruly as a coiled spring, into the tiny slit in his diaper was a battle I increasingly lost. The shit on my shirt and in my hair delighted Samuel, provoking his own defiance, making it difficult to diaper him. Maybe this was the evidence Elaine was hoping for, proof that George was a provocation, not a solution. I worried that Samuel might regress to smearing his feces on the wall. My experiment was failing, yet I didn't know how to end it without harming Samuel further.

The fourth night I was jolted awake by a scream so piercing that for an instant I thought I'd dreamed it. I stumbled to my feet and rushed to the sun porch. Even in the faint illumination of the night lamp, I saw that Samuel's bed was empty. I flipped on the overhead light. The cage door was open. Samuel was curled up on the floor inside. George cowered at the back, half whining, half crying, hiding behind a blanket he'd pulled over his head. He's killed our son, I thought.

I shot into the cage and knelt beside Samuel. His tiny body was shaking, heaving in uncontrollable spasms of fear. Or maybe it was grief. When I picked him up, he was damp in my arms. Then I saw it wasn't tears but blood that was darkening my hands.

"Oh, Samuel, what's George done?" Elaine cried as she rushed into the sun porch.

I carried Samuel to the kitchen to find the source of the bleeding. There was a small wound, the size of monkey teeth marks, just above his wrist where George had bitten him. Samuel must have entered the cage during the night to be closer to him. Scared or threatened, George did what wild animals do when frightened. However it happened, for whatever reasons, the blame was mine as much as George's. My crazed attempt to make Samuel speak had harmed him after all. I couldn't meet Elaine's eyes as she washed and bandaged his wrist.

"It's okay, Samuel. The bleeding's already stopped," she murmured, caressing his trembling body.

Tears welled up in his eyes as if he understood all the distress and sadness that we were feeling. Suddenly, he thrust his hand forward and pointed.

Elaine and I both turned to see George hovering uncertainly in the doorway. With the cage door open, he'd followed us to the kitchen.

"Gorge sorry . . . sorry," Samuel stammered. "He promise to be good."

I was stunned by both the line he remembered from the book and his generosity. If he could forgive George so easily for biting him, perhaps he could forgive his parents' confusion and our fumbling efforts to help him when his struggles were so much greater than our own.

Tears came to Elaine's eyes as well. "It's easy for little monkeys to forget." She recited the next line from the book, her voice thick with emotion.

As if he understood, George thumped his long black tail in response, then leaped onto the table.

Samuel gripped Elaine's hand and pushed it toward the monkey. She held back a second, then gave in and let him guide her hand toward George; together they gingerly patted his lowered head. George squeaked happily in reply.

Something broke in me as I watched. I, too, had promised to be good. But I'd let my disappointment, my guilt, my desperation to fix Samuel prevent me from fully embracing our delicate, sensitive son. For so long all I saw was the trapped, tongue-tied boy whom I foolishly believed a capuchin monkey could free.

I took Samuel from Elaine and clasped him to my chest with a tenderness so sharp I felt its ache. "I love you, Sammy. I really do," I murmured.

"Daddy . . ." He looked up as if seeing me for the first time. "Daddy . . ." he repeated.

I had no idea what would happen next, whether Samuel would ever speak another sentence, or what Elaine and I would do about George or our marriage. For the moment it didn't matter. In his bright hazel eyes, I glimpsed the father I might yet be.

Reason enough to have children.

Trail's End

The boy wriggles in his scratchy sheets and blankets, unable to sleep. One month past his seventh birthday, he's never been away from home before. He misses his soft sheets and thick mattress and the familiar traffic noises drifting up to the bedroom window of his family's third-floor apartment on West 72nd Street. Tomorrow his parents will visit for the first time and discover all his postcards have been lies. An owl hoots outside the cabin—Boo-hoo! Boo-hoo!—mocking his misery.

He wants to get up and pee to prevent his thin mattress from stinking in the morning, but the soft chatter of his counselors binds him to his bed. He finds their hushed voices comforting, like a night light in the dark. His narrow bed is close to theirs, which are near the cabin door so they can enter at night without waking the six boys in their charge. He's too young to fully understand what they're saying, and memory is unreliable.

What we choose to recall or forget or invent about the past always reflects our present needs. Still, as I picture David, the boy I was then, this is what I remember.

Art is talking in a low voice, barely above a whisper. "We rowed to that far bend in the lake, out of view of camp. There's a little beach there, very private, that I discovered last year. A beautiful spot to swim and sunbathe . . ."

"And skinny dip," Howie interjects.

"You're rushing this. Going way too fast. I like to take things slow. We had all afternoon together. After we swam, we lay on our towels, drying in the sun. She was wearing that pink V-neck bathing suit that clings to her body. I watched drops of water slide down her face and neck and disappear between those lovely breasts . . ."

"You're such a romantic," Howie says.

"Well, it was a perfect moment. How many more will I have? She looked so beautiful. I leaned over and traced her cheek with my finger down her neck to her breast . . .'You know I might not make it back, I said.'"

"You told her that?"

"It's true. Who knows what could happen?"

For a moment the only sound is the hiss of the kerosene lamp that casts Art and Howie in shadows.

"What did she say?" Howie asks.

"She started crying."

"Of course she'd cry. What did you expect?"

"At least it gave me a chance to comfort her."

David can imagine Art comforting another person. He plays the guitar and leads the singing in his mellow voice at the Friday night campfires; and Art's kind to him when he wets his bed.

"Pretty soon we had our bathing suits off," Art goes on.

"Finally!"

"I told you, it takes time."

David has seen Art before without his clothes, but he can't quite picture the naked woman with him. Perhaps she's Annie, the swimming counselor; he's seen Art with his arm around her.

"'But we have no protection,' she said. 'I know that,' I said, 'but there are other things we can do.' I took her hand and gently sucked one of her fingers. 'You know how much I care for you,' I said. 'Maybe . . . maybe you could kiss it . . .'"

"You didn't?"

"'This could be our last time alone like this,' I said. 'When

I'm over there, at least I'll have it to remember . . .'"

"You're shameless," Howie chuckles.

David doesn't know why this could be a last time or why Art's ashamed of kisses, but he doesn't like hearing Howie laugh at Art. He's caught Howie rolling his eyes before when he lets a fly ball glance off his glove, or when his sheets are wet in the morning. He turns his back to the counselors and pulls his blanket over his head.

* * *

At breakfast, all the boys in the Iroquois cabin talk eagerly about what their parents will bring them this Sunday. David's parents left for France and Italy shortly after they delivered him to Trail's End and haven't been back since. His mother mailed him picture postcards of the Eiffel Tower and Roman Colosseum and other "magnificent" sights they saw on their vacation. In return, he sent his parents the plain, pre-addressed postcards the counselors made them write each week. He carefully printed the same message on every postcard: "Dear Mother and Father—Everything is fine here—I miss you—David." He hopes now the mailman lost them.

Parents start arriving in late morning while they are playing softball. There are three cabins of seven to eight-year-olds—the Iroquois, Navajos, and Mohawks—eighteen Jewish Indians, enough to form two baseball teams. Whatever team he's on, they stick him in the outfield. Today he's positioned deep in right field, where few boys can hit the ball over his head. Before camp he had no interest in baseball; now he really hates it.

He watches the visitors trickle in from the parking lot. Most of his bunkmates' parents are younger than his; they wear brighter clothes and drive flashier cars than his father's black Pontiac, and they tote picnic lunches from Zabar's, corned beef and pastrami sandwiches, and chocolate babka and bags of candy his mother frowns on. He doesn't want any of their treats or sweets; he wants his parents to pack his trunk and take him home. Since they're back from Europe, they no longer need a place to dump him. He doesn't care if the other boys call him "momma's boy" or "fraidy-cat," or "quitter." He never wants to see any of them again.

The game is almost over when he spots them. While most of the fathers wear short sleeves and khakis, his father is dressed in pressed tan slacks and a blue sports jacket; thankfully he's skipped the tie. His mother has armed herself against the sun with oversized sunglasses and a wide brim, floppy hat that seems better suited for the jungle. He fears the other Iroquois will think his parents old and odd, another excuse to make fun of him. They wave at him in the outfield and sit in the rickety wooden stands to watch. Mercifully, no one hits the ball toward him. His team wins and they run onto the field to high five each other. He skips the celebration and walks to the stands.

His mother hugs him, smelling of the lilac perfume she wears when his parents go out at night. "I've missed you so much," she says and holds him at arm's length to examine him. "I think you've grown," she exclaims.

His father squints at him through his silver-rimmed glasses. "About an inch, I'd say," and pats him awkwardly on the shoulder. Baseball doesn't interest him—he wouldn't know Mickey Mantle from Roger Maris—instead he asks what he really cares about. "I'm eager to see you in the water," he says.

David ignores the comment. His father will discover the truth soon enough.

Only half the boys in his bunk eat lunch in the mess hall; the rest are picnicking with their parents on the grassy slope leading to the lake. Since his parents ate on the road, they use the time to visit "Uncle" Chic, the owner of the camp, who came to their apartment to persuade them that a summer at Trail's End was a "character-building experience" every city boy should have. David would hike, swim, come to love sports and the outdoors and return to Manhattan stronger, healthier, and more confident. "Sounds great, doesn't it?" said his father, who played no sports and rarely even ventured into Central Park, but he was pleased to provide David an opportunity his own parents couldn't afford when he was a child.

"I thought your parents were gonna show up today," Robbie Ungar says at lunch. Robbie is the best ball player in their group and his chief tormentor.

"They did," he answers.

"How come you're not eating with them? They too busy changing your sheets?"

Two other boys at the table snicker at Robbie's lame joke. Robbie's parents didn't visit today or last Sunday, which may be why he's picking on him again.

"At least my parents are here," he says so softly that Robbie isn't sure he heard. Robbie circles an ear with his hand. "What did you say?"

David changes his mind. "I said pass the potato salad, please."

"You say diapers? Pass the diapers please?" He piles the potato salad on his own plate, leaving almost nothing left in the bowl. "Bedwetter," he sneers.

If Art were at their table, David knows he would've stopped Robbie's heckling. But Art has this Sunday off, so David can only pretend he hasn't heard.

After lunch he meets his parents outside the dining hall and leads them to his cabin. His mother keeps running her fingers through his curly hair and rubbing his shoulders as they walk, until he pulls away, afraid others will see her coddling and petting him. Inside the cabin, she inspects his bed and cubby and rearranges his clothes, which she carefully name tagged at home to make sure they wouldn't get lost in the camp laundry. She's brought him a T-shirt from Paris with a picture of the Eiffel Tower and a package of new underpants, "in case you run out," she says. The underpants make him think that Howie has reported that he pees his bed at night;

if he has, she doesn't mention it. Or maybe counselors lie to parents the same way he does.

When they exit the cabin, they find Howie quietly conversing with his father on the porch. Both men shift uncomfortably, as if caught saying something David shouldn't hear. "You know Howard goes to the same law school I did," his father says and looks down at his shiny, tasseled leather loafers. The fancy dress shoes his father wears to camp shame him as much as the conversation he suspects they're hiding. He wishes Art were here instead of Howie.

His parents walk to the lake with him for the afternoon swim. Although there is no breeze this afternoon, David feels goose bumps rising on his skin. Every time he nears the lake, fear prickles the back of his neck. The second week of camp he fell—or was pushed—off the dock. Unable to swim, he panicked. Water flooded his nose and mouth as he gasped for air and thrashed his arms and legs to reach the ladder, kicking and kicking to keep afloat. Then darkness closed around him. The next thing he knew he was sprawled on the dock, coughing and spewing water, and gazing at the whistle dangling from the lanyard around Annie's neck as she hovered over him in her pink bathing suit. "He slipped. I saw him slip," Robbie kept yelling as David puked up the water he'd swallowed. Robbie's nervous ranting made him wonder if he really stumbled or if Robbie pushed him.

Because Annie feels responsible for his falling into the lake—even though she dived in to save him—she's made it her mission to teach him to swim this summer. So far, she hasn't succeeded. He's still confined to the crib, a wooden enclosure for those who can't pass the deep-water test. The crib has a wooden floor where he can stand and not worry about drowning.

His parents watch as most of the Iroquois head for the roped-in swimming area on one side of the dock, and he and Lucas step into the crib on the other side. Lucas, a Mohawk who is a year older, can do the dead man's float and dog paddle, but he isn't a strong enough swimmer to leave the crib. David can float on his back when Annie's with him, yet whenever he puts his face in the water and holds his breath, his lungs feel about to burst and he panics again. Today there are no lessons, just free swimming. He lowers himself to his shoulders and splashes around a little at the far end of the crib, clinging to the edge and kicking, hoping his parents will think he's practicing his strokes.

At last, Annie blows her whistle and the boys emerge from the water, making way for the girls who will follow. As they dry themselves and put on their sandals, he sees his father walking toward Annie and knows he will ask why he can't swim yet.

"You're shivering," his mother says, wrapping his towel tighter around his shoulders. It's not the chill but fear of what Annie will say that makes him tremble.

He can't read his father's face as he walks slowly back from the dock. "Your swimming counselor says you're making progress, that you'll be out of the crib by the end of the summer," he says as they climb the slope to his cabin. He looks at David for confirmation.

David can't meet his eyes. He doesn't know why his father thinks it's so important that he learn to swim. There's no pool in their apartment building, and they never go to the beach. In fact, he can't remember ever seeing his father in a bathing suit. "How old were you when you learned to swim?" he asks.

His father doesn't answer for a moment; he glances toward the lake. "Actually, I never learned. That's why I want to make sure you do."

Hearing his father's reluctant confession, David knows he's doomed to repeat his failure.

Sensing his discouragement, his mother puts her arm around David's shoulders again. "If the swim teacher is confident, so am I," she says, refusing to accept her husband's legacy.

His parents don't stay much longer. They've talked to his counselor, heard what they wanted, ignored the rest, and are impatient now to avoid the Sunday traffic on their way back to the city. He's relieved they won't return until camp's end. His father's tasseled shoes and his mother's floppy sunhat and excessive hugs only confirm his oddness.

* * *

A few days after his parents' visit, Art takes him aside after arts and crafts, where he teaches campers to weave multicolored laces into lanyards and sculpt flowers from Popsicle sticks and pipe cleaners. "You remind me a lot of myself when I was your age," he says.

"Did you suck at sports too?" David asks.

"Pretty much. Stickball was what we played. I wasn't very good, always the last to be picked on any team. I was a skinny kid—'broomstick' they called me—and I got pushed around a lot. There was this bully Marvin Firestone, who picked on me all year when I was in second grade. Marvin was really scary— he'd light matches and throw them at you, or walk over and suddenly punch you in the stomach. I was his favorite target."

"I guess I'm Robbie's favorite too."

"I've noticed that."

David shrugs. "Everyone has."

"You know you don't have to put up with it."

David swallows hard. "What did you do?"

"I convinced my parents to get me boxing lessons. I wasn't going to be Marvin's punching bag any more. The summer after second grade, I spent a lot of time at the gym. I can teach you what I learned." Art reaches beneath his workbench and pulls out a pair of red leather boxing gloves. "We're going to have a tournament in two weeks and I want you to take Robbie on. In the ring."

"But I've never hit anyone before."

"Well, I'll be there to step in if you hurt him too much." Art grins and hands him the gloves. "Try them on. See how they feel."

David gingerly slips his hands into the gloves and Art tightens the wristbands.

"Go on, you can practice on me." He holds up his hands for David to hit.

David tentatively punches with his right hand, then his left.

"Punch with your whole body, not just your hands. You have to throw your weight behind your fists."

David punches harder this time. He strikes again and again, imagining he's pummeling Robbie's face. The counselor finally lowers his hands; his palms are almost the color of the boxing gloves. "You're a natural," he says. "You're going to surprise everyone with how well you do."

David's hands sting as he takes off the gloves, yet he feels strangely excited. "Is this how you stopped Marvin?" he asks.

Art sighs. "I wish. When school started in the fall, I was ready. But the first day of third grade, I learned his family had moved away. I'd missed my chance to stand up to him. I don't want you to miss yours."

The next two weeks David careens between anticipation and dread. When the tournament is announced, all the Iroquois, Navajos, and Mohawks are amazed to hear he's going to fight Robbie. "If you can't hit a baseball, how you gonna hit me?" Robbie sneers as he bobs and weaves to prove the point.

"Your head's bigger than a baseball," David says with more confidence than he feels.

"We'll see about that, bedwetter."

In the evenings after dinner, Art continues coaching David, teaching him to defend himself. "Don't pay any attention to Robbie," he says. "He talks trash because he's scared. He only volunteered to fight because he thought no one would get in the ring with him. He hasn't taken boxing lessons. No one's punched him in the face before."

No one's punched David in the face either and he isn't eager for the experience. But he likes spending time with Art, shadow boxing and listening to his stories about Marvin and the tough girls and boys he grew up with in Brooklyn. "Boxing lessons taught me I was stronger than I thought. So are you. You don't have to let anyone push you around." Practicing the left jab and the right cross, over and over again with Art, David almost believes he can pay Robbie back for all his meanness. Lying in bed at night, though, he runs his fingers down his face, wondering if his nose and mouth will be the same once the fight is over.

A few nights before the fight, when the urge to pee wakes him, David overhears Art and Howie talking about the coming match.

"I don't know why you pushed him into this," Howie says. "Robbie's just going to beat the crap out of him."

"You underestimate the rage of the humiliated," Art counters.

"Is this from some psychology book, or your own experience?"

"Both," Art says tersely.

David lies rigid until he's sure they're both asleep and then creeps to the bathroom to make sure his sheets aren't damp in the morning.

The day of the tournament, he's too nervous to eat. He keeps going to the toilet to empty his bladder or bowels. All that's left inside him is a jangle of nerves. He's sorry now he's let Art talk him into this. Shadow boxing isn't the same as real fighting. Even if Robbie is just boasting to hide his fear, he's still bigger and stronger. If he does beat the crap out of him, he'll keep on bullying him for the rest of the summer.

Whether they box or not, all the boys attend the matches. Girls are excluded because they're considered too delicate to watch boys smash each other in the face. The ring is set up in the middle of the camp's auditorium. The matches begin with the youngest campers and advance to the fourteen- and fifteen-year-olds. David's happy that the first fight is between two Mohawks so he can see how hard they hit. He watches closely as they circle each other. They jab cautiously, mainly striking gloves or shoulders or elbows before they dart away. The brass bell rings and the boys retreat to their corners. The second round, they are a little bolder, but both seem too afraid of being hit to do much damage. Watching them dance around the ring, David thinks maybe he can do the same and stay just outside Robbie's reach. When the match ends, the counselor who is refereeing raises both their arms to signal a tie. They smile and bang gloves again, almost as hard as they did fighting.

Then it's his turn. The pit in his stomach feels as if he's already been punched there. Art is in his corner, Howie in Robbie's. Art tightens his gloves and inserts his plastic mouth guard. "Remember, this is your chance, buddy. Show him who you are."

The referee brings them together to tap gloves, then steps aside. David bites down hard on his mouth guard and assumes the boxing stance Art has taught him. Robbie mirrors his stance and rushes toward him. David wards off his first jabs with his gloves and backpedals. The light blows swat away his fear.

Robbie attacks again, as he has all summer. David raises his gloves to defend himself. Robbie punches him hard in the stomach. David drops his hands a second and Robbie hits him in the face. The blow glances off his cheekbone. Water blurs his eyes as he skirts away. Robbie glares at him, his face as clenched as his fists, ready to knock him to the mat the way he pushed him into the lake.

David crouches to protect himself. When Robbie lowers his fists to strike again, David swings wildly and smashes him squarely in the nose. Robbie's head snaps back; his eyes cross momentarily. David hits him in the face again. He hears the cheers of the other campers and keeps thrashing, windmill-ing and side-arming Robbie in a frenzy of blows that seem to emerge from another person. Robbie hunches to cover up, his legs wobble, and he drops to a knee. The referee quickly steps in and raises David's arm. Robbie swipes a glove at the trickle of blood dripping from his nose and looks at him incredulous-ly. David is as astonished at his own explosion of fury. His eyes burn; his face smarts; he feels a wave of nausea as he stumbles to his corner of the ring. "What a puncher," Art says as he pulls his gloves off. "You fought like Rocky Marciano tonight."

David spits out his mouth guard. "I never want to box again," he says.

"Then, like Rocky, you can retire undefeated." Art massag-es his bony shoulders. "I'm so proud of you, David. You were very brave."

David feels something stirring in his chest for which he has no words. No one has ever called him brave before.

Later, when they all walk back to the cabin, even Howie compliments David on the fight. If Robbie hears the praise, he ignores it. He jokes with the other boys, as if a bloody nose is no worse than a knee scrape. Still, when they undress for bed, Robbie skips his nightly warning to David to keep his pajamas dry. Art shoots him a pleased look as he turns out the cabin light, as if to say, "Didn't I tell you?"

***

The next Saturday, when David returns from lunch, he finds Art packing clothes into a worn tan suitcase on his bed. "Where are you going?" David asks.

"I've been meaning to tell you . . ." Art stops as if searching for the words.

David's stomach does a somersault. "Are you leaving?"

The counselor's solemn, unshaven face confirms it.

Two boys bang the screen door as they enter the cabin and

rush to get their baseball gloves. Either they don't notice Art's suitcase or don't care that he's packing to leave.

"But camp's not over yet," David protests.

"It's not my choice." He closes the suitcase and puts a hand on David's arm. "Come outside," he says.

They go out to the porch and sit together on the creaky wooden swing. "You've heard of Vietnam?" Art says. "You know we're fighting a war there."

David nods. He's seen planes dropping bombs and soldiers marching through the mud and jungle on TV.

"Well, the army needs a lot of men to fight there. And my number's finally come up."

An image of a helicopter lifting a wounded soldier on a stretcher flashes in David's mind. "You'll come back, won't you?"

"I'm certainly planning to."

He can hear the doubt in Art's voice. It's not the way he talked about boxing. Tears rise unexpectedly in David's eyes. He clutches the lanyard around his neck to hold them back. He remembers what he overheard Art telling Howie. "Can I kiss it?" he says softly.

"What?"

"You know. What you asked Annie."

The swing jerks backwards so violently that David grips Art's leg to keep from falling.

"I want to kiss it too . . . so you'll remember me."

"Oh, David, that's not something . . ." The alarm on his face tells David he's said something terribly wrong, a secret that should never be revealed. Art gently detaches David's hand from his leg. For an instant there's an agonizing silence. Then Art puts his arm around his trembling shoulders and pulls him closer.

"Of course I'll remember you. How could I forget? The Rocky Marciano of our camp."

David leans against his chest and sobs into his Trail's End T-shirt.

* * *

It's a gray December Sunday as I descend the slanted stone path to the Vietnam Veterans Memorial in Washington. Despite the threatening rain-clouds, the memorial is crowded with visitors, come to grieve and honor the more than 58,000 men and women lost to a war the U.S. should never have fought. The density of names on the granite slabs is numbing, as incomprehensible as hieroglyphics. I search for one name— Arthur Cohen. I find it in the middle of a panel on the east wall of soldiers killed in 1968. Like others who mourn, I run my fingers over the letters engraved in the cold black stone. Standing back, I see my distorted image reflected ghostlike in the mirrored marble, hovering over Art's name. I think of Springsteen's song: "If your eyes could cut through that black stone/ Tell me would they recognize me?"

I'm thirty-five now, a Legal Aid lawyer in San Francisco, married with a four-year-old son I can't imagine ever sending away from home as young as I was. Although this is the first time I've visited the monument, I often think of that summer with Art. The next year I refused to return to Trail's End. I didn't want to play baseball or box again or even learn to swim. I learned of Art's death by chance, from an accidental meeting with Lucas in the dinosaur hall at the Museum of Natural History when I was ten. I remember standing underneath the Tyrannosaurus rex skeleton when he told me. I was too stunned to cry.

The database of casualties says PFC Art Cohen was killed in a firefight in Gia Dinh Province at the age of twenty-five. I wonder what went through his mind as he lay dying in that rice paddy. Was he thinking of Annie? Or Marvin, the bully he failed to confront as a child? Was he wondering if standing up for yourself meant you had to stand up for your country, too? I don't even know if he believed Vietnam was worth dying for. "Sometimes you don't get to choose," he told me the afternoon he left camp. But that contradicted what he tried to teach me that summer. You always have a choice whether to fight back.

A middle-aged woman in a green raincoat kneels to place a wreath of flowers at the foot of the granite slab. Visitors leave all kinds of tributes to their fallen friends and loved ones: dog tags, photographs, letters, American flags, combat boots, helmets, military and religious medals, and other remembrances that the National Park Service collects each night. Over 400,000 artifacts stored in some giant warehouse in Washington. I've brought only a pair of shiny red kid's boxing gloves to leave at the memorial.

The air begins to mist as I ascend the path and emerge into the pale winter light. I don't believe there's one experience, one defining moment in childhood, that shapes who you are or will become. I overcame my fear of drowning several years after Trail's End and now enjoy the swimming I dreaded. I never boxed again, and I don't watch fights on television. It's not because Art helped me face Robbie, or the confidence that gave me, that I've come here today. It's because he saw in me what no one else did then. I loved him for it, a love he generously returned.

Misfits

A shrill screech, like metal scraping metal, assaulted Morris as he emerged from the elevator. He scanned the dim underground garage for its source.

The girl was crouched beside a black Mercedes SUV. Sixteen at most, he guessed, with frizzy chestnut hair and a schoolgirl's backpack. The blade of a pocketknife flashed in her hand.

"You shouldn't do that," he said. An impotent reprimand for a crime already committed.

She rose to face him with an expression he couldn't decipher—chagrin or maybe defiance. Her T-shirt proclaimed "Every Day is Earth Day" above a blue-and-green drawing of the planet. "Yours?" She nodded toward the SUV.

He shook his head.

"Good." She closed the red Swiss Army knife and slipped it into her ripped jeans.

"It's hardly the way to save the earth," he said.

"You going to call the cops?"

He'd been too surprised to think of it.

She quickly stuck a card beneath the windshield wiper of the SUV. "The assholes who drive these should suffer for their sins."

"You think keying them will make them repent?"

"If they don't, we're all going to fry."

"I know the climate's warming, but . . ."

"Then you should do something about it." She headed toward the stairway exit, pausing as she opened the door. "Dare to be a force for nature," she urged and disappeared.

Morris moved closer to the Mercedes to inspect the damage. Two jagged scratches scarred the side door of the G Class SUV. He read the carefully hand-lettered card she'd left on the windshield: "Your Car is Fucking Up the Planet."

He hastened to his BMW—his wife's choice of cars not his—to avoid any connection to the girl's crime. The encounter rattled him. He felt that he'd somehow failed to rise to the occasion, although what the occasion demanded wasn't really clear. Should he have tried to detain the girl? A citizen's arrest? The idea seemed as foolish as her juvenile protest. Still her rebuke rankled. She had recognized his passivity at a glance.

* * *

As soon as Sofia hit the street, she broke into a sprint, trying to make her legs keep pace with her heartbeat. When she finally slowed to a walk on the Santa Monica promenade, her heart kept racing, like an alarm clock that wouldn't stop ringing. That had been close, closer than she'd ever come to getting caught before. In the faint fluorescent light, she hadn't been able to see the man clearly. Fortunately, his surprise had given her time to escape. Men like that were cowards, too satisfied with their lives to take bold action. She was pleased she called him out before she fled. Whatever car he drove, maybe he'd remember her next time he filled his tank.

* * *

Two weeks later, the girl startled Morris again. Entering Starbucks on the ground floor of the five-story Wilshire Boulevard office building where he worked, Morris discovered her sitting alone, drinking something iced, and reading a paperback copy of Edward Abbey's *The Monkey Wrench Gang*. Absorbed in her book, she displayed no sign of malice. In her white Oxford shirt, dangly silver earrings, and freckled innocence, she looked more like a girl whose parents drove a Mercedes than a delinquent who went around defacing them. The contradiction led him to the empty seat across from her.

"That's a bad influence," he said.

She put the book down, surprised either to see him or that he'd read the novel. "I haven't finished it yet."

"It romanticizes misfits."

"Leo DiCaprio is making a movie of it."

"It figures."

She gazed at him a moment, as if appraising him. He was suddenly conscious of the soup stain on his shirt and the plastic pocket protector that held his pens. Whatever the girl assumed from his appearance, she reached for her backpack on the floor.

"I hope you're not headed for the garage," he said.

"You drive a gas guzzler too?" She jammed the book into her backpack.

"It's not my car I'm worried about."

"No?" She stood, scornful, impatient.

"I'd hate to see you do something you'll regret later."

"You only regret what you aren't brave enough to do." She slipped her backpack over her shoulder, turned, and swept out of the coffee shop.

Morris remained at the table, feeling even more inept than he had in the garage.

He purchased a slice of lemon cake for his wife and went upstairs to their fifth-floor offices where they worked together in their boutique accounting firm, Fishborne and Associates. He was Fishborne, Evelyn the associate. They'd worked together and been married now for twenty-seven years. Accounting was the occupation he'd fallen into, not his ambition. He'd imagined something more adventurous—a naturalist, a river guide—but his father's heart attack at forty-nine, dying without life insurance or savings, had forced him to drop out of Santa Monica College to support his mother and two sisters. A sixty-year-old tax accountant had taken him under his wing and changed the trajectory of his life.

"Something wrong?" Evie asked, when she saw him at his desk, leaning back in his chair, staring at the mounds of papers atop his file cabinets that blocked the wildlife and nature photographs hanging on the walls.

"We need to digitize more of these files."

"All in good time," she said, reclaiming her lemon slice he'd absently been eating. "You know that's not good for you."

"A lot of things aren't good for me," he said, thinking of all the vicissitudes that had led him to such a mundane, conventional life.

She came around the desk and massaged his neck. "You've been working too hard lately. You could use a break."

A faint sadness he couldn't identify rose in his chest as she rubbed his shoulders. "You're right," he said. "It would be good to get away."

They took a long weekend in Laguna Beach, strolled along the beach, imbibed the ocean air and several good bottles of Pinot Noir. The sun and wine brightened his spirits, but at night the crash of waves outside their hotel window thrummed a constant refrain of regret. *You've settled. You've settled. You've settled for less.* The frizzy-haired girl reminded him of youthful passions, paths not taken, opportunities he'd ignored or failed to seize. If Evie had been able to bear children, they might have had a daughter the same age as the teen. Evie had come to terms with her infertility years ago, though, and with nieces and nephews to dote on, he'd accepted her decision not to adopt. Now he wondered if he should have pressed her more.

Wednesday was the day he'd found the girl at Starbucks, so the next Wednesday afternoon he ambled downstairs for a cappuccino and some pound cake. She didn't appear that Wednesday or the next, which led him to buy coffee other afternoons as well. Evie kept reminding him that they had a coffee maker in the office. "But not a cappuccino maker," he said.

He didn't know if the girl frequented the coffee shop after school or if their two meetings had simply been an accident. He hoped that lecturing her hadn't scared her away. He wasn't sure exactly what he wanted from her, perhaps just a chance to change her perception, to present a bolder, more daring version of himself. She had given him no chance to explain himself, rejecting him as peremptorily as an IRS auditor who refused to hear any argument for a tax deduction a client was claiming. Their two encounters left him irritable and dispirited, unable to concentrate at work or fall asleep at night. He hated the image he imagined she'd formed of him.

* * *

Her mind wandered, as usual, to catastrophe. The ice caps were melting, the rainforests burning, drought and famine in Africa, floods and hurricanes in America, polar bears disappearing as fast as elephants, mad men firing assault rifles, terrorists blowing themselves up in crowds, a future so dark and bleak that it was almost impossible to bear, yet Sloan kept droning on about Calvin Coolidge and the Revenue Act of 1924.

"Are you with us this afternoon, Sofia?"

She quickly closed the notebook in which she was drawing the teacher's effigy and looked up to see him hovering over her like his cheap cologne.

"Taking notes for your paper?"

She placed her thick political science textbook squarely on top of her notebook. Seeing that it would take force to wrest the notebook from her, Sloan stepped away. "Have you decided what you're going to write about yet?" he asked.

"I'm still thinking about it."

"I certainly hope so, because you haven't given much thought to anything else in this class."

"How do you know what I'm thinking? Can you read my mind?" From the rustle in the classroom, she knew everyone had turned to listen.

"You don't seem to care much about this subject."

"You're wrong. It sucks that the rich don't pay their fair share of taxes," she bristled, "but that's not the way you're presenting it."

She saw his mouth twitch and knew she'd gotten to him.

"Well, your term paper will give you a chance to convince me." He turned to the blackboard and changed the subject.

A few desks ahead of her, Clarice flashed a surreptitious thumbs-up. The school's renegade bad girl had struck again. Sofia's pleasure was short-lived. Now she would have to write something substantial enough to change Sloan's opinion of her and avoid flunking the course.

The Archer School for Girls hadn't been her choice. But the elite Brentwood prep school was one decision her divorced parents agreed on, even if for different reasons. Her father believed single-sex education would encourage her to be independent and fearless. Her mother just wanted to protect her from the lust of teenage boys. Both her parents had misjudged the school. Many of her classmates, like Clarice, were already having sex; and the social pressure to get into the right college discouraged dissent as much as her teachers' flat earth views of the world. When she failed trigonometry as well as chemistry, her mother sent her to a psychiatrist to insure that she would graduate.

Her first session the shrink sat back in his leather chair, in his dandruff-flaked turtleneck, listening impatiently to her complaints about her stifling school as if he'd heard them all before. When she moved on to the evils of predatory capitalism, he stopped her. "And exactly how does that affect you, Sofia? Is that why your parents divorced?"

She didn't want to talk about her parents' ugly breakup or her mother's pitiful search to find another husband. "Exploitation affects everyone—even you," she said. "Do you know how little the Chinese worker who made your iPad earns?"

The shrink looked down at the tablet-sized computer in his lap. "Global inequities are certainly an important issue," he said, "but I don't think they're the reason you're having so much trouble at school." Then he started scrolling through a list of symptoms on his tablet: How often did she feel sad? Did she feel she had no one to talk to? Did she ever feel hopeless? Worthless? Did she worry that she might hurt herself? Though Sofia felt an urge to shock, to say something scandalous enough to make him drop his iPad, she mainly lied. When she left his office, she rode the elevator straight from the fifth floor to the garage and keyed the first SUV she saw, hoping it was his.

Their second session, the doctor delivered a diagnosis of depression and prescribed Prozac and monthly appointments to monitor the drugs. She didn't want to take anti-depressants, and she didn't want to come back again, but her mother watched to see that she swallowed a pill each morning. To avoid another blowup, and because she was also curious to see its effect, she took the Prozac and waited for the "sunshine" it was supposed to bring.

The miracle pill only made her more anxious and distracted during the day; at night she found it difficult to sleep. The doctor's response was to switch to Zoloft. "Drugs alone aren't the answer," he told her. "I see how much you're hurting, Sofia. If you persist in blaming everyone else for your problems and don't look at how you may be contributing to them, there's little chance things will change." Like her mother, he believed the fault for her unhappiness was all her own. She blinked back her tears. She wouldn't give him the satisfaction of seeing her cry.

* * *

Morris watched the third-floor elevator door slide open, startled to discover the girl again. This time she was slumped in the back corner with her backpack. She flinched as if he'd struck her. *Not you again?* her glare protested. He stepped in the elevator despite it.

She dropped her gaze and stared at her day-glow orange tennis shoes. From her puffy eyelids, Morris guessed that she'd been crying.

"Are you all right?" he asked.

She dabbed at her eyes with the back of her wrist.

None of the lines Morris had rehearsed fit the tears leaking down her cheek. She pulled up the neck of her black T-shirt to dry her face. Inscribed on the shirt was the day's battle cry: "Question Everything."

The elevator door opened. "Is there something I can do?" he asked.

She brushed past him in silence. He followed her into the lobby. "I'd be happy to call someone."

"Not your problem." She motioned for him to go away.

"But you seem upset."

She turned abruptly and faced him. "Look, one shitty shrink's enough for today." Then she opened the glass door and stepped into the street.

Morris hesitated a second, then went after her.

"I'm not a shrink. I'm a tax accountant."

"Yeah?" She didn't slow her stride.

He quickened his pace to keep up. "It's what I do, not who I am."

"Nobody's who they say they are." She altered her path to avoid a homeless man pushing a shopping cart filled with his dirt-encrusted belongings. Morris passed around his other side.

They stopped at a corner for a red light.

"You going to follow me all the way to the Metro?"

"I am heading in that direction," he lied.

She glanced at the traffic light, then back at him. "You know I finished the book last week. In the end Hayduke lived. He got away with it."

"It's fiction, not reality."

"Life imitates art, doesn't it?"

"Not in my experience," he said and instantly regretted it. He was sounding dreary and unimaginative again.

The light changed and he crossed the street with her. They walked another block in silence. Morris no longer knew what to say. It wasn't how he'd envisioned meeting her again.

"I suppose I should thank you for not ratting me out," she said, as if she'd been thinking about it for the last block.

"I didn't see the point. I sympathize, though I can't say I approve of your tactics. I'm not sure what you're trying to accomplish . . ."

"Just trying to wake people up. It got your attention, didn't it?" They reached the entrance to the Metro. "What's your name anyway?" she asked.

"Morris Fishborne. And you?"

She shook her head. "Better to keep that to myself, Morris."

She glided through the turnstile and disappeared from view.

Walking back to his office, he found himself whistling. He wasn't sure what had possessed him to follow her, but he was pleased he had. He'd acquitted himself much better this time. If he never saw her again, he could still take satisfaction from the gallantry with which he'd treated her. He may not have been a force for nature, but at least she recognized that he'd been understanding, kind. Passing the homeless man again, Morris pulled out his wallet and handed him a ten-dollar bill. It wasn't going to end poverty or save the planet, but it was something.

* * *

Riding the bus from school to Santa Monica, Sofia considered whether to keep this week's appointment with the psychiatrist.

She hated the numbing meds he'd prescribed, and she'd tossed them a week before. The Zoloft was worse than the Prozac; it made her feel as if everything had slowed and dulled, that she was watching an old black-and-white movie with fuzzy sound. If she told the shrink that she'd ditched the pills, he would just alter the dosage or prescribe another anti-depressant. What good was it to change your chemistry if the world remained as corrupt and ugly as before?

She fingered the Swiss Army knife she carried in the pocket of her jeans. Her cinematographer father had given it to her as a birthday present when she was ten, just before he ran off to London with his pretty camera assistant. Her father had grown up next to a forest, where a knife had many uses, and he still carried it with him to the many threatened ecosystems where he filmed around the world. The Swiss knife was about all that still connected Sofia to him, although she doubted he would approve of the way she used it. But better to cut a Mercedes than herself. She'd tried that once and it had only brought more pain.

Exiting the bus, she felt the urge to wield the knife again. A block from the shrink's office, she passed a public parking lot. Six or seven floors of cars to choose from. She took the stairs, searching for an empty vehicle that deserved trashing. Maybe a Porsche this time or a Lexus LX 570 like the one her mother's latest loser boyfriend drove. An oversize Cadillac Escalade caught her eye. There was no one else in sight. She waited until a car passed, leaving the garage; then she opened her knife and approached the SUV. Suddenly the elevator sounded, and a middle-aged woman stepped out holding her keys. Sofia quickly closed her knife and scrambled down the stairs.

She stood outside the parking structure, breathing heavily. It was too dangerous to keep doing this in garages. Across the street a homeless man stared walleyed at her as if he knew her secret. A few doors away a figure lay sprawled in a doorway covered by a filthy blanket. Everywhere she looked was pain and misery. The shrink had no meds to cure it. He wanted her to shift her gaze, take responsibility for her own unhappiness, as if she'd created the fucked-up world around her.

There was no point going back to see him. He had no good answers for the mess that adults had made of the world. She needed to find someone else to explain why people acted so selfishly and cruelly.

* * *

Morris sat at his computer working on a complicated late tax return involving schedules A through D and forms 1116, 6251, 4562, 8959, and 8960, with more to come. There was a satisfaction in the work, a comfort in its rigor. Immersing himself in the numbers, he could forget the deceits and evasions of his clients. Focus on the figures, add them up, calculate the percentages, mark them down, neat and precise. The numbers were a discipline, a practice that shut out the venality and corruption of the world, made it easier to live with himself and the frequent avarice of his clients.

Evie opened his door a crack. "There's a young girl here to see you, something about a research paper . . ."

Morris tried to look past her to see who was in the outer office of their suite.

"She says she met you at Starbucks."

"Yes . . . of course." He felt a flush of pleasure, instantly dampened by embarrassment at what Evie might think. "Yes, send her in." He stood to greet the girl.

"You didn't expect to see me again, did you?"

"I don't even know your name."

"It's Sofia." She slipped off her backpack, plopped down in the chair opposite his desk. Her T-shirt today declared "Apathy Kills." Morris wondered if she'd worn it especially for him.

"I want to know about tax policy," she said.

"Tax policy?" It seemed an unlikely reason for her visit.

"I have to write a paper for my poly sci class. It's supposed to be original research. Not Wikipedia. We've been talking about taxes in class, and I want to understand more about them."

"Like what?"

She looked around his office at the Sierra Club photos that lined his walls. "Like you care about the environment, right?"

"I do."

"So how come you're helping rich people destroy it?"

"What makes you think I am?"

"You help people avoid paying taxes, don't you? Isn't that your job, to help them get away with it?"

"No, that's not what I do," he said curtly. There were deductions he refused to defend, fraudulence he would not abide.

"It's just a question, Morris. I don't pay taxes. That's why I'm asking. You work for rich people. I thought you'd know their secrets and why they don't give a shit about any of the damage they do." She looked at him expectantly, as if he really understood greed and selfishness.

"I think the psychiatrist or psychologist you're seeing might have a better explanation."

"I'm not seeing him anymore."

"What happened?"

"He wasn't a very good listener."

"That's not a good quality for a shrink."

"No shit."

Morris looked out his half-opened door to see if Evie was listening. He considered closing the door, then thought better of it. "You really want to know about taxes?"

"I'm trying to understand why everything's so screwed up." She paused a second. "I don't know any other adults to ask."

Morris felt the tug of her appeal, even flattered that she'd turned to him for help, but also alarmed that she was asking him, a stranger she barely knew, to provide answers other adults had failed to give her. What truths could he offer when he was often unsure how much his clients were lying or hiding from him? The intricacies of the tax code hardly addressed the questions he sensed Sofia was asking. Stalling for time, he rummaged through the papers on his cluttered desk until he found a copy of the annual newsletter he sent his clients. "Here, this might help, a piece I wrote about the new changes in the tax law." He read the opening lines: "Whenever tax laws are rewritten, the effects are uneven. Some of you will see your taxes rise, others decrease significantly . . ."

"You mean all the billionaires and gazillionaires who run the country." Sofia took a notebook from her backpack and began to write.

* * *

Sofia's visits to Morris produced a paper on tax policy that even Sloan couldn't dismiss. Though she imagined he had to grit his teeth when grading her, he ended up giving her an A. "Excellent research," he wrote. "Happy to see such a thoughtful analysis of a complex subject. Wish you would share more of this in class!"

Pleased with her work, Sofia left the paper on the dining room table to prove she was doing better at school and no longer needed the pills; and also to postpone the inevitable fight when her mother discovered that she'd stopped seeing the shrink. To prevent the psychiatrist from calling, she'd sent him an email from her mother's computer firing him for failing to help her "very unhappy daughter." She knew eventually her mother would learn the truth—probably when the shrink failed to send his monthly bill—but by then maybe her grades would be good enough to demonstrate that she'd been cured.

Meanwhile, she continued to visit Morris at Starbucks on Wednesday afternoons. Their conversations cheered her. She took pleasure in castigating him for his failure to live according to his beliefs. "You say you believe in global warming, yet how does hanging Sierra Club photographs on the wall change anything?"

"I could say the same of defacing SUVs."

"It's a warning to climate deniers and polluters. You could join me, Morris. Be a Hayduke. Rebel."

"I'm afraid changing the world's a lot more complicated."

Her father had said something similar when he left them. "I don't expect you to understand this now. At your age life is black and white. When you get older, you'll see how gray it is."

She told Morris what she wished she'd said then to her father. "That's just a cop-out, an excuse for acting badly. It's *way* too complicated. People always say that when they know they're wrong."

"But life is complicated," he replied with a resignation that made her want to goad him even more.

"I think you're just afraid, Morris, afraid that if you really take a stand, you'll be a misfit like me."

He stared a moment at the cappuccino cradled in his hands, as if considering her accusation. He took a last sip of the coffee. "There's a price to pay whatever you choose." He brushed the crumbs of lemon cake from his shirt and rose abruptly. "I should go. I have work I need to finish."

Watching him leave, Sofia felt a hollow opening up inside her that she couldn't explain. No other adults would let her speak to them the way she did to Morris. She didn't know why he put up with her.

Her mother had her own suspicions. "Who's this accountant you interviewed for your paper?" she asked.

"You actually read it?"

"Of course. I'm interested in what you're learning. Where did you find this accountant?"

"At Starbucks."

"Did he approach you?"

"Yeah, we started talking."

"Sofia, you don't know anything about this man or his intentions."

"We just talk about the environment and tax policy."

"You're being naïve, Sofia. You're an extremely attractive young woman. You need to be careful with men you know nothing about. I don't want you to see him again."

Clarice was even blunter. "You having sex with him?" she asked one day as she walked Sofia to the bus stop after school.

"You sound like my mother."

"Well, how come you're seeing him instead of your shrink?"

"I like talking to him."

"He's probably just waiting to fuck you."

"He wears a pocket protector to hold his pens."

"If he's that careful, then he won't get you pregnant."

"You're sick," Sofia said.

She worried, though, that she might be missing something about him. Why had he walked her to the Metro that afternoon? Did he have motives she failed to perceive? Is that why he put up with all her taunts and insults? Could he be a perv as her mother or Clarice suspected? She didn't trust either of them very well when it came to men. But then she didn't trust her own judgment either. All adults confused her. Why did Morris prefer meeting at Starbucks instead of his office? She needed to see how he acted with other people, outside the coffee shop.

"My teacher was impressed by your comments in my paper," she told him the next time they met. "He's interested in your speaking to our class. You know so much about tax policy, and you explain it so clearly. It'll be a relief from our teacher, and I'll get extra credit for bringing you."

And a chance to see Morris with other people, a way to test her own faulty instincts.

* * *

Morris hesitated before accepting Sofia's invitation to speak at her exclusive prep school. Her description of her classmates—

"spoiled sluts and anorexic airheads"—didn't suggest an audience interested in the tax code. Still, it obviously mattered to her that he visit, that he see for himself why she felt so alone and miserable at school.

He never expected her to appear in his office and was surprised each week when she returned to rail against the destruction of the planet and chastise him for his failure to combat it. It was hard to defend himself against her accusations. He wasn't the person he wanted to be.

Evie had little patience for his regrets. She was twelve when her parents emigrated from Lithuania, and she immediately fell in love with the good life America promised. The U.S. offered so much more than she'd experienced growing up in Lithuania that she considered any qualms or misgivings he had as petty; so he kept them to himself and Sofia away from Evie.

"Who is this surly girl, and how did she end up on your doorstep?" Evie asked after Sofia's first visit.

"She was seeing a psychiatrist in the building."

"You're an E.A., not an M.D."

"I know the difference. She needed help with a school paper."

"How noble of you to come to her rescue. A pretty girl in a short skirt."

"Don't be ridiculous. I'd do the same if we had a daughter."

"Well, we don't, and she looks like a poor substitute to me." Her face tightened and she turned away.

He saw that he'd hurt her, but her imputation offended him. He was flattered that Sofia kept returning. The idea that their conversations might offer her some value pleased him.

"Exactly what do you want me to talk about to your class?" he asked.

"The truth, Morris. Not the usual crap our teachers feed us. Shake them up for a change. Make them think about something else besides boys and clothes."

"And what truth is that?"

"Fires are going to incinerate their Malibu estates, and the ocean is going to wash away their fancy beach houses."

"And how is that connected to taxes?"

"It's why they can afford their multi-million-dollar homes, isn't it? If they paid what they really should, we might still have a chance to save the planet."

"I don't think the world is coming to an end just yet."

"Maybe not your lifetime," she countered, "but certainly in mine."

Though he feared it might be a fool's errand, he finally agreed to visit her school, a small act of solidarity in her battle against apathy and authority. Pulling into the parking lot of the sprawling Spanish-style campus, he saw immediately why she felt in enemy territory. The lot was filled with the kind of expensive vehicles she targeted, BMWs and Audis and Range Rovers that had to be the students' cars. The only vacant space was a narrow slot between an adobe wall and a Porsche Cayenne, which left him barely enough room to fit his outdated BMW. The license plate on the SUV spelled RICHGRL.

Sofia was waiting for him by the side door with a friend she introduced as Clarice. "So you're the secret Sofia's been keeping," she said.

"He's not a secret."

"Not anymore, no." Clarice offered Morris her hand. "I'm glad she's finally found the courage to introduce you."

Sofia rolled her eyes. "Ignore her."

"Sometimes silence reveals more than lies," Clarice said.

"And sometimes you're so dumb," Sofia retorted.

She grabbed Morris's arm and led him through the Spanish-tiled halls to their classroom and introduced him to the teacher, an earnest young man who seemed to have balded prematurely. He took Morris aside. "I appreciate your coming. It's good of you to take such a strong interest in Sofia," he said, as if suspicious why Morris might aid such a rude and truculent girl. Then he retreated to a chair in the back. The wall behind him was lined with posters of women who had rebelled long before Sofia: Eleanor Roosevelt, Rosa Parks, Susan B. Anthony.

The teacher turned the class over to Sofia. "This is Morris Fishborne," she announced. "An expert on our screwed-up tax system. He was the source for my term paper, which you'll be amazed to hear, received an A. So he clearly deserves your attention."

Sixteen teenage girls turned their faces toward him.

"It's true our tax code is very complicated," Morris began. "And I certainly agree it's in need of reform. But I think it's important to understand how we reached this point and how our tax system has evolved over the years. It's often said that taxes are the price of civilization . . ." It was not the fiery warning that Sofia had urged, and the girls' attention quickly flagged. One stared out the window; another opened a book. Clarice seemed to be texting something on a cell phone in her lap. He quickly skipped from Andrew Mellon's theory of "scientific taxation" to the present.

A pony-tailed girl impatiently tapped a pencil on her desk. Unable to restrain herself, she flung her hand in the air. "My father says 48% of the people in this country don't pay taxes, so people like my parents pay way too much, and most of it's wasted."

"Yeah, that's what's so screwed up," another girl added. "It's high taxes that keep people from starting new companies and creating more jobs."

Morris saw Sofia scowl. "That's not what's screwed up, is it, Morris?" she said.

"No, Sofia's right." He was happy to come to her defense. "Economic growth can take place even when taxes are high. In fact, there's no real evidence that lower tax rates create more jobs."

"That's not what I meant," Sofia corrected.

Morris didn't understand.

"It's all screwed up because rich people don't pay their fair share."

"It's true, the present tax code is designed in their favor."

"Yeah, but they also cheat, don't they? They pay people like you to find ways to hide their money."

The girls swiveled in their seats to hear his answer.

It was a charge she'd made before, but never so publicly. "It's not a crime to use every legal means to minimize your taxes," he said.

"But you've said yourself, it's the rich and powerful who've rigged the tax code. If you work within a corrupt system, you're part of the problem. Admit it, Morris, you're an enabler. You help the rich keep the money they've gotten by screwing the poor."

His chest constricted and his stomach plummeted. "I don't file false returns. And I don't condone cheating," he said as evenly as he could. "I help people pay what they legitimately owe the government. That's what honest tax accountants do."

"Maybe you think it's legitimate to help the rich and greedy," she continued. "But I don't. I think it's really fucked up."

"Sofia!" Her teacher rose to intervene.

Morris waved him off. "No, let me answer." Was this the real reason she had brought him here? To humiliate him? "You want the truth, Sofia?" He gazed directly at her. "You can't make the world a better place by trashing it and other people. That's not how those women changed the world." He stabbed at the posters on the wall. "What you call rebellion is just destructiveness. It might feel good for a moment, but —and I think you know this—you still hurt the same the next day."

She flinched as she had that day she saw him standing at the elevator door. Not the truth she wanted, but what he should have said to her from the start. He scanned the room for the reaction of the other girls. Several were smiling, either at his or Sofia's distress. Their smugness infuriated him. What did any of them know about the compromises life exacted? He nodded toward the flustered teacher. "Thanks for inviting me. I hope it's been useful." He headed for the door before anyone could stop him.

He slammed out the building and squeezed into his car, choked with anger. Why had he ever believed he could make a difference in her troubled life? He'd tried to help her and this is how she'd repaid his generosity.

He jammed the car in reverse, stomped on the accelerator, and shot out of the parking space. CRUNCH! The rear of his car caught the bumper of the Porsche with a thump that shuddered through his body. He glanced back at the SUV's smashed fender and dented RICHGRL license plate. Fuck her for parking like that. Her Cayenne deserved the mutilation. But how unjust that he had to pay the price. When the IRS caught his clients' deceits, the clients always blamed him for the audit. Why did he put up with it? He unbuckled his seat belt and turned to open the door. Then he saw the parking lot was empty. Not a witness to report him. He hesitated. What point was honesty in a world of greed and selfishness?

* * *

Sofia didn't wait to hear Sloan berate her. She didn't need anyone to tell her she'd made a mistake in driving Morris away. She didn't know why she'd acted so meanly, but she knew she had to catch him before it was too late.

She reached the door to the parking lot just in time to see him decimate the Porsche. More damage than she'd ever gouged with her knife. She started to run toward him to celebrate the destruction, then saw him emerge from his car, jot something on a card and stick it on the windshield of the mangled car. "Oh, Morris, why waste such an opportunity when you're already halfway there?"

She dashed to the Porsche as he peeled out of the parking lot and quickly replaced his business card with one of her own handcrafted cards. It was the least she could do to make up for her meanness.

She wasn't sure what to expect when she invited him to

speak. But she saw now that whatever hopes she had for him were foolish. Morris would never be a Hayduke. Or a real ally. He was no different from any of the other adults who'd failed her. At least her father had left her a Swiss Army knife to remember him. She crumpled Morris's business card as she watched his BMW vanish around a corner knowing he was disappearing from her life forever.

Layover

"American Airlines flight 245 to Los Angeles has been delayed. It will now depart at 6:15."

"I wouldn't count on it," a female voice scoffed at the announcement.

Lionel looked up from the *New York Times* to locate the skeptic. Sitting in the row of seats across from him in the terminal was a young woman with short, dark hair and angular features that gave her a severe, forbidding appearance. She wore a black leather jacket over a black tank top, a purple micro skirt, and black mesh stockings, which called attention to her long, slender legs.

"Check the sky." She pointed. Teal nails matched her startlingly blue eyes. "If the plane doesn't get here in the next fifteen minutes, I bet they scrap it."

Lionel followed her gaze to the dense clouds darkening the airfield. He thought of all the patients he'd have to call to rearrange his crowded schedule if the flight were canceled. From the churning in his stomach, he knew his cortisol was rising.

Although he traveled frequently, Lionel hated flying. Every time he stepped on a plane there was a chance that the engines would fail, the plane plunge into the ocean, or suicidal terrorists would grab control and ram the jet into a skyscraper. He knew the improbability of such catastrophes, but as a psychiatrist, he also understood how feeble reason was to quash his fears. Long lines at security, overzealous TSA officers, the dread of an explosion 30,000 feet in the air, always triggered his anxiety. And now there was the added danger that the plane might have to take off in a thunderstorm.

The half Xanax he'd taken on the way to the Reagan National Airport wasn't going to be enough. He wheeled his suitcase over to a water fountain and swallowed the other half of the pill, which he'd been saving until he boarded.

When he returned to his seat, there was a new announcement: flight 245 would now depart at 7:30 p.m.

The micro-skirted woman shook her head. "They never tell you the truth until the last moment."

"So what's your guess?" he asked. "When do you think we'll leave?"

The gathering rain clouds were moving faster now than the workers on the airfield. "I think we're fucked," she declared.

Lionel picked up the *Times* again and waited for the Xanax to kick in. The woman retreated to her smart phone. From time to time, she looked up from whatever she was doing on the phone and caught him watching her. He quickly averted his eyes. Whether it was the unanticipated delay or the leggy woman, he found it difficult to concentrate.

His thoughts wandered, as they often did in airports, to past insults and affronts. The hundreds of passengers milling about en route from one destination to another led him to imagine bumping into people whom he rarely thought of otherwise— colleagues he'd argued with, women who'd spurned him in college and medical school, patients who'd left him. Maybe it was the sense of mortality that flying evoked that made him fantasize about meeting them again. Or maybe ruminating about old slights and injuries was a reaction to the benzodiazepine not noted in the literature—a possible subject to consider for further research. Whatever the cause, it was satisfying to think of encountering these doubters and detractors who'd long since vanished from his life. How surprised they'd be to see how badly they'd misjudged him, how assured and successful he'd become.

"So what brought you to D.C.?" the woman asked.

He put down the newspaper to see her staring directly at him with an expression he couldn't quite read.

"A medical conference," he said.

"You're a doctor?"

"A psychiatrist."

"A shrink." She nodded as if she suspected it all along.

"I prefer to think of myself as an expander." He used an old line. "I create possibilities for people, open the way to a richer life."

"You mean you give them drugs."

He couldn't tell if it was a question or an accusation. "Yes, I prescribe medications."

"Got anything with you now? I sure could use something."

For a second he thought she might be serious; then her lips widened into a grin that softened her features, made her more approachable than she first appeared.

"No drugs," he lied.

"Well, I guess I'll have to go to the bar then." She picked up her oversized silver purse. "Want to join me?"

Her offer caught him by surprise. She was at least thirty years younger than he, closer in age to his two teenage daughters. It seemed foolish to think she might be attracted to him. But his mouth was dry—a side effect of the Xanax—and conversation might make the tedious wait for boarding go faster.

"I suppose we have time," he said.

They wheeled their carry-on bags to the Jet Rock Bar and Grill, the nearest restaurant where they could sit. A hostess seated them and they formally introduced themselves. Lorraine lived in Hollywood and was returning now from a friend's wedding in Virginia.

"And what do you do?" Lionel asked.

"I'm an artist. Multimedia, video, installations . . . but right now I'm working as a waitress to make ends meet. I dropped out of Otis a year ago. Wasn't worth the debt I was racking up. The longer you stay in school, the more enslaved you are to the fucking banks."

Her vehemence made Lionel wonder if money was the real reason she'd dropped out of art school. "What kind of videos do you make?"

"Collages mainly. I collect images and combine them in unexpected ways. The piece I'm working on now mixes fashion, porno, and roadkill. Only you don't know it's roadkill at the start. The images are abstract, ambiguous, until the end when everything becomes clear."

Her description confirmed what he suspected. Easier to blame the banks than admit her own lack of talent. "Interesting," he said.

"It's much more than that!"

"I guess it's something you have to see."

"Not see, experience," she said emphatically.

The waitress arrived and they ordered drinks—Lorraine a Long Island iced tea, Lionel a Diet Coke.

"You don't drink?" she said.

A single malt was what he really craved, but benzodiazepine didn't mix well with alcohol. "Not when I fly."

"I doubt we're leaving tonight."

"Then I will need a stiff drink."

"You might as well start now," she advised.

Lionel didn't know if it was her brashness or naiveté or her mesh stockings that stirred him. Maybe it was just the disinhibiting effect of the Xanax.

"So you're a pill pusher," she said.

This time there was no mistaking the accusation. He'd heard the charge many times before; it always irritated him. "That's a gross mischaracterization of psychiatry. You seem more intelligent than that."

"So, Doctor, tell me why I'm so ignorant," she laughed.

He saw that she was mocking him; still, he felt a need to defend himself. Who was this art school dropout to question what he'd devoted so many years to mastering? Psychopharmacology was not the path he'd anticipated when he began his psychiatric residency at UCLA. That was before he spent three humiliating years in analysis—three times a week, forty-eight weeks a year—picking at the scabs of all his early wounds only to discover how many of them were self-inflicted. "Your parents may have caused your wounds, but they're not the ones who keep reopening them," his analyst constantly reminded him. Lionel realized something else during all those agonizing hours on the couch: he couldn't possibly spend the rest of his life listening to patients wallowing in the same kind of misery.

Fortunately, in the age of neuroscience, the "talking cure" was a relic of the past. Insight may have been the best tool available to Freud, but a century later, drugs were much faster and more effective. Everything he learned about brain biochemistry and neuroanatomy confirmed his belief that Freudians were mired in the dark ages. When he terminated his analysis—prematurely his analyst warned—he committed himself and his future to biological psychiatry. If Freud knew what today's neuroscientists did about the brain, Lionel was sure the Viennese doctor's view of life would have been much less gloomy.

Calmly and carefully, he explained to Lorraine the scientific principles on which he based his practice. Mental illness was fundamentally a biological problem, a real disease that required a medical solution. The mind didn't exist except as a property of the brain. To understand mental suffering, she needed to understand biochemistry and genetics and neuroscience. Neuroimaging had revolutionized the understanding of the brain and enabled psychiatrists, finally, to build a bridge from neurochemistry to behavior.

He continued as the waitress brought their drinks. The speech was one he often gave his patients, but Lorraine's facile description of psychopharmacology provoked him into unusual eloquence tonight.

She toyed with her glass as he spoke. "So what you're saying is that we're just a bunch of chemical interactions."

"That's a crude over-simplification," he said, dispirited by her response.

"But it's hard to believe that all my thoughts and feelings are just products of my biochemistry."

He tried another way to explain it. "Have you ever taken drugs?"

"Sure, I've dabbled. Who hasn't?"

"And what was the result?"

"Sometimes you see the world in a different way."

Lionel nodded as if she had proven his point.

"But it never lasts," she said. "You wake up the next morning and you're still as fucked up as the day before."

"Self-medication is usually a mistake."

"So, instead, I should entrust someone like you to prescribe pills that would make my life richer and happier?"

"Appropriately prescribed, yes. Look at what lithium has done for people who're bipolar, or antipsychotics for schizophrenics. If you're depressed, miserable, unable to get out of bed in the morning, altering your serotonin imbalance can certainly help."

"So just like that, you're ready to give me meds?"

"No, not just like that. I don't know enough about you to prescribe anything. I'd have to take a family history first, do a complete medical exam."

"You mean a physical?"

"Of course."

"That your way to get me naked?" she said brazenly.

Was she taunting or inviting him? Whatever her intentions, he felt a spark of sexual arousal. He reached for his Coke to defuse it.

"You're not my patient," he said. "If you're looking to see

someone, I can suggest several excellent psychiatrists in L.A."

"You really think I need a shrink?" Again she seemed amused. "Is that your considered professional opinion?"

"Not at all," he denied.

"Am I too forward for you? Do I say fuck too much?"

It wasn't the expletive that confused him. Although trained to uncover what words often disguised, Lionel wasn't sure what she was implying. Was she really signaling sexual interest?

A public address announcement saved him from having to decide. "All passengers on American Airlines flight 245 to Los Angeles, please report to Gate 32."

"Finally," he said with relief. He waved to the waitress for the check.

"We'll see," Lorraine cautioned.

As they walked back to the gate, Lionel saw that rain was now pelting the windows of the terminal. Disgruntled passengers crowded around the airline counter. The LED screen at the gate explained their anger. Flight 245 to Los Angeles had been canceled.

"I knew it," Lorraine said with a satisfaction hardly warranted by the cancellation. "We'd better go right to the service counter." She abruptly turned and wheeled her suitcase in the opposite direction. Lionel quickened his pace to keep up with her. From past experience he knew the stranded passengers on flight 245 would all be vying to get a seat on the first plane out of Reagan in the morning. A few were already on their phones dialing the airline to make new reservations. The scramble to reschedule, the uncertainty about tomorrow, roiled his stomach again.

To his surprise, Lorraine seemed strangely sanguine about the need to reschedule. "Where are you going to stay tonight?" she asked as they waited in line.

"I have no idea," he said, trying to control his agitation.

"Well, make sure they get a hotel reservation for you. Least they can do. When they cancel because of weather, they don't even give you a fucking voucher."

The agent called her next. "Good luck," he said.

She touched his arm lightly. "I'll wait for you."

The brush of her hand produced another erotic charge. Watching her at the counter, he imagined her without her skirt and stockings. The image of her bending over, naked, both excited and disquieted him. He wanted to be sure he wasn't misreading the situation. Professional success and recognition had made him more confident with women than he had been in his youth, but loyalty to his wife, or a still lingering timidity—he wasn't sure exactly which—kept him from seizing opportunities that women he met at conferences sometimes seemed to offer.

After several minutes, she turned and lifted her thumb in the air. She had secured a seat on a plane the next day.

"They have rooms at the Hilton in Alexandria," she said when he stepped to the ticket counter to take her place.

"I need to get on the first plane to Los Angeles tomorrow," he told the agent, whose graying temples marked him around the same age as Lionel. "And I need a room for tonight."

The man looked up from his computer to assess him. "The same hotel as your daughter?"

"We're not related." Lionel felt his cheeks flush.

"Then it doesn't matter which hotel?"

"No, no, I'd like the same hotel . . ." Lionel lowered his voice in embarrassment.

"Well, let's see if we can find you a room there." The agent picked up the phone and called the Hilton. "I'd like to book another room for tonight . . . If possible, the same floor as the young lady I just called about." He smiled at Lionel, clearly enjoying his unease.

Lionel avoided looking at the agent while he secured him a seat on a morning flight to L.A. "I hope you enjoy the hotel, Doctor." The agent smirked when he handed Lionel his new boarding pass.

Lorraine rose from the chair where she was waiting for him. "The Hilton?"

"You said that's where you were staying."

"Good, let's get a cab." She hooked an arm through his as if they had known each other for years. Lionel felt his pulse quickening at the contact.

Rain was still falling heavily as they joined the line waiting for a taxi. They huddled under the airport overhang to keep dry. Lorraine hunched her shoulders and shivered in the autumn chill, her short leather jacket flimsy protection against the damp. Pearls of water trickled down her cheek and neck. In the rain and gloom she seemed far more fragile than she had inside the terminal. What did he really know about her? What kind of woman picked up a stranger she'd just met at the airport? Was her boldness a mask for something else? He regretted that he hadn't asked her more about herself. If she'd come to him as a patient, he would certainly have asked more probing questions. The thought of his patients reminded him that he would have to cancel tomorrow's appointments once he got to the hotel. His wife would also be expecting him home tonight. He took out his cell phone and texted her that he'd be returning a day later. Then he turned the phone off.

Finally, they reached the head of the line and a cab slid to the curb in a spray of water. Rain spattered Lionel's pants and seeped into his shoes as they clambered inside the back seat of the taxi. Lorraine stared at the rivulets of rain streaking the side window as if they formed a pattern she could decipher. The steady thrum of the windshield wipers magnified the awkward silence between them.

The cab splashed through a large pool of water in the street. "I hate the fucking rain," she said. "Rain doesn't wash away anyone's sins, does it?"

Lionel didn't know how to respond.

"Do you even believe in sin?" she said pointedly. "Isn't it all just chemical interaction to you?"

Her sudden shift in mood startled him. "I don't understand. What does rain have to do with sin?"

She looked at him a moment, then laughed suddenly. "That's a shrink question, isn't it?" She reached across her shiny silver purse and squeezed his hand. "Oh, Lionel, don't try to figure me out. I'm not a patient."

He held her hand a moment and squeezed back. He wasn't sure what she wanted from him. She was sending contradictory messages to his brain and to his groin.

The taxi pulled up to the hotel, and the driver flipped open the trunk. Lorraine grabbed her bag and wheeled it inside while Lionel paid the fare and considered what to do next. Should he offer to share a room with her or was that too forward, as she might say? Too crass? He had little prior experience to guide him.

Lorraine was waiting just inside the entrance, looking impatient. Still, he hesitated, afraid to make a fool of himself. Seeing his indecision, she took his arm and leaned close to him. "I'm sorry to have to ask," she said in a voice barely above a whisper, "but I'm really strapped. My credit card's maxed out and all I have with me is $25. Since the airlines don't give vouchers . . ." She gazed at him with her azure eyes.

"You want me to pay for your room?" He felt a flash of anger at his own stupidity. So this was why she'd been leading him on.

"I was thinking more like we could share a room . . . if that's not too much trouble . . . I don't want to be a problem for you."

The desk clerk looked at them expectantly, waiting for their decision. Lionel didn't know whether it was her mixed signals or the lingering effects of the Xanax, but his brain felt like cotton and he was unable to think. A single room seemed the easiest choice. To avoid any misunderstanding, he asked for double beds loudly enough for Lorraine and anyone else in the lobby to hear.

They rode the elevator to the fifth floor in silence. Lionel felt his stomach tighten as they rose. Coming to the same hotel with her had been a mistake, a lapse of judgment he would not compound. He opened the door to their room and turned on the lights. "Pick your bed," he said. "I'm going to wash and go to sleep. I asked the desk clerk for a wake up call at six tomorrow." He untied his soggy shoes and headed for the bathroom.

Staring at himself in the mirror, he saw what an easy mark he was: a middle-aged man with a neatly trimmed beard, colored to hide the growing gray; an expensive Italian shirt and designer glasses to compensate for his homeliness; and a woeful lack of skill with women. What a vulnerable target for a long-legged girl in a micro skirt. He had made a fool of himself, after all. Now he had to decide how to retain some dignity when he returned to the bedroom.

Lorraine was stretched out on the bed by the window, hands behind her head, leaning back against the pillows as he emerged from the bathroom. For a second he imagined her lying there without her clothes. He blinked to dispel the image.

"The bathroom's yours," he said, hoping she would use it now so he could strip to his boxer shorts and slip between the sheets.

"Thanks." She made no effort to move.

He sat down on the far side of the other bed and took off his damp socks. "It's been a long day and we have to get up early tomorrow."

"I know, but it's hard for me to fall asleep in a new place. You have anything that could help?"

"You mean sleeping pills?"

"Whatever."

Her beliefs were as labile as her emotions. "I thought you didn't like drugs," he said.

She turned on her side and propped her body on her elbow to face him. "I'm not looking to change my life, just for a good night's sleep. Don't you have anything in that psychiatric bag of yours that could do the trick?"

Lionel had the Xanax and some Rozerem and a few other drug company samples in his shoulder bag. Rozerem was designed specifically for people who had difficulty falling asleep. If one pill could make her drowsy, it would be easier for him as well.

Lionel went to the desk, searched through his bag, and brought the Rozerem over to her. "This should help," he said.

She took the pill and examined it. "Aren't you going to ask me any questions first? Allergies? Other drugs I might be taking?"

"This is a commonly prescribed sleep medication. It's safe, non-addictive."

"How can I be sure? You said you always took a medical history before you prescribed anything, but you haven't asked me any questions."

He didn't know whether she was mocking him again. "Is there something I should know?"

"If you asked more questions, maybe you'd find out," she said coyly. She patted the bed in a gesture for him to sit.

Lionel resisted the temptation. "If you take this now, in a half hour you can be asleep."

She looked at the capsule again and placed it on the night table on the other side of her bed. "It's hot in here, isn't it?" She suddenly pulled off her tank top, exposing a black sheer lace bra that barely concealed her breasts.

Lionel drew a sharp breath. She was offering herself after all.

"That's better. Now where were we?" She patted the bed beside her again. This time he sat. Her wet hair gave off an herbal scent, which mixed with the faint odor of sweat. He wasn't sure if it was hers or his.

"Okay, ask me anything you want now," she said.

"Is there something you want to tell me?"

"Well, aren't you curious why I'm so attracted to older men?"

"Tell me." He reached over, running his fingertips lightly down her arm.

She shivered at his touch and pulled away. "There's too much light in here." She shaded her eyes with her hand.

Lionel rose and turned off the lights in the room, switched on one in the bathroom, and closed the door halfway. When he turned back, he saw she was lying naked on the bed, her lanky torso all that was visible in the reflected light. He had examined countless women in his years as a doctor, but the sight of a lovely female body never failed to move him. With her slender, boyish figure and shaved pubis, Lorraine looked more like an innocent schoolgirl than the mercurial seductress who had enticed him to the hotel. Still, the gift she was presenting was one he could hardly refuse.

"I'd feel more comfortable if I wasn't the only one without clothes here," she said.

He fumbled with the buttons on the shirt he'd bought in Milan, glad that the light was dim enough to hide his underdeveloped chest and flabby belly. He couldn't quite make out her face in the shadows; her long legs and the flare of her hips dried his throat, making his breath come faster. He dropped his pants to the floor and then his shorts. She slid over to make room for him on the bed. Despite the Xanax, he was so aroused he was ready to part her legs and enter her. But she turned on her side, offering only her back.

He tentatively ran his hand down her spine and over her buttocks. She lay there, inert but unresisting. He continued to caress her body, growing more and more excited as he kneaded her hips and ass until he finally slipped his hand between her thighs and felt her wetness. She turned, reached for his cock, and started stroking it. The move was so unexpected, her fingers so insistent, that he was unable to stop himself and he came shuddering in her hand. He fell back against the pillow, ashamed.

Lorraine bolted upright, smeared her hand across the sheets and reached underneath her pillow. Suddenly, a light exploded in his face, blinding him. She raised her hand, and the flash went off again. He tumbled off the bed, instinctively covering himself with his hand. "What the hell are you doing?" he shouted.

"Collecting images." The light flashed again.

He tried to grab the cell phone, but she quickly leaped to the other side of the bed. They stood there naked, breathing heavily, the bed between them. His whole body clenched with fury. He lunged for the phone again, sprawling ludicrously across the bed. He rose unsteadily. "Give me the phone," he seethed.

Lorraine backed up against the wall and rapidly twirled her thumbs over the phone. "Too late! It's in the cloud now."

Everything about him shriveled. "Why are you doing this?" he groaned.

"For my collages."

He tried to make sense of what was happening, but all the synapses in his brain seemed to be misfiring. He slumped backward onto the other bed and closed his eyes to steady himself. Lights and colors whirled around his head. When he opened his eyes again, she was still standing against the wall, brandishing the phone like a gun.

"I wish I had this when I was a kid."

He fumbled for his shorts in the dark, dazed, uncomprehending.

"Maybe that would've stopped my father from creeping into my bed at night."

Lionel's throat constricted, and he felt a wave of nausea.

"Your father molested you?"

"I was ten, ten when he started. He went to a shrink like you to stop. But it didn't help."

The queasiness in Lionel's stomach rose to his throat. "I'm so sorry," he said.

"Sorry! That's all you can say?" She grabbed the Rozerem on the night table and threw it at him. "I hated him for it. Hated him. Fathers aren't supposed to do that to their little girls."

He had a sudden image of a little girl lying in her room

at night, alone and frightened, as she waited for her father to sneak into her bed. Now here he was, another man who couldn't control his lust, as weak and hateful as the father who'd defiled her.

"I didn't realize . . . I thought . . ." he stammered.

"What? You thought what? That I wanted you? Even my father didn't believe that. He knew it was wrong, but he couldn't stop. Finally, he couldn't live with himself any longer. I came home from school one day and found him hanging in my closet. Do you have pills for that, Doctor?" She sank to the bed and turned away, her shoulders heaving.

Lionel watched her sob, as he watched so many of his patients, mute, tongue-tied, unable to relieve their pain. He felt a desire to reach across the bed, place a consoling hand on her bare shoulder; still he hesitated, fearing her reaction. As if sensing his intention, Lorraine curled her body into a fetal position and pulled the covers over her head.

He gathered up his clothes and quickly dressed. He couldn't spend another minute in that hotel room. Slipping into his wet shoes, he picked up his suitcase and shoulder bag and moved quietly to the door, afraid Lorraine might spring up again to photograph him. But she'd accomplished what she wanted and remained buried with her cell phone underneath the quilt.

He wheeled his suitcase down the empty corridor and waited for the elevator.

There was no point in getting another room. He carried no pill strong enough to let him sleep that night. His mind raced from one image of disaster to another—his wife or daughters or a patient walking into an art gallery and seeing his naked portrait splattered on the wall like roadkill.

A man was still tending the bar in the lobby when he entered. Lionel ordered a double scotch and downed it. Numbness was worth risking the nausea that mixing alcohol and Xanax could bring. Better to lacerate his stomach than think about all the mistakes and failures that led him to the hotel that night. He remembered something he read once—"without a wound, there is no artist." He'd failed to perceive Lorraine's wound; he'd probably misjudged her talent as well. Her collages were just the kind of work to gain notoriety in a world that craved sensation. He couldn't let that happen. He couldn't let her transform his humiliation into art. Her art might be her therapy, but he wasn't her therapist, and he wasn't about to let her pain ruin everything he'd worked so hard to build. Whatever figure she named, he'd pay to destroy those photos. The cost couldn't be higher than what he already paid that night.

The Mink Coat

In the winter of 1970, a few months after I moved from Boston to Montreal, my mother sent me her prized mink coat. It arrived, without warning, by insured mail in a plain brown box. The classic, full length, mahogany mink with ruffled collar and cuffs was carefully wrapped in a cloth garment bag that bore the faint smell of my mother's cedar closet. Along with the coat, a cryptic note: "Know I'm thinking about you. Mom."

My mother and I had spoken only once since I'd moved to Canada to marry my college boyfriend. A day before his induction, Terry had fled in protest against dying uselessly in Vietnam in a war we both considered immoral. My father had fought in Guadalcanal during World War II and thought Terry a coward and a traitor. Better he should be in prison than living free in Canada. I deserved the same fate for marrying him. He forbade my mother to talk to me.

Although my mother generally deferred to my father, occasionally—though often surreptitiously—she defied him. I gave her our Rue de Bullion apartment address and phone number, hoping my willingness to stand up to my father would encourage her to do the same. One night shortly before Thanksgiving, she telephoned, a slurred call from what sounded like a restaurant or bar, as if a few drinks had given her courage or recklessness to dial my number. Was it much colder there than Boston? she asked. Was I keeping warm?

I assured her I was fine.

"And what about the Quebeckers? Is their French as bad as people say?"

"It sounds a little like mine when I've drunk too much."

"You shouldn't follow my example."

"It was a joke, Mom . . ."

There was silence on the other end of the line.

"Is he treating you all right?" she finally asked. It was difficult for her to even say Terry's name.

"Why wouldn't he?"

"I just want you to be happy, Brenda."

I didn't answer.

"Well, I should get back to your father." She ended her brief rebellion.

The mink arrived a few weeks later.

I knew the coat held a privileged place in my mother's wardrobe because she wore it only on those rare nights when my parents dressed in evening clothes, or when my father wanted to impress insurance clients. As a child, I loved to watch her as she carefully "put on her party face" for these engagements. When she took pains with her appearance, she appeared especially glamorous.

Photographs of her before her marriage show a slender woman, with pale-blue eyes and a smile that could be either shy or coquettish. After three pregnancies—two of them miscarriages—her face and figure had coarsened some, but she could still turn heads when she entered a room. The mink helped. It wasn't Blackglama—too expensive even for my father—but the finely tailored, knee-length coat provided a Lauren Bacall haughtiness missing from her life as suburban housewife and mother. In her pale-blue evening gown that matched her eyes, diamond pendants dangling from her ears, and the fur draped casually over her shoulders, she seemed a different person from the mute, distracted woman I'd often find at the kitchen table, restlessly smoking and playing solitaire.

Each April, in a spring ritual as regular as Easter, she would send the mink back to the furrier to be cleaned, glazed, and stored until reclaimed for the company's annual New Year's Eve party. The coat transformed her into a mysterious and inaccessible woman I barely recognized. Now she'd given me the most elegant possession in her life. The gift both touched and puzzled me.

I tried it on and looked at myself in the mirror. The mink flattened my hips as it had my mother's, made my frayed jeans look hip, stylish. The fur was luscious, velvety despite its years. Its warmth took the chill off our drafty second-floor apartment.

When Terry returned home that night from his bookstore job, I was wearing the mink.

He stepped back from my embrace as if the coat was toxic. "Where did you get that?"

"My mother sent it."

"It figures. It's obscene."

"I thought you liked obscenity." I opened the coat to reveal that I was wearing nothing underneath.

He put a hand in front of his face as if to block my nakedness. "Do you know how many animals they have to kill to make a coat like that? Sixty? Seventy? They spend all their lives crammed into these tiny, filthy cages. They go nuts, start cannibalizing each other."

"I didn't buy it. It's a gift."

"So what. It's like the war. You support it, you have blood on your hands."

"Not everything is Vietnam. Do I call you a murderer because you wear leather boots?"

"Send it back! It's disgusting."

I flung the coat at him and retreated to the bathroom, slamming the door behind me. A crack in the frosted window made the bathroom the coldest room in our apartment. I shivered on the toilet seat until I could bear it no longer. When I emerged, Terry had hung the coat in the closet. "I'm sorry," he apologized, handing me his flannel nightshirt. "I have a problem with anything to do with your parents."

"At least my mother's making an effort."

"What? To bribe you to come home?"

I threw his nightshirt back and pulled a blanket from the bed to cover myself. "You think the worst of everyone. In case you haven't noticed, it's really cold here."

"Well, you don't have to be a fucking martyr. Turn up the heat!"

Whether rebellion against Terry or loyalty to my mother, I kept the coat, my badge of defiance. It was also the warmest garment I owned. I wore it, though, only when I went out alone. In a city whose language I never spoke fluently, and where I always felt out of place, the mink was a protective covering that helped me blend in with the fashionable Quebecois shop girls in their faux furs and miniskirts. I knew I should feel sorry for the dozens of hapless minks who'd died for my comfort, but I felt no collective guilt for their murder, no shame for wearing a coat I hadn't bought myself. You can only protest so many things at once, and fur coats didn't top my list.

* * *

The 1973 Paris Peace Accords stopped the fighting in Vietnam and American troops began coming home. Six months later Terry and I officially dissolved our marriage. With the war and draft ended, we no longer shared a cause strong enough to bridge our differences. Terry stayed in Canada to work with U.S. military deserters, and I moved to Chicago. Northwestern offered a scholarship to graduate school in psychology and I eagerly grabbed it—a ticket back to the United States that bypassed Boston and a chance to explore why I'd made such a mistake in marrying Terry.

I packed my Friedan and Millett and de Beauvoir, my bell bottoms and tie dyes, and the mink, and left everything else behind. Like my mother, I'd stored and cleaned the coat at a furrier each April and reclaimed it in November. Although the fur was not quite as supple as before, reglazed it still retained its luxuriant sheen, its aura of glamor. I felt bolder, freer somehow whenever I wore it.

Terry would have hated Chicago, railed at its hypocrisy and political corruption, but I fell in love with the city almost from the start. Unlike Montreal, divided by class and language and ideology, Chicago was a place where contradictions were more easily tolerated, where rich and progressive weren't viewed as antithetical, where you could wear expensive Italian boots and still rail against capitalism. Here my mink evoked admiration, not scorn. I was wearing it when I first met Bryan.

It was a frigid January night; wind stung my face and eyes as it whipped across the lake. I was trying to hail a cab in front of a North Shore apartment building after leaving a party of graduate students where I'd drunk too much and insulted too many earnest men who reminded me of Terry. Cold had emptied the streets and the few taxis that passed were all occupied.

Bryan emerged from the building, hatless and gloveless, in a black overcoat with a sable collar. He was in his late thirties, with the self-assurance of a man who enjoyed striding bare-headed into the wind.

He looked me over. "You waiting for someone?"

"A taxi."

He shook his head at my grim prospects. "Fortunately, you've got a great coat to keep you warm." He reached out and ran his hand lightly over my sleeve. "Did you know minks make love for six hours at a time?"

"Don't they get bored?"

"I wouldn't."

"Is that a boast or a dare?"

He looked at me again. "Where are you going?"

I told him.

"My car's just down the block," he said. "Let me drive you."

On the way to his car, we stopped for a drink at the James Hotel, and then another, and, in the end, took a room for the night. Though he wore no ring, I probably knew that he was married. I didn't care. I wanted to be desired again, not judged, swept away rather than measured. He made love to me in my mink and although he could not live up to his claims, he made me feel beautiful, alive.

In the morning he told me about his wife, who was in New York that weekend with their two young children, visiting her parents. He said he no longer loved her; even if he had told me otherwise, I would have seen him again.

We continued meeting, in my apartment, at night in his law office, and over heady weekends in New York, San Francisco, once even Paris, where his international law firm sent him. When we were together, I wore my coat as often as the weather warranted, flaunting it, as he flaunted me, his decade-younger mistress, elegant or vulgar depending on your taste. In my mink and French lingerie he bought me, I felt alluring, not tawdry, a woman of the world, with secrets, mysteries. Weeks when he was occupied with work or family, I worried that he was using me, that there was no future in our relationship, but I loved his extravagance, his romantic recklessness, so different from my father, his ease and sophistication in the world, so different from Terry. I saw in him what I wanted and ignored the rest.

* * *

At the beginning of April 1976, my father called from Boston. It was the first time we'd spoken in years, but his peremptory tone hadn't changed. "Your mother's ill. You need to come home."

For my father to call, it had to be grave. The diagnosis was esophageal cancer. Doctors were treating it aggressively, but they'd caught it late. I didn't ask the prognosis.

Although my mother and I now talked a few times a month on the phone, I hadn't seen her since I left Boston. President Carter pardoned draft dodgers the day after his inauguration, but my father still hadn't forgiven me. My mother relayed his view: "They broke the law and betrayed the country. As far as I'm concerned, they can all rot in hell."

I flew, unannounced, to Boston and took a taxi to our house in Newton. The front door key was still hidden on the ledge, and I let myself in the house. Mother was alone in the backyard, lying in a lawn chair, covered with a blanket even in the warm spring air. She was thinner than I'd ever seen her, thinner than the pictures of her in her youth. Her pinched face was capped by a black turban to hide the wasteland chemotherapy had made of her hair. When she reached to embrace me, her papery arms were as gaunt as the branches of the still-bare trees.

"Your father tried to get me to quit smoking for years," she said. "I guess I should have listened." One of her small mutinies against him.

I told her she could beat the cancer.

But she already knew the truth. "I can see the doctors' faces. I'm a lost cause."

"I don't believe that, Mom."

"You sound like your father. You two are more alike than you think."

"You can fight this. You can't give up." I tried to sound more confident than I felt.

"At least it's brought you home again. I'm happy for that." She looked me over with her restless eyes, the only familiar feature in her wan face. "It hasn't been easy for you, has it?"

"I'm doing fine."

"That man you're seeing, how's that going?"

"Fine," I said again.

"He's married, isn't he?"

Somehow she'd managed to detect that even on the phone.

"I suppose he's promising to leave his wife."

"As a matter of fact . . ." I started to explain.

She cut me off. "You know they never do."

"You learn that from soap operas?"

"We all make our own mistakes. I'd hate to see you keep repeating them."

I wanted to lash back—Bryan wasn't at all like Terry—but she shivered and pulled the blanket up around her shoulders. Stricken by her frailty, I knelt and took her hand. Its coldness chilled me. I thought how the mink could have warmed her. "When I was in Montreal, why did you send me your coat?" I asked.

"Do you still have it?"

"Of course."

She looked pleased. "I hope you're storing it during the summers."

"Just like you did. But I still don't understand why you gave it to me. You had more reasons and places to wear it."

She paused before she answered. "I thought you needed a good winter coat, and I wasn't sure you could afford one."

"It was more than a winter coat. It was the nicest thing you owned."

"It was a wedding present. If you'd had a proper wedding, I would've bought the bridal gown. I wanted to give you something that would mean as much."

It struck me again what it must have cost her to give away my father's most expensive gift to the daughter he'd disavowed. My own rebellion had cost much less. I'd discarded Terry, but she still lived with my father. I squeezed her hand and kissed her chilled cheek. "Has he forgiven you for sending me the coat?" I asked.

"I never told him."

I wanted to ask why she'd married such an unforgiving man, but like my mother, I found it easier to avoid the question. Besides, I told myself, she needed to think about the future, not the past. I'd come home to bolster her spirits, not darken them with regrets. So I did what I often do when I feel emotions building that I can't control: I cooked. Chopping, peeling, measuring helped to focus my attention elsewhere. My mother sat at the kitchen table watching me, as I'd watched her when I was a child, offering occasional instructions for dishes she could no longer eat. Despite her loss of appetite—or maybe because of it—I filled the refrigerator with familiar soups and casseroles, as if her old Good Housekeeping recipes might restore a time when we were closer and make up for the lost years between us.

My father ate the food I cooked for dinner and helped clean up afterwards. Otherwise we avoided each other. I didn't even know if his summons home had been his idea or my mother's. The first night, when he returned to the den after seeing my mother to bed, I asked him. "Why did you wait so long to tell me she had cancer?"

"This has been hard enough for her. She needs all her strength to fight this."

"You thought I'd make her worse?"

"Six years. It's been six years since you ran off. Where have you been all that time?"

"Exactly where you wanted me. In exile."

"You know how much grief you've caused your mother . . ." He swallowed whatever words were rising in his throat. "We're going to get through this. We will. All of us."

I didn't argue or contest his view of the past or future. Denial was the default coping mechanism of our family, and we quickly lapsed into familiar silences. After three days I could bear them no longer. Pleading obligations at school, I booked a flight back to Chicago, promising to return within a few weeks.

My father was as relieved as I that I was leaving. The divide between us made it even harder to accept the imminent loss of the one person who bound us together.

* * *

Shuttling between Chicago and Boston, I stopped working on my thesis. I could no longer focus on reasons middle-class girls became delinquents. I told Bryan I needed to know where we stood.

He was understanding, supportive—he had lost his own father two years before—but he appealed for more time. He was a good lawyer and his arguments always sounded reasonable. It was the wrong moment for either of us to make such a big change. He was fighting a political battle for control of his law firm, and because of tension with his wife, his son was acting out at school. I should focus on my mother and my dissertation, while he would work to resolve his office and family problems. Then we could be together.

I wanted to believe him, so I agreed to wait a little longer. Between my trips to Boston, and the stress of his work and family, we didn't see each other as often as before. And, when we did, I was no longer the uninhibited mistress who met him in his office late at night, without underwear, or unzipped his pants again as he drove me home in his Corvette.

One night, after we hadn't seen each other for almost two weeks, he agreed to dinner at my apartment before returning home—a rare occurrence now. Needing a distraction, and wanting to please him, I spent the afternoon cooking, trying Julia Child recipes I had never made before. He arrived over an hour late, ruining all my careful preparation. The spinach soufflé had fallen, and I feared the *poulet* à la *diable* was overcooked.

He put his arms around me as he apologized and slipped his hands underneath my blouse.

I pulled away, wanting to get to the table.

"We can heat the food up later," he said.

The ease with which he dismissed my hours of work irritated me. "No, everything's past done."

He wasn't interested in the menu and pulled me back. "What happened to that sexy girl in mink I met three years ago?"

"She's been standing at the stove all day cooking for you." I tried to extricate myself from his grasp.

"You know the two most overrated things about marriage?" He grinned. "The other is home cooking."

I hit him in the chest with my fist. And then slugged him harder before he pushed me away. "You should go. Now."

He glared at me with an expression I'd never seen before—a fury that must have mirrored my own, or maybe it was just recognition of a truth we'd both been refusing to accept. "You want more than I can give right now," he said.

Terry had said much the same when I told him I was leaving. The pain was just as sharp. Bryan turned without another word and walked out of the apartment. The click as the door latched was louder than I'd ever noticed before.

Would I have relented if he called the next day, or the day after, or even the week after that and pleaded for another chance? Perhaps. But the call never came.

* * *

Mother died a few weeks later. She took her last breaths while I was still in the air circling over Logan airport. It wouldn't have mattered if I had been at her bedside. I had flown back to Boston several times during those last months, but we never spoke more openly than the first day I'd returned, either about my mistakes or hers. On one of my final visits to the hospital, she mentioned a suitcase that she was leaving for me in her closet. "Promise you won't open it until I die," she said. She struggled to sit up to make her point. "After you've gone through it, burn everything!" I promised to honor her request. Whatever secrets the suitcase contained, neither of us had the courage to face them while she was still alive.

Her funeral was a bleak, dry-eyed affair. A modest number came to pay their respects—neighbors, acquaintances, colleagues of my father. It was all decorous and proper. "As your mother would have wanted it," my father said, as usual attributing his own desires to her.

I found it hard to measure the depth of his grief. Maybe all these last months he had been preparing himself, or maybe my parents had lived such separate lives for so many years that her actual loss made little difference. Guadalcanal had taught him to cut his losses and move on. He was as incapable of talking about my mother's death as he was the war. Two days after the funeral, he went back to his office to work. His absence gave me a chance to open her last gift.

I found the worn canvas suitcase hidden behind a stack of shoeboxes in her cedar closet. Inside was a carefully preserved scrapbook of my mother's life, neatly sorted stacks of letters, cards, and yellowed newspaper clippings, all tied together by different colored ribbons. According to the newspaper accounts she'd saved — their wedding photo, a picture of my father in military uniform, an article about my mother's fund-raising activities for the local library, a story about a golf tournament my father won—my parents were a prosperous, civic-minded, American couple. Greeting cards confirmed the public record—a proper sentiment for every occasion—birthdays, anniversaries, Valentine's Day, Mother's Day, including all the hand-made cards I was forced to make at school. She'd dutifully saved them all, as if throwing them away might have exposed their fraudulence.

The letters told a different story. My mother's youthful beauty had attracted many men. She had been admired, desired, pursued. "I dreamed of you last night, your eyes as blue as the sky . . ." "I can't stop thinking about you and the fleeting touch of your lips on mine. Why did you run away?" "If you gave me a chance, I'd make you the happiest woman in the world." "Your braking my heart," another wrote in touching misspelled prose. "Why are you so mean to me?" Although she'd flirted with many, she seemed to have denied her favors to all.

Somehow, meeting my father had changed all that. Why

she'd fallen in love with him was impossible to tell from the letters in the suitcase. They had met while he was in basic training, shortly before he shipped out to the Pacific. The only letters from him she'd saved were ones he wrote during the war. Many had portions blacked out by military censors. Others were constrained by my father's reticence. "I think of you so much, but I never seem to be able to put my thoughts on paper." "So much has happened, and it is still forbidden to tell all that it makes letter writing very difficult." Even in his stiff prose, though, my father's feelings were clear. "I think of you constantly. You are what keeps me going through all this mess." "I have seen all I want here. All I want is to see you again." That was as much passion as my father allowed himself to express. But perhaps his reticence was a perfect fit for her own remoteness. "Your heart is as cold as ice," one of her early admirers had written her.

Whatever my parents had sensed in each other in their first meetings seemed to have been reinforced by their correspondence during the war. Soon after my father returned from the army, they married—the censored letters and Hallmark greeting cards the only record of their attachment.

At the very bottom of the suitcase was a large pack of letters she had written to her older sister Bea, who lived in San Francisco with another woman. My father didn't approve of my lesbian aunt, so she and my mother didn't see each other often. I didn't know my aunt well because she died when I was ten, but she was evidently the one person my mother could confide in. My mother must have found the letters after Bea's death and kept them to document the full story of her life.

The letters were hard to read—the handwriting often illegible, the ink blurred with time and maybe tears. "Long, empty days. Stan working late again. Brenda busy with her friends and me alone as usual . . ." The discontent and entrapment she felt were often more implied than stated, as if she were reluctant to admit her feelings even to herself. "Drank too much sherry and burned dinner tonight. Stan late at work anyway. Brenda content with macaroni."

Finally, she could no longer ignore or deny her suspicions of my father's infidelity. In a letter written when I was in third grade, she reported to my aunt irrefutable evidence of a long-running affair my father was conducting with an office secretary. Several phone calls must have followed, for in the next letter, she wrote: "Took your advice and spoke to Stan. He's agreed to end it, swears he will never see her again. Can I believe him?"

Three days later, she wrote again: "Today he brought home a mink coat as an apology. As if that makes up for all his lies. I can't bear to put it on. Wonder if it was really meant for me."

Then another scribbled note, dated two days later. "This morning I made my decision. Better to keep the family together. Am I making a terrible mistake?"

There was no record of my aunt's reply. Maybe my aunt didn't support her decision, or maybe in deciding to remain married, my mother felt she had abrogated her right to complain, for her letters to my aunt ended shortly afterwards. Still, she saved them for me, wanting me to know the truth at last. The letters, like her wedding present of the coat, were her final revolt against my father.

When I finished going through the suitcase, I burned all its contents in the fireplace, as she had wished, turning all her pain to ashes.

All the next day I tried to think what I could say to my father. Wasn't that the reason she'd saved the letters all these years? So I could speak in her place, say what she'd been unable to. Or were the letters just meant for me, a cautionary tale about marriage and men, delivered too late? Or was this her way of forgiving me for my own mistakes?

The morning I was to leave, my father offered to drive me to the airport. It was the chance I'd been waiting for, yet in the car I still didn't know what to say.

"What now?" he broke the palpable tension between us. I

wasn't sure if he was asking himself or me.

"I read her letters to Bea," I blurted out. "She wanted me to know how badly you hurt her. She saved those letters so I would know." I was trembling as I said it.

He kept his eyes fixed on the road. "I loved your mother," he said quietly.

"Then why did you see other women?" I lashed out. "There were other women, weren't there?"

His silence confirmed it. "You don't understand . . ." he started, then fell silent again.

"What? What don't I understand?" Yet even as I asked, I think I knew. We all make choices that fit our needs, I no more than my parents.

"Despite what you may think, we had a good life together," he finally said.

"You . . . *you* had a good life, but she deserved more."

He lifted one hand from the steering wheel as if to ward off the accusation, but then dabbed at his eyes instead.

At the airport, he got out of the car. "Will you come back?" he asked as he handed me my bag. The catch in his voice caught me by surprise. Sorrow deepened lines in his face, eroding its stoniness.

My mother had been willing to accept his contrition and confine her regrets and injuries to a suitcase in her closet, but forgiveness was as difficult for me as it was for my father. "I don't know," was all that I could say.

* * *

I didn't reclaim my mother's coat from the furrier until the middle of November. A few days later, on a crisp fall day, I put it on to join six other fur-clad women in front of a window display of mink coats at Marshall Field's, two blocks from Bryan's law offices in the Loop.

At a given signal, we shed our coats and picked up huge

hand-lettered signs to cover our nakedness. "I'd rather go naked than wear fur," one poster proclaimed. Another asked: "Would You Wear Your Dog?" Mine read: "Stop the Pain!"

A crowd of bystanders gathered, a few to cheer our sentiments, others to try to glimpse the nudity behind our placards. Newspaper photographers clicked away. Television cameras rolled.

Despite the sun, you could feel the start of winter in the air, a perfect time to give our coats away to the homeless. Terry no doubt would have felt vindicated to see that I finally recognized the immorality of the coat. Even Bryan might have appreciated the flamboyance of the gesture.

But it wasn't the poor minks I was thinking of liberating as I posed for the cameras in the chill autumn air. I only wish my mother could have been there to cheer me.

The Cactus

Cary noticed the *Echinopsis* the first week he began jogging through Beverly Hills. It caught his eye because he had grown several of the same variety. The cacti had flowered, and so had his fortunes. Then Margo left and took them with her, confirmation that his luck had run out once more.

He'd bought the cacti for the balcony of his second-floor apartment to celebrate the start of a new career in stunt work. A month later he met Margo, a life coach with a growing list of entertainment wannabes. They were both rising, behind-the-scene players in Hollywood, working to sustain the fantasies of moviegoers and the dreams of hopefuls struggling to break into the business. Until everything went to shit again.

When she walked out, he thought of buying new cacti to replace the ones she'd meanly appropriated. But it had taken a year for those to flower, and he didn't have the heart to start over again. He was sure they would wither under Margo's care. In their three and a half years together, had she even watered them half a dozen times?

The Beverly Hills succulents were clustered together in a cracked pot by the driveway of a McMansion with towering front doors and faux Doric columns. The house was too big for its lot and the multi-stemmed, columnar cacti had outgrown their container. Cary couldn't tell whether the owners had left the pot for the gardener to replant or just abandoned it.

He stopped to catch his breath and peer through the dark curtained windows for occupants of the house. Whoever lived there remained hidden. He'd started running again to vent his anger at Margo, yet crossing the city line from West Hollywood into Beverly Hills only fueled it. The metal-gated driveways, the "Armed Response" signs for security services, warned that he was an intruder in this neighborhood. The foot tall *Echinopsis* kept him returning anyway. He varied the times of his run, hoping to encounter someone to ask about the cacti, but the only person he ever saw descending the marble steps was the mailman.

Every time he passed the house, he imagined the dormant cacti blooming on the balcony outside his bedroom. Although he didn't think of himself as a thief, the cacti were too beautiful to be left to die. What harm could come from snatching the pot? Would anyone even notice it was missing? And if they did, what would they do? Summon a Beverly Hills cop to investigate? Still, he hesitated—until the morning he discovered a realtor's For Sale sign casting an ominous shadow across the plants. The sign brought him to an abrupt halt. He stood there, sweat-soaked, breathing heavily, contemplating his options.

He wasn't about to grab the clay pot in broad daylight and run with it back to his apartment. Wiser to wait till nightfall. All day he felt heady with anticipation. It was the same intoxication he'd felt doing stunt work, the mix of excitement and fear, a leap into the unknown with only faith in himself and the future to rely on, a confidence he hadn't felt since Margo left him, and in truth, for a long time before.

He sat at his desk in the Venice insurance agency where he worked now, unable to concentrate on the forms on his computer screen. When his career in stunt work collapsed, he started selling insurance. If life had taught him anything, it was this: hope for the best, but protect against the worst. He could wax poetically about home break-ins, fires, earthquakes, mudslides, all the hazards of living on a fault line in southern

California. You could never have too much insurance. All cacti had spines. He kept imagining everything that could go wrong that night: a patrol car passing by, barking dogs waking the owners, a neighbor peering out the window.

Too distracted to focus, he left early to buy two large terra-cotta pots and the special soil mixture he used before: 60% pumice, 10% peat, 20% Supersoil, 5% sand, and a few lava rocks for the bottom of the containers. He set his alarm for two in the morning, but couldn't sleep. Impatient to set off, he dressed in dark pants and a black hoodie—it's what burglars wore, wasn't it?—and left the apartment at one. Crossing Sunset Boulevard, he drove slowly toward the house on Oxford Way. At 1:30, the windows were dark, the house at least fifty yards from the nearest streetlight. He turned down Lexington Road and parked. No cars passed, no private security guards, no police looking to ticket vehicles without a residential parking sticker. Exiting the Honda, he quickly approached his prize. When he lifted the plants, they were heavier than he anticipated. He cradled the pot and strode rapidly to the car, expecting at any moment a window to fling open and someone to yell "thief." But he seemed the only witness to his crime. He placed the cacti carefully in the trunk, wiped the dirt from his hands, and drove away to his own applause.

As soon as he reached his apartment, he repotted the *Echinopsis* in the two large terra-cotta pots. In the morning he placed the repotted plants on his balcony, with its perfect southeastern light. Margo would have thought his theft harebrained, as reckless as the actions that destroyed his movie career, and baseball hopes before that—what she called "self-sabotage"—but his late-night burglary boosted his confidence, renewed his hope in the future.

* * *

Three weeks afterwards, he met Sheila. She telephoned the insurance office from her cell phone, and he answered the call.

Though she was a client of his agency, they'd never met before. His office was only a mile away, so he arrived immediately.

She was standing on the curb on Amoroso and Lincoln, her unruly red hair as tangled as the wreckage of her red Mazda Miata, which had just been broadsided by a Lexus SUV. A quick assessment of the damage told him the car was unsalvageable.

"Wow, that was fast!" she exclaimed when he introduced himself. She seemed surprisingly buoyant in the face of disaster.

"We do our best," he said. "Are you all right?"

"Not even a nose bleed." She shrugged to indicate the improbability of it. "I loved that car, but I guess our time together is over."

"It's why you have insurance."

"Great insurance! You showed up faster than the tow truck." She flashed a dazzling, gap-toothed smile. He quickly looked away. It had been a long time since anyone gushed at him like that.

The officer who responded to the accident approached to get more information. Meanwhile, his partner was shoving the female driver of the Lexus into the back seat of their patrol car.

The cop studied Sheila over the top of his notepad. "She's lucky she's in one piece." He nodded toward the other driver. "Her blood alcohol level measured .20. That's criminal negligence . . . She must have been drinking all afternoon."

"The world's a dangerous place," Cary said.

"You don't have to tell me."

The flat beds finally arrived and cleared both cars from the intersection. The police drove the DUI to the station, and he was left alone with Sheila. "Can I take you to a rental agency?" he asked.

"I don't know if I want to drive again tonight," she said, perhaps more shaken than she appeared.

"I'll be happy to drive you home then," he said.

"I'd appreciate that." She smiled again in gratitude.

"Maybe you should get something to eat first, something to settle your stomach . . ." He surprised himself with the offer.

"I didn't know that was in my policy," she laughed.

"We're a complete service agency."

"In that case, I accept. Lead on, Sir Galahad."

He took her to Lula's Mexican Cocina, whose Cadillac margaritas with Grand Marnier he always liked. He ordered one for each of them. Sitting across from her in the tiny booth, he found it difficult to avoid gazing into her sea-green eyes. She didn't look away.

"You look familiar," she said.

"Maybe you saw me at the office."

"No, I bought my policy over the phone. Were you ever on TV? The movies?"

He felt himself blushing. "As a matter of fact, I did work in movies for a time. But you never saw my face. I was a stunt man . . ." He looked up from his drink. "Doubled once for Tom Cruise."

"Shut up!" she laughed.

"It's true. He was feeling sick that day. So I ruined my shoulder hanging from a ledge for him."

"You really are Sir Galahad," she said admiringly.

He looked down at his glass, embarrassed. "And here I always thought it was just bad luck."

"No such thing! Bad luck, good luck, they're just names for things we can't explain."

"Well, my life could use some explaining. It's been a little rocky lately," he confessed.

"Tell me," she encouraged.

He ordered another round of the Cadillac margaritas to make it easier to recount his streak of misfortunes. "It started in my second year in college when I crashed into a fence chasing a home run ball I should've given up on. A futile gesture. We lost by ten runs anyway."

"I like people who don't give up."

He took another sip of his margarita to avoid her gaze. "Unfortunately, I tore my rotator cuff crashing into that fence. The surgeon promised my shoulder would be even stronger when he repaired it. He never mentioned how I'd hit. After the operation, I couldn't catch up to a fastball anymore and the coach didn't wait around until I could. He gave my scholarship to a better prospect."

"His loss," she said.

"Maybe, but other coaches felt the same. No college was willing to give me a scholarship, so I dropped out . . . Then a friend suggested stunt work. He said anyone willing to run into walls for a baseball was crazy enough to leap from rooftop to rooftop or ride a motorcycle through flames. He was right. I loved it—the planning, the preparation, the satisfaction of a perfectly executed stunt. Then one day I hung too long from that second-story window ledge and wrecked my shoulder for good. Only 70% mobility now." He raised his right arm to demonstrate.

"Tom Cruise should be filled with gratitude."

"I'm still waiting for his get-well card."

She reached across the table and took his hand. "Well, I'm grateful," she said.

Impulsively, he raised her hand to his lips.

"Maybe you should drive me home now," she said.

* * *

The first time Sheila visited his apartment she raised the blinds in every room. "You need to let the sunshine in. No one thrives in gloom." Then she opened the sliding doors to the balcony and discovered the *Echinopsis*. "Wow, these are really beautiful. You must have been growing them a long time."

He wanted to explain their provenance, but their relationship was too new, too uncertain. Instead, he tested the soil with his fingers. "Needs watering," he said. "The more light they get, the more you need to water. If you take good care of them, they reward you with magnificent flowers." He pointed to the tiny buds just beginning to appear on the plants. "It won't be long now. Most cacti bloom once a year, but an *Echinopsis* can flower multiple times."

"I'm eager to see," she said, throwing her arms around him.

A month later she moved in, replaced the blinds with curtains, re-covered his drab gray couch in coral, and repainted each of the beige rooms a different color—daffodil yellow, cornflower blue, and moss green. A beautician who spent her days making plain women glamorous, she had a gift for beautifying everything she touched. She viewed life the same way she did the women who came to her salon: whatever their flaws or deficits, with the right hairstyle, the right makeup, they all could be beautiful.

It was this gift, he thought, that explained how she'd survived the losses of her own childhood. The evening they packed up the last few possessions in her Venice apartment, they strolled along the beach and she told him about her parents. When she was four, her mother walked out the door one day and disappeared forever. Her father drank to numb the pain and lost one job and then another until finally alcohol and despair defeated him.

When she was eight, he sent Sheila to stay with an aunt one evening, closed the garage door, and turned on the car engine. She recounted all this as matter of factly, as emotionlessly, as if it had happened to someone she barely knew.

"That must have been so painful," was all he could say.

She stopped a moment and gazed at the slate-gray ocean as if hoping her memories would recede with the ebbing tide. At last she turned to him. "They could barely take care of themselves. How could they take care of me too? What's the point of brooding about it? You can't change what happened. I don't like talking or thinking about it, but I thought you should know."

Her lack of rancor made him ashamed of the resentment

he harbored for his own vicissitudes, which paled compared to hers. She exemplified what Margo preached to all her clients: no matter what circumstances you face, you control your own fate. But where Margo used her philosophy to castigate his faults, Sheila saw his failures as a sign of his resilience, his ability to keep bouncing back. It terrified him to think he might fail again and lose her.

One night, as they were lying in bed watching the eleven o'clock news, a female newscaster appeared in front of a burned-out house to report a fire that killed a mother and father and their two young children. Glancing at Sheila, Cary noticed tears running down her cheeks. In the four months he'd known her, he'd never seen her cry. His first reaction was to protect her from the pain that stirred her tears. He searched for the remote. "I see enough tragedies at work. We don't need to watch more at night."

Sheila stayed his hand. "But look how loved they were." She pointed to the neighbors placing cards and flowers in front of the charred home. "That's so beautiful."

"You always find the best in everything," he said.

"It's because I've known the worst."

He held her while she wept. Behind her on the TV, another reporter, illuminated by the alternating red and amber lights of an ambulance, described a four-car pileup on the 405. Cary muted the sound. "We should get married," he proposed.

She wiped her eyes with the collar of her T-shirt. "I've been wondering if you'd ever ask."

A week later they went to Santa Monica City Hall. A few friends witnessed the brief ceremony. Sheila wore a white pantsuit, ruby blouse, and white headband to bind her rebellious curls; Cary wore the dark suit he kept for weddings and funerals. She carried a bouquet of peonies, lilies, and roses he'd carefully picked out. Two of Sheila's friends from the salon threw rice at them as they descended the steps of City Hall. A colleague from his insurance office clapped him heartily on his damaged shoulder as he reached the street. "She's quite a catch," he marveled. "You're a helluva lucky man, my friend."

The sudden twinge in Cary's shoulder made him wonder how long the luck would last.

* * *

When you were hitting or pitching well, you never risked your streak by changing bats or gloves or chewing gum. It was the same performing stunts. Who knew what slight misstep could ruin your future? The day Cruise decided at the last moment not to drop from that ledge, Cary had to abandon his usual habits. So he stuck faithfully to the routine that had brought Sheila into his life. Every morning he'd go out to the balcony and tend the cacti, watering or fertilizing them as needed with concentrated tomato food or bone meal. Three mornings a week he still jogged north of Sunset, although careful to avoid Oxford Way where he'd stolen the *Echinopsis*. He'd return in time to kiss Sheila goodbye before she left for her salon. Then he'd shower, eat the same Cheerios for breakfast every day and drive to his Venice office where he was selling more insurance than ever.

It was nights when he worried that it might all come crashing down again. Often, he would wake in the darkness in a cold sweat from a recurring nightmare from his stunt days of jumping off a skyscraper without a parachute or diving off a cliff into a bottomless abyss. To keep from disturbing Sheila, he would throw on a sweater and slip out onto the balcony to still his fears.

One night when he couldn't sleep, Sheila put on her robe and joined him on the balcony. She stood behind him and massaged his neck. "What's keeping you up? Is your shoulder bothering you again?"

He didn't want to burden her with his dark thoughts. The cacti he'd bought to celebrate the start of his career in stunt work hadn't prevented it from ending. Though the new *Echinopsis* had restored his luck, he worried that stealing it somehow tainted the good fortune it brought, that eventually there would be retribution for his theft.

"Don't you ever worry about the future?" he asked.

"Sometimes, but you have to deal with whatever curves life throws you."

He grabbed her by the waist and pulled her toward him. "Curves like these?" He slid his hands down her hips.

"You have no trouble handling them."

"Everything should be this easy."

She pulled away. "What if my curves expand?"

"What do you mean?"

"I think I'm pregnant."

The suddenness of it was like a gust of wind in the chill night air. "You sure?"

"I haven't taken the test yet, but I know my body."

"You really want a child right now?" He felt a stab of fear. Why alter their present happiness?

"It's one way to shape the future. I know you'll make a great father."

He groped for a response. Though they'd talked about having children, he'd always imagined it years away.

"I know it's sudden," she said. "It was a surprise to me too."

He was too stunned to absorb the news.

"You don't have to say anything right now," she said. "Just love me. And love the child we've made together."

He took her in his arms and held her. The warmth of her body reassured him. "Of course I will," he said.

* * *

The *Echinopsis* blossomed, and so did Sheila. The flowers were incredibly intricate with several layers of petals, each layer a different hue of pink or white. Sheila's complexion radiated the same beauty. The flowers only lasted a few days, but Sheila continued to bloom. The more her body swelled, the more radiant she became. Her flame-red hair seemed to deepen in color; her pale skin glowed. Lying naked beside her in bed, he felt dizzy with happiness. He would place his lips on her pillowy belly and whisper to the son they'd created together—he was certain it was a boy—and wait for the baby to respond.

"What are you whispering?" she asked one night.

"That's between us. Father and son."

"What if it's a girl?" She'd insisted the obstetrician not tell them the sex of the child.

"Then it's between father and daughter."

"Tell me," she said. "You know I don't like secrets."

"I have no secrets from you. You know everything about me. What haven't I told you?"

She sat up suddenly in bed. "Only you would know that."

It seemed a ridiculous trifle to withhold, but he was ashamed of what he'd done, a rash act in a troubled time. It was not the way he wanted her to see the father of their child.

"I was a different person before I met you. I can't even remember that person anymore."

She wrinkled her face, not quite believing him, but let it pass.

"Well, I'm very happy that you're the person who replaced him."

* * *

Two weeks later, Sheila woke up to discover blood dripping down her leg. Her obstetrician, Dr. McKenna, met them in the emergency room. He asked Cary to remain in the waiting room while he examined her. When he finished, he invited Cary back into the exam room. Sheila was sitting up on the examining table, pale as her hospital gown. He took her hand.

"We have a complication," the doctor said, fingering the

stethoscope dangling from his neck. "Both your wife and the baby are at risk."

The doctor was younger than the surgeon who'd operated on his shoulder, not that long out of medical school, Cary guessed. He spoke quickly, as if trying to reassure himself as much as both of them. Sheila had a rare condition called placenta previa: the placenta covered the opening of the cervix, which could lead to massive internal bleeding.

Cary tried to take in everything he was saying, but all he could focus on was the blood on the sleeve of the doctor's white coat.

He tightened his grip on Sheila's hand. "If you're in that much danger, maybe we should terminate the pregnancy."

Sheila looked to the doctor.

"This is a serious complication, but it's manageable," he said. "We just need to take the right precautions."

"Meaning what?" Cary tried to quell the fear flooding his body.

"I want your wife to remain in the hospital so we can monitor her until the baby's ready to be delivered."

"If that's what's necessary," Sheila said.

Cary felt the old ache in his shoulder as she squeezed his hand.

"Good, I'll arrange it," Dr. McKenna said.

"It's going to be fine," she reassured Cary when the doctor left.

"You don't think we should get a second opinion?"

"I know he's young, but I believe in him. I have good instincts about people."

He didn't want to shake her confidence in the obstetrician, who'd been recommended by a co-worker at her salon, so he didn't insist on consulting another doctor. Her faith in other people brought out the best in them.

* * *

He visited Sheila every evening in the hospital and all Saturdays and Sundays. She bore the bad food, the back pain, the boredom with few complaints. This would all be over soon and she would return home with a new addition to their family. She even found unexpected benefits in the daytime TV she watched—ads for products that would make her a more capable mother.

Though Cary tried to remain as positive, he found it difficult to accept the precarious situation of his wife. Sheila never smoked, barely drank, was careful about what she ate, exercised regularly, was a perfect candidate to bear a child. Yet suddenly she was on bed rest, monitored twenty-four hours a day, at risk of hemorrhaging at any moment. How to explain this cruel twist of fate? Although he sold insurance to protect against incalculable forces like earthquakes, hurricanes, and floods, he was unprepared for the irrational event that had swept down on them.

One night, after she'd endured another episode of bleeding that soaked the bed and took frightening minutes to stanch, he found her uncharacteristically discouraged. "I know they say everything happens for a reason," she said. "I don't know why this is happening to me. Women have babies every day without problems. Why can't I? Tell me."

Cary struggled for an explanation. "You know the good-luck cacti on our balcony, the ones you like so much . . ." he began haltingly, hands clenched in the pockets of his jeans, a penitent beside her bed. "I lied to you about them."

"What do you mean?"

"I stole them."

"Why? How?" She looked confused.

"They were in a pot in the driveway of an ugly house in Beverly Hills. I didn't think anyone was taking care of them. So late one night I snatched the pot and took it home and replanted the cacti." He glanced at her to see his own disgust mirrored in her face. All he saw was puzzlement.

"You didn't steal the plants. You rescued them."

"I never thought of it that way before," he said.

"I don't know why. How can you steal something that someone else abandoned?"

The relief he felt overwhelmed him. He shed his shoes, lay down on the hospital bed, and wrapped his arms around her. The luck the *Echinopsis* had brought them would hold.

* * *

The closer Sheila came to giving birth, the more Cary started to worry again. Playing ball and doing stunt work, at least he had some measure of control. Now Sheila and their child's fate was in the doctor's hands, not his. His powerlessness increased his fear. Routine was all he had to cling to. So he continued monitoring the cacti every morning, jogging the same streets on his runs, eating the same breakfast, driving the same route to his Venice office. Passing Lula's restaurant each day reassured him. Like the cacti flowering on their balcony, Lula's had brought them together. Their lives were intertwined now; she was his good luck, and he hers.

Then one morning, driving to work on Pico Boulevard, the BMW in front of him stopped suddenly to avoid a youth skateboarding across the street. Cary slammed on the brakes and avoided hitting the BMW, but the Ford behind him rammed into his Honda. And a Prius rear-ended the Ford. The damage to his bumper wasn't great—$1600, Cary immediately estimated—and he felt no whiplash from the collision; still, the three-car pileup jarred him and took a long time to untangle. When he finally turned down Main Street to pass Lula's, he was further rattled to discover a pipe had burst, blocking the street, and he had to take a detour to his office.

Visiting Sheila that night, he ran into Dr. McKenna coming out of her hospital room. Though the obstetrician checked on her on his daily rounds, Cary rarely saw him. The few chance encounters they had, the doctor assured him everything was under control, as he hurriedly did again. "We're watching her very closely, waiting as long as we can to operate," he said before he rushed away. The doctor appeared to be a careful, cautious man, who trimmed his close-cropped beard every day. Cary wanted to have faith in him, yet he was bothered by the doctor's social awkwardness and the way he constantly fingered his stethoscope.

The doctor's quick escape and the unexpected alteration of his morning ritual alarmed him. He took them both as warning signs of impending disaster. "Luck doesn't just happen to you; you make your own luck," Margo kept telling him before she left. And maybe she was right all along. It's why he'd taken the *Echinopsis* after all—to change his fortune. He needed to do something as bold as that again.

He asked the cheerful Jamaican nurse on the night ward for the name of the best obstetrician at the hospital. "Dr. Wang the best. No question," the nurse answered without hesitation. Two days later, Cary stopped by the hospital cafeteria at lunchtime and spotted the doctor sitting by herself, absently eating a salad and reading a paperback. He bought coffee and a turkey sandwich and nervously approached her table. The petite, gray-haired doctor lowered her book and peered at him over her reading glasses. Cary asked if he might join her. She gestured for him to sit.

He quickly introduced himself, explained his wife was a patient in the hospital, on bed rest, waiting to have their baby. "I've been told you have a lot of experience with difficult cases, that women with high-risk pregnancies come from around the world to have you deliver their babies."

"I've been a doctor a long time," she said. "I've treated all kinds of complications."

Cary described Sheila's condition, the severe bleeding she suffered. Dr. Wang listened attentively and asked the name of her obstetrician.

"I know Dr. McKenna," she said. "Your wife's in good hands. Her bleeding can be managed."

"Yes, he told us that."

"But you're not convinced."

"I want to make sure we're doing everything we can."

"You want reassurances?" She sipped her coffee, then cradled the paper cup a few seconds before replacing it on the plastic tray. "Are you religious?" she asked.

The question caught him by surprise. "No, I don't believe there's a God who's aware of my existence or has any interest in my life."

"I don't believe that either. But there are things medicine, science, can't explain."

"Luck!" he uttered.

She smiled. "I wouldn't call it that. I prefer 'mystery,' what the writer of this book says language and speech are powerless to convey." She lifted her book to reveal the title: *The Case for God*. "I often feel that mystery, forces in the universe we can't explain. You can call it God if you want, or luck, or fate . . . inadequate words really for something we don't understand. It's why I keep reading books like this. And delivering babies. Every birth reminds me of the uncertainty we all live with, for which there are no guarantees, no easy answers."

It wasn't the second opinion he hoped for.

"But you didn't sit down to discuss religion with me, did you? I'm sorry that you caught me in a particularly reflective mood."

She glanced past him toward the entrance of the cafeteria. "Ah, there's your doctor now."

Cary turned to see Dr. McKenna staring at them from behind the salad bar. He hoped the obstetrician wouldn't see his speaking to Dr. Wang as a betrayal, an effort to replace him.

Dr. Wang picked up her book and tray and rose. "You should speak to Dr. McKenna about your fears. He's a very capable doctor. He'll do all he can to insure your wife has a safe birth and healthy baby."

Cary watched her dump her half-eaten salad into the trash and nod to McKenna as they passed. He was relieved when McKenna sat down with two nurses at another table.

Cary pushed his untouched sandwich away. His stomach was already filled with fear.

* * *

The thirty-seventh week of Sheila's pregnancy, McKenna decided it was finally time to perform the C-section. He set nine in the morning for the operation. Cary awoke before dawn, drenched with perspiration from a nightmare he often had before, where he was running to catch a fly ball, straining to reach it, and finding his legs could barely move. To counter his dream, he went for an early morning run. Dashing home, he quickly showered, watered the cacti, and drove to the hospital. Sheila was standing by the window when he arrived, a blade of sunlight slanting across her swollen belly. "It's a beautiful day to bring a baby into the world," she said. He had no words adequate for the love he felt for her. He put his arm around her shoulder; together they watched the sun slowly rising above the distant ocean.

A nurse entered with hospital scrubs for him to wear so he could be with Sheila during the birth. He held her hand as the orderly wheeled her toward the delivery room. Dr. McKenna stopped him at the sliding doors.

"This is delicate," he said. "It's better you not come in."

He started to protest. "The nurse said fathers could . . ."

Sheila squeezed his hand to stop him. "It's okay," she said. "We're both going to be fine." Her smile was almost as radiant as the one that dazzled him the day they met.

Cary brushed back her unruly curls and kissed her cold forehead. "I'll be waiting for you both," he said. He watched the gurney vanish behind the sliding doors.

There were no other fathers in the tiny waiting room, only a gray-haired man and woman, waiting for the birth of a grandchild, he assumed. The woman smiled kindly as he entered in his scrubs; the man barely turned from the baseball game on the TV screen. The Dodgers were playing the Orioles in Baltimore in an inter-divisional game. He couldn't watch. He walked downstairs to the cafeteria and bought a cup of coffee. His hand shook as he tore the sugar packet, knocking over the paper cup and spilling the coffee on his pants. He wished he believed in a God he could pray to.

When he returned to the waiting room, the baseball game was over and the elderly couple gone. He turned off the television, closed his eyes, and tried to imagine bringing Sheila and their son home, wrapped in the blue blanket they'd purchased together months before. The image wouldn't hold.

He rose, paced the hall, sat again. He gripped the armrests as tightly as he could to keep from feeling that he was jumping out of his skin. He tried to envision his son growing up, teaching him softball, watching him become the athlete he'd wanted to be. But other images kept intruding: crashing into that outfield wall, the surgeon peering down at him on the operating table, the obstetrician barring him from the delivery room.

At last he heard footsteps approach. He leaped up to meet the doctor. His scrubs were spattered with blood, his face drained of color. We lost her! Cary thought. He lunged for the chair to keep from falling into the chasm that opened up beneath him.

The doctor took his arm to steady him. "Your wife's very brave. She wanted so much for this baby to live. 'If you have to choose,' she said, 'choose the baby.'"

Cary sank into the chair, unable to speak.

The doctor bent beside him. "But we saved them both. They're both fine," he said proudly. "You have a healthy baby daughter."

Cary didn't know whether to laugh or cry or scream. He felt a wave of gratitude for the doctor and shame for how he'd misjudged him. Sheila had been right to trust him, after all. "Can I see her?" Cary asked.

"Of course. They're just bringing her into the recovery room. But you can see your daughter now."

Dr. McKenna led him to the nursery. A nurse brought over a tiny bundle wrapped in a pink blanket and held it out to him. She shifted the blanket so that he could have a better view. The baby had a tuft of red hair, as untamed as her mother's. Cary looked down at her with an overwhelming mixture of humility and awe.

The nurse again offered his daughter for Cary to hold. Gingerly, he took her. The baby was so light in his hands that he felt an ill wind could sweep her away.

He had found Sheila, almost lost her, then received this wondrous gift. Good luck, bad luck, dumb luck couldn't explain any of it. Maybe it was what Dr. Wang struggled to describe. A mystery beyond his comprehension or control.

The baby stared up at him with Sheila's pale-green eyes. Her arms flailed and her delicate hands opened, as if reaching out to him. A wave of anguished tenderness washed over him. Who could predict what joys or tragedies awaited her?

He would name her Mirabelle, for the rare *Echinopsis mirabilis,* the Flower of Prayer. He hoped the name would give her courage to confront whatever life would bring.

Doubles

It began innocently enough. "Can I buy you dinner or a drink this week?" R asked as we walked to our cars after our regular Sunday tennis game.

"To make up for today?" We'd been partners and he played poorly.

He shifted his tennis bag from one shoulder to the other. "I need some advice, and I thought you could help."

"About what?"

He glanced at other players returning to the parking lot of the Cheviot Hills public courts where we played. "I'd rather not talk here."

His invitation and secretiveness intrigued me. Although we'd been playing doubles every Sunday for years, we never socialized outside the courts. I suggested we meet at Musso & Frank in Hollywood. Whatever counsel he was seeking, I thought their martinis might make it easier to tell me.

We met two days later, at three in the afternoon, early to start drinking, but I figured he chose that hour because there would be fewer people in the restaurant. Although we sat in the back, in one of Musso's scarlet leather booths, he kept glancing furtively toward the front, as if any minute someone might enter who recognized him. In his dark tailored suit and striped silk tie, he looked like any affluent businessman who drank here; it was the tentativeness of his eyes that betrayed him.

"You seem on edge," I remarked.

"Is it that obvious?" He gulped rather than sipped his martini.

I didn't say anything. As a journalist, I'd learned that others usually rush in to fill awkward silences.

"You know I read your book. You're a good writer."

I'd written a book about a Chicano gang that attracted a little attention when it was published, but had been out of print for several years. "I'm surprised you can still find it."

"You can find anything on Amazon."

He'd shown zero interest in the book when it first appeared; I waited to see where his sudden discovery of my writing led.

"How many years have we been playing tennis?" he asked.

"Seven, eight. I don't remember anymore when we started."

"Neither do I. But we've been friends a while, haven't we?"

Friends was hardly how I would've characterized our relationship. We shared little in common besides our inconsistent U.S.T.A. 3.5 tennis ranking. We'd met playing on the Los Angeles County Parks and Recreation public courts. There were six in our doubles group; with six we always had enough to field a match on Sunday. It was an odd group, connected by chance and tennis skill rather than occupation or common interests. I knew R's strengths and weaknesses as a tennis player—his ferocity at the net and his tendency to choke at key moments in the match—yet little else about him. I'd written him off as a dull, Century City tax attorney with rich clients, a pretty, stay-at-home wife, and the usual soccer-playing children. Maybe that was because he was so uninterested in me.

He emptied his glass and scanned the room again for eavesdroppers. Then he dropped his voice to almost a whisper. "I've gotten into a rather uncomfortable situation . . . a woman . . . not my wife . . ." He checked my face for judgment.

I hoped I didn't display surprise. He seemed an unlikely candidate for adultery. Still, I was hardly one to judge.

"It's ended badly, very badly. And now she's threatening me . . ."

An old story—a cheating husband, a vindictive mistress—a woeful tale that countless men must have lamented over martinis in the hundred years since the restaurant opened, the day Prohibition ended. Chaplin, Fitzgerald, Faulkner, Chandler, Bukowski, all regulars here, could have provided R better advice.

"What does she want?" I asked the obvious question.

"A lot more than I can afford." He sloshed the remainder of the martini from the sidecar into his glass; then immediately drained it.

"Maybe she's bargaining."

"No, I've tried. She'd rather ruin me." He grimaced the way he did when he smashed an easy overhead into the net or double faulted at match point, unforced errors that suggested a character defect that might have led to his current problem.

"I appreciate the delicacy of your situation," I said carefully, wondering what defects he'd seen in me that led him to believe I could help.

He stared at the olives in his empty glass as if debating whether to continue. "Look, I made a terrible mistake. I let my prick do my thinking. Stupid, I know. And I regret it. More than I can say. But it's over. Finished. Except she has something of mine that I need back, something that could destroy my family, my reputation—my whole life, really." He finally looked up at me. "I have to get it back."

I tried to imagine what could be that damaging, or if it was simply revelation of his affair that he feared. "Have you tried a private detective?"

"No, no detectives. I can't risk anything like that." He lowered his voice again. "But you know people. You could introduce me."

"What people?"

"The gangbangers you wrote about."

"That's a bad idea," I said.

"It's nothing you need to get involved with. I just need a

name, a phone number. I don't know anyone in that world. You do. All I'm asking is you connect me with someone who can help me retrieve what that bitch refuses to sell me."

He caught the eye of a red-jacketed waiter and ordered another round. I probably should've stood up then and left, or simply refused to discuss the subject further. But I was hooked. He had a secret, and I was curious to know more. A writer's appetite for scandal? Or maybe a baser desire to uncover someone's sins that are worse than your own.

"It's been a while since I wrote that book," I demurred when the waiter departed.

"I'm asking as a friend. All I want is an introduction. You write down a name on a piece of paper and we don't ever have to speak about it again. I'll make it worth your while," he added, a little sheepishly I thought at having to resort to bribery. But maybe the embarrassment was mine that I was still listening.

"I'm not even sure where most of the people I wrote about are now. I haven't spoken to them in a while."

"I'm desperate," he implored. "I don't know where else to turn."

* * *

Though I'd stayed to hear R's plan, the sober light of morning clarified its madness. How could I suborn people who trusted me to break the law for a man I knew mainly as a tennis player? I had more loyalty to the homeboys who confided in me than R. I thought they might be amused, though, to hear that a successful west side lawyer was looking to hire them as burglars. I dialed C, my chief informant in the gang, whom I hadn't spoken to in months. Since all the *cholos* used cheap, throwaway phones, I wasn't surprised that his number no longer worked. With nothing else to do that morning, I drove down to the Pico-Union neighborhood to see if I could find him.

We're all good at explaining or justifying our behavior,

whether or not our explanations are true. Who really understands his own motives? At the time I was "in between assignments," my freelance career was going nowhere, and my ex-wife and I were fighting over the shared custody of our four-year-old son. R's request provided an excuse to reconnect with the subjects of my one modest success as a writer.

While working for an online news service, I'd stumbled onto an 18th Street set of one of L.A.'s four hundred street gangs and gradually gained their trust. Raised by a single mother who worked at a bakery to provide for my sister and me after our father left us, I understood what it was like to grow up poor and an outsider. At the snobbish prep school I attended on scholarship, I sold pot that I grew in our backyard to spoiled classmates who received birthday gifts of BMWs when they turned sixteen. If the teacher who caught me hadn't given me a second chance, I might have ended up on the same self-destructive path as most of the gang members. Still, I was drawn to their bravura and fuck-all disdain for social norms and conventions. However self-defeating their choices, I shared their contempt for the rich and privileged they sold drugs to. Hanging with them, I fed off the danger and unpredictable violence they faced from cops and rival gangs—the symbiotic relationship between journalist and subject, the pilot fish and the shark.

C was the principal character in my book, although I'd disguised his identity enough to protect him. Bright, magnetic, a natural leader; if he'd grown up in Palos Verdes or Pacific Palisades, or received any of the breaks I had, he'd be a lawyer now instead of selling drugs to law students at USC. Our relationship cooled after the publication of the book, which he first pronounced as "mad real," recognizing only what he wanted to see in my account; later, though, I think he came to regret the book. The last time I saw him, he lived near MacArthur Park in a cluster of rundown apartments with salsa blaring from the windows and laundry hanging from the sills.

I found a parking place halfway up the block and walked toward his building, feeling as self-conscious as always in this neighborhood of Mexican and Central American immigrants. Children kicking a soccer ball, women conversing animatedly in Spanish, a gray-bearded man smoking a cigar in a folding lawn chair, all turned to stare as if trying to decide whether this unfamiliar gringo might be a despised agent of La Migra.

Living in the Hollywood Hills, it was easy to forget that whites are a minority in Los Angeles, less than thirty percent of the ten million people in the county. As my blue-eyed, blonde ex often joked, in another twenty-five years the only place in L.A. where you'd be able to find women like her would be museums.

"You lost, homes?" A buff Latino in sunglasses and a blue do-rag studied me from the scruffy front yard of the building. His white wifebeater revealed tattooed flames flaring up both his forearms to his impressive biceps. With him was a younger, skinnier youth with a beginner's mustache and a wispy goatee. Both were strangers to me. I told them who I was looking for.

They surveyed me while they toked joints they were smoking. The pungent odor reminded me of the many nights I'd spent stoned in this neighborhood.

"He's away right now, vacationing in Pleasant Valley," Do-rag finally replied.

"When?" I asked, dismayed to hear he was in prison.

"A couple of months ago," the starter mustache said. "He got into a fight and sliced someone."

I was ashamed I hadn't known. C once told me he expected to be dead or serving time by twenty-five; he laughed when I suggested there were other options.

The two *cholos* regarded me with suspicion. "And who the fuck are you?" Do-rag said.

"An old friend."

"That *vato* got no gringo friends," the starter mustache scoffed.

"It's been a while since I saw him."

"You buy weed from him? Before it was lee-ga-lized?"

I ignored the question.

"If it's weed you're looking for," the older one said, "you've come to the right place. You want a taste, *hombre*?" He extended a tattooed arm to offer the joint. The crudeness of his tattoos and ripped body suggested that he'd also spent time in places like Pleasant Valley.

"No thanks."

He took another toke and extended the joint again. "This is good shit, man. You pay a lot more for it in those fancy shops on the west side."

"Yeah, bougie boy, you can buy it much cheaper from us," his sidekick echoed. His eyes were like a smeared window.

"Thanks. Another time." I turned to leave, regretting that I'd come.

"What's your hurry, homes? You don't like the hood?" the tattooed *cholo* jeered. As if dancing to some music I couldn't hear, they moved in unison to block my way. Dope or their own boredom encouraged them to mess with me.

"Okay, maybe just one hit," I said, not wanting to provoke them. I took a modest drag of the joint. The pot was stronger than expected. "It's good shit." I passed the joint back. "But I'm not looking to buy."

"Maybe you're looking for something harder. Snow, ice, cotton candy."

"Or maybe he's a narc." Do-rag weighed the possibility. "*Quien sabe* the *pinche* assholes the cops are hiring these days?"

I reached into my wallet and handed him an old business card from my former online employer to show I was a journalist, not a cop. I explained that I'd written about C in a book and that I was looking for him again. The book drew blank expressions—it was clear they'd never heard of it—but my business card impressed them.

Do-rag studied the card a moment. "You got one for Luis?"

I found another for his sidekick. "We should get cards like this. You know, advertise. You Want Primo? Come See Pedro. Yeah." He laughed at his burst of freestyle. He fished a pen out of his baggy pants, wrote a number on my card, and passed it back. "You ever want quality shit, give me a call. Have a nice day, bougie writer." They stepped apart and let me pass.

* * *

The news of C's arrest depressed me, reminding me why I hadn't visited Pico-Union in months. My romance with gangsta life waned with the publication of my book. The book didn't do much to advance my career, and it certainly didn't change the lives of any of the 18th Street set. Reviewers from both sides of the ideological divide attacked me. A few critics charged me with "cultural appropriation," exploiting the lives of my subjects. What did a white writer, who attended UC Santa Barbara, know about growing up in the *barrio*? Conservatives accused me of glamorizing gang life, portraying the homeboys as rebels instead of the violent criminals they were. I assumed it was their disdain for the law that made R think they'd be willing to steal whatever his mistress was holding. I waited until our Sunday tennis game to tell him I couldn't help.

We both arrived early. "I'm afraid I can't find anyone," I said.

"I guess I misjudged you." He smashed his racket hard against the net, snapping a string. He flung the broken racket across the court.

I'd seen him erupt before, but never this fiercely. His rage, or desperation, was much greater than I'd imagined.

"What's going on, gentlemen?" The ophthalmologist in our group eyed us curiously as he opened the gate to the court.

R looked at me, the writer, to come up with a convincing lie. I explained that he'd just discovered his racket was broken and hadn't brought a backup. Fortunately, the aerospace engineer, the other member of the day's foursome, carried a replacement. R crossed the net to team with the ophthalmologist against the engineer and me.

Despite our diverse professions and social status, we were all evenly matched at tennis. Our games were spirited and sweaty, the sets always fiercely competitive. In between games, we engaged in typical male "locker room" banter: who was the better player, Nadal or Federer; which NFL or NBA teams would make the playoffs; which female star would you rather do. We rarely discussed anything personal or even political. We didn't come to the courts to talk.

The ophthalmologist served and R smashed the first volley of the game directly at my head. I ducked and the ball sailed well beyond the baseline. R was going to make me pay for my failure. A little over six feet, he was an imposing presence at the net, ready to poach any ball within his reach. Today he was particularly vicious, slamming most of his forehands at my body. After a few games, I retreated to the baseline and started lobbing balls over his head. That only infuriated him more. As often happened when frustrated, he began hitting balls long or into the net, double faulting, and cursing his unforced errors. We won both sets handily.

"Well, you brought your F game today," his partner cracked, referring to the number of times R uttered fuck.

"It must be the racket," the engineer said as R returned it.

"Not my day." R glared at me.

He walked with me to the parking lot. "I thought we had an understanding," he said, re-litigating my decision. All he wanted, he'd confessed over our third martini at Musso's, was someone to break into his mistress's apartment and retrieve an incriminating video. He knew where she kept it and the hours she was away. No need for strong-arm tactics; nobody would get hurt. Just a simple burglary. But he thought it too risky to hire a detective. A gangbanger from East L.A. was another story. They committed crimes like this all the time. And they lived in the same side of town as the greedy bitch who was blackmailing him.

"I'm really disappointed. I thought you were a friend," he said.

I don't know whether I felt contempt for him at that moment, or pity, or if I was still angry for all the balls he'd slammed at me, but it suddenly struck me that he and the two *cholos* I'd met deserved each other. I took out my wallet and found the business card on which Pedro had scrawled his number.

"This is all I got, a drug dealer. I don't even know his last name. But maybe he can help you."

* * *

R didn't play tennis the next Sunday—it was the insurance broker's turn in our rotation—and he didn't call or email. I didn't expect him to. Now that I'd provided him a contact, I assumed he wanted to distance himself as much from me as I did from him. I wasn't proud that I'd succumbed to his bullying pleas; I should have refused his request at Musso's. Now I didn't even want to play tennis with him again.

Meanwhile, *Los Angeles Magazine* had responded positively to a query I'd sent proposing an article about nanny agencies that catered to the wealthy. I'd discovered the subject in searching for childcare for our son. The assignment provided a purpose and deadline and hope that I might yet revive my faltering career as a journalist. My unstable employment and paltry income had been one of the reasons our marriage foundered. My wife and I met while she was finishing her pediatric residency at UCLA and I was writing political screeds for the *LA Weekly*, when it was still a viable weekly. I think our marriage was her last rebellion against her upper-class Boston family, from whom she was estranged. After a few years, as I moved from one online journal to another, she grew impatient with my failure to live up to the promise she first saw in me.

Neither the *New York Times* nor *Washington Post* was calling. She wondered if it might be my choice of subjects. "Writing about the poor and alienated keeps you impoverished too," she claimed. It didn't help either that she caught me cheating with an intern at the news service.

Although we'd been separated for more than a year now, we hadn't finalized our divorce or custody agreement. She and a nanny were caring for Gideon during the week, and I was taking him every other weekend. I picked him up at the house in Westwood we could only buy because of her income. She met me at the door in a black sheath dress and heels, wearing the antique silver earrings I'd scraped to buy for our first anniversary. The light above the door fell on the earrings and accented the soft curve of her neck, the luster of her skin. For a second I remembered why I'd fallen in love with her.

"They still look lovely on you."

Embarrassed, she reached up as if to remove an earring.

"Don't." I stayed her hand though it hurt to see her wearing what I could barely afford for another man. Maybe the same thought struck her, because her eyes glistened. She turned away to compose herself and called Gideon. He was standing a few feet behind her in the hallway, diffidently clutching his stuffed monkey to his chest and furiously sucking his thumb.

I entered the house and scooped him up. "I'll take good care of him," I promised and fled toward the street. Gideon wriggled in my arms, waving goodbye to her all the way to the car. She stood in the doorway in the fading evening light, watching until we pulled away.

At McDonald's, Gideon took his thumb out of his mouth long enough to eat half a burger. I managed to coax a smile, then laughter from him, pretending that the monkey was behaving badly, throwing his silverware on the floor, refusing to eat anything but ice cream. Gideon and I both enjoyed the monkey's rebellion—acting out that was safe for both of us to do.

I drove back to the one-bedroom apartment I rented, parked

in the basement garage and carried Gideon up the stairs. Two shadowy figures in hoodies were sprawled on lounge chairs by the courtyard pool.

"You don't answer your phone, homes." Pedro rose and flicked his cigarette into the pool.

"You didn't leave a message."

"We wanted to talk in person."

Instinctively, I clamped my hands on Gideon's tiny shoulders and pulled him closer. "Well, here I am," I said as evenly as I could, wondering how they'd got past the locked entrance.

"We came to thank you." The huge grin that stretched Luis's mouth made his wispy mustache look even more ridiculous.

"For what?" Although I already knew.

"We figured it was you who recommended us."

"Yeah, that's some piece of work, that *gabacho* friend of yours," Pedro said.

"But now he's shitting in his expensive pants," Luis added.

"You shouldn't say shit." Gideon giggled.

For the first time they appeared to notice him.

"He yours?" Pedro asked.

"Yes, my son. Gideon."

"Well, Gideon, there's nothing wrong with shit. You shit. I shit. Your dad shits. *Mierda.* It's a part of life. You can't escape it."

"Yeah, shit is shit," Luis confirmed the fact. "Don't let your father tell you different."

"It's a lesson I'm sure he'll take to heart." I tightened my grip on Gideon's shoulders. From experience, I knew I needed to be careful. Violence is never completely random. There's always a provocation somewhere.

"We got that porno tape your hotshot lawyer wanted. Whew!" Pedro fanned the air as if clearing a foul odor. "No wonder he wants it back."

"You watched it!" I shouldn't have been surprised.

"Hey, that *puta* was there when we tried to steal it. She was happy to show it to us."

Luis whipped out his phone. "You want to watch, homes? For a big man, he's got a little package."

"That's the least of it," Pedro said with disgust.

I waved the phone away, appalled at what I'd instigated. "So you didn't return it to him?"

"Not for what he's paying. It's worth a lot more than that. Check it out." Luis thrust his phone toward me again. I backed away, pulling Gideon with me. He lifted his thumb to his mouth for protection.

Pedro gestured for Luis to put the phone away. "You don't want to watch this *basura*. Thirty seconds was enough for me. You got to talk to your *gilipollas* friend. Tell him he's fucking with the wrong people."

"You can get a hundred grand for a sex tape like this," Luis said.

"But your piss ant friend's not taking our calls or answering our texts. He's disrespecting us," Pedro said. "What kind of *pendejos* does he think we are? You think that *puta* didn't make a copy too? We're all in this together now. Either he pays up or we sell the tape to someone else. She don't care either way. A porn site's just more advertising for her."

"It could go viral, homes," Luis said gleefully.

"If he's really your friend, talk to him. Convince him we're not fooling around. He has till Monday. Otherwise, fuck it . . ." Pedro shrugged.

"You know how to find us," Luis said. "And we know how to find you." He looked up at the lighted windows of the apartment building. "I bet some real hot chicks live here." Then he bent to address Gideon. "Remember, *niño*, it's okay to say shit, cause the world's full of it, and you might as well wise up to that now."

"Fucking right," Pedro said. They spoke a few rapid words in Spanish that I didn't understand, then high-fived each other and split.

When they were out of sight, Gideon removed his thumb

from his mouth. "What does fucking mean, Daddy?"

"It's just an expression. Not to use with your mother."

He looked up in puzzlement and raised his thumb to his mouth.

"It's what you say when everything's gone to shit," I tried to explain. "When no other word will do." Which was exactly how I felt. When I was hanging out with the 18th Street home-boys, a few never trusted or liked me. Wary of their hostility, I was careful to avoid them. Why the fuck hadn't I done the same with these *cholos*?

* * *

I thought of texting or calling R the next morning to convey Pedro's message, but finally did neither. I wanted to extricate, not involve myself further in R's problems. He didn't need me to confirm their threats. How he responded to their extortion was his problem, not mine. Sex tapes were ubiquitous on the internet. Pamela Anderson, Paris Hilton, Jennifer Lawrence, Kim Kardashian and how many other celebrities had their sex-capades hacked, or leaked the tapes themselves. I didn't know where Luis came up with the hundred-thousand-dollar price tag; I couldn't imagine that R's adulterous activities would interest more than his wife or the lawyers of his white-shoe firm. But maybe Pedro's disgust suggested something more disturbing about the video. If so, I was glad I hadn't viewed it. Why was R allowing himself to be videotaped anyway? In the age of cell phones and the cloud, how could he not realize there would be more than one copy? Maybe there was more going on between R and his mistress than I'd suspected.

We were both scheduled to play tennis on Sunday. I wavered about finding a last-minute substitute. I couldn't avoid R forever and it would be easier to meet him again, if he did show up, surrounded by other people. He arrived at the courts a few minutes late with a new racket and buoyancy I hadn't expected. "New racket, new game," he said. He pointed his racket at me. "How about you and me play together?" Was this a sign of solidarity? Had he paid the *cholos'* price and ended their extortion? Or was he partnering with me to gain my support to resist their demands?

Whether it was uncertainty or trepidation, I played badly, hitting the ball long or wide, or straight into the rackets of the engineer and the insurance broker who was playing instead of the ophthalmologist that day. "Not your usual game," R commented when I muffed a particularly easy overhand. As if inspired by my mistakes, he upped his play, chasing down balls with the zest of a twenty-year-old, or maybe a man freshly liberated from disaster. Despite my string of unforced errors, we just narrowly lost the first set, 7-5.

"C'mon, focus, we can beat these guys," he said, emboldened by his own intensity.

"You brought your A game instead of your F game today," the engineer said after R managed to whip a wicked backhand past him at the net.

"Yeah, some days are like that," R said, fist bumping me to celebrate. We won the second set, 6-4, and would have won the third if time hadn't run out.

"Walk with me," he said when the others had left.

I followed him to his Lexus, which he'd parked on the street today. "I know those assholes spoke to you," he said.

"I assumed you got their message."

"You were right at Musso's. She was just bargaining. I shouldn't have panicked and hired your friends. A huge mistake. But we've worked everything out now. In the end everyone has a price."

"I'm glad it's over."

"Almost over. I still need someone to deliver the money in return for the video." He looked at me.

"Forget it."

"I don't trust those guys. They screwed me once. How can

I be sure they won't again?"

"It's your mess, not mine."

"But they're your gangbangers. You hooked me up with them. And now they've switched sides and joined forces with her."

"You hire drug dealers, what do you expect?"

He gestured for me to lower my voice, although there was no one near us on the street. "I'm afraid this is your mess too," he said.

"No more. I'm out of it."

"Almost. I already told them you're making the exchange. If you back out, I'll tell them I gave you the money, and you're holding out on them. You want them back in your life?"

The bribe he'd offered me at Musso's hadn't tempted me. So now he was resorting to intimidation. Either the *cholos* had stiffened his spine, or his desperation had hardened him.

He popped the trunk of the Lexus and handed me a shopping bag of old tennis balls. "Don't open it now," he said. "At the bottom's a phone number and a manila envelope. Call the number and set up a meeting. Bring the video back next Sunday."

He had it all worked out, confident that I'd comply. He'd sensed some weakness in me from our tennis games that convinced him I would help. My failure that day confirmed his judgment. He knew he could coerce me into making the exchange.

* * *

I called the number at the bottom of the shopping bag. A woman answered. I told her that R wanted me to deliver a package for him. She named a Panera Bread restaurant in Cerritos and told me to be there at eleven the next morning.

The next morning I drove to Cerritos, a southeast suburb of Los Angeles wedged between the 5 and 605 freeways. I'd passed through the community before on the way to other destinations but never had reason to stop there. The first billboard

I saw when I exited the 5 was for tattoo removal, suggesting that the middle-class suburb had changed significantly since Pat Nixon grew up here.

I arrived at the restaurant early, found a table in the back, and ordered coffee. It seemed ironic that a dubious scheme hatched over drinks at a legendary Hollywood restaurant should end in a chain bakery-café in a suburban mall. Or maybe I was just trying to convince myself that the errand I'd agreed to carry out was an everyday occurrence. Didn't all adulterers try to cover up their affairs? Was my caving to R's pressure so craven? Didn't I want to see how this story ended anyway?

I was checking my phone for messages when I looked up to see a long-haired Latina in jeans and a black turtleneck standing in front of the table. My first thought was she was a waitress; then she slid into the chair across from me.

"Not what you imagined?" she said.

My face must have registered my surprise. "You, ah . . . startled me. I . . . I thought I was meeting Pedro and Luis . . ."

"I decided to come instead."

She was older than I'd expected, maybe in her early forties, and considerably less attractive. Her lipstick was too red and her eyebrows arched too high, as if she were trying either to camouflage or accentuate how life had bruised her. It was hard to believe this was the woman R had fallen for.

My discomfort amused her. "Did you imagine someone younger? Whiter? How did he describe me?"

"He didn't."

"But you had fantasies."

I shook my head.

"All men have fantasies. Most just lack the courage to act on them." She smiled seductively.

"And that's what you do? Help men act out their fantasies?"

"Yes, I liberate them, help them get in touch with their true desires. Didn't your friend tell you how much freer he is now?" She reached into her jeans and pulled out a cell phone.

"You want to see?" She extended the phone.

The relish with which she offered the phone reminded me of Pedro's reaction to the video. Her relationship with R was clearly more complicated and sordid than I'd realized. I pushed her hand away.

She gave a little laugh and took the phone back. "For a voyeur, you're very squeamish."

If she was trying to provoke me, she was succeeding. "Whatever's on that phone is between the two of you. I'm just here to make the exchange." I took the sealed manila envelope out of my shoulder bag and laid it on the table, wanting to end this as quickly as I could.

"You're such a good delivery boy. You could work for FEDEX or UPS."

"I don't think blackmail is part of their job."

Her laugh was full-throated this time. "You think that's what's going on here?"

"Isn't it?"

"You're blinder than I thought, stumbling around in the dark without even a flashlight to guide you."

"So what am I missing?" I said, stung by her comment.

"Why your friend can't end our arrangement any more than he can leave his wife and children. He tried—he even hired those fools to scare me—but then he realized how much he missed me. I'm the reason he can live the lie he does." She put the phone on the table and slid it toward me. "Maybe you'll find it easier to enjoy this in private. To see how delicious it is to give up control."

I let the phone lie there as she reached across the table and took the manila envelope. "I hope some of that is going to Pedro and Luis," I said, "because if either of them shows up at my apartment again I'm calling the cops."

My threat only made her smile. "Don't worry. Your part's over. And so is theirs. You got drawn into a game whose rules none of you understand. For some men, surrendering money can be as pleasurable as whips and chains. Resistance is just foreplay." She placed the envelope in her purse and rose. "You might try it sometime."

Anger drove me to my feet as well. "I'm not looking for what you're offering."

"Too bad. It would be much more satisfying to have me punish you than doing it yourself."

"I doubt it."

"Then what are you doing with *vatos* like Pedro and Luis? What's in the *barrio* you can't find at home? I could help you discover your true desires." She smiled again, and I realized my first impression of her had been wrong. She was more attractive than I'd thought.

* * *

The video on the cell phone may have been the original, but of course she'd made other copies. I sealed the phone in a box and left it with R's secretary that afternoon. I had no desire to speak to him again. A week later, I received an anonymous email with a link to a video. A few seconds was enough to confirm the participants. I quickly deleted the email; I didn't need any more reminders of how obtuse I'd been. Maybe R had truly wanted to sever his relationship with his dominatrix when we met at Musso's, or maybe he'd just wanted to up the stakes, add a new frisson to the elaborate game of domination and submission they were playing. Or maybe he'd seen me as someone with whom he could share his degradation. Whatever his reasons, I had my own actions to contend with. How can you understand other people if your own motives remain a mystery?

Claiming a shoulder injury, R dropped out of our doubles group and has given no sign that he expects to return. His name rarely comes up on Sundays now. We all have our own lives, our own *mierda* to deal with, which we'd rather keep to ourselves. Better to continue arguing about Federer and Nadal and whacking the ball as hard as we can at each other.

Tikkun Olam

The lawyer's phone call was one she'd been expecting—dreading, really—for the past two years. What surprised her was that Deshaun wanted to see her again. Why? "I have no idea," the public defender said. "You're the only one he asked for."

Roz debated several days whether to drive to the Riverside County Jail. Was she the only credulous person left he could call for help? Or was he summoning her there to blame her for everything that led to his incarceration? The need to resolve that uncertainty made the decision inevitable. The drive from Brentwood took two hours, more time than she wanted to ponder all the mistakes she'd made with him.

Her first impression, when he'd entered Juvenile Court in his black Nike jacket, tight jeans, white T-shirt, and white sneakers, was that he was the kind of handsome, reckless youth she should immediately flee. The swag clothes and slight smirk on his lips, as if he were superior to everyone who'd dragged him there, warned her to stay away. She'd gone out with men with the same cockiness and self-regard; it always ended badly.

The white-haired judge appeared to share her skepticism. He'd detained Deshaun in juvenile hall for three weeks for smoking marijuana and assaulting a staff member in his group home. Deshaun had completed his detention, but remained on probation, and the judge continued to question his behavior. Deshaun's parole officer, a man with a hardened, acne-scarred face, reported that Deshaun was uncooperative at his new group home and he'd tested positive again for pot. His public defender, a petite Latina who seemed fresh out of law school, reminded the judge "drug relapse is common." The judge acknowledged the fact but said if there were another relapse, he wouldn't hesitate to aid Deshaun's recovery by locking him up again. The case lasted five minutes.

Afterwards, the L.A. public defender hurriedly introduced Deshaun to Roz and left them in the crowded juvenile court waiting room. Roz explained that she was a CASA, a court-appointed special advocate who'd been assigned to his case.

"You another lawyer?" he asked, as if she were as useless as the rest.

"I'm a recovering one," she said. "I used to write contracts for a record company that no longer exists."

"Spotify, huh?" He summarized her recent history. "So how come you doin' this?"

Though others had asked the same question, she still hadn't formulated a simple, satisfying explanation. "I'd like to help," she said.

"You wanna help?" He lowered his voice conspiratorially. "Can you get me some weed?"

For a second she wasn't sure if he was serious. Her reaction made him laugh. "You really think I want that judge to put my ass behind bars again? Lighten up, lady. You feel me."

He rose from the plastic chair. "I gotta get the hell out of here." He nodded toward a burly, dreadlocked man hovering by the entrance. "My chauffeur be waitin' for me." Then he strutted out the door.

She called the CASA office a few hours later and asked if they might have made a mistake in assigning Deshaun to her. When she volunteered to become an advocate, she imagined becoming a compassionate mentor to a sweet, twelve-year-old foster girl who needed a shoulder to cry on, or advice about boys or schoolwork, or simply an occasional treat to lunch and a movie. It's what she'd craved growing up, support and encouragement from an adult who would listen sympathetically to her complaints about her taciturn and unresponsive parents. With no children of her own, and no longer work to occupy her, she finally had time to become the warm, indulgent figure she'd wished for as a girl.

Deshaun was *not* what the CASA training had prepared her for. If the non-profit, which had long experience at this, had a good reason for matching them, she didn't detect it. "The courthouse is a difficult place to meet," the young woman who answered the phone counseled. "I can understand why he'd want to rush out of there. Why don't you arrange another meeting in a more comfortable environment?"

She didn't want to admit that she hadn't liked him. Besides, persistence was a quality she prized in herself; she didn't want to quit because the boy had made her uncomfortable. So she called his group home and arranged to visit him at the end of the week.

The home was in Ladera Heights, a middle-class Black neighborhood beginning to attract white buyers looking for affordable residences. The house was a typical two-story suburban dwelling from the 1970s, still in good condition, with pink and white azaleas blooming in the front yard. There was no gate, no bars on the window, nothing to suggest that delinquent teens lived there.

Inside, the dreadlocked staff member she'd seen at the courthouse sat at a desk that separated the foyer from the living room, where another co-worker in his early twenties was drinking a Coke and watching Judge Judy on a large-screen television. He reluctantly rose and went upstairs to fetch Deshaun.

Deshaun appeared wearing earbuds and bopping to some music on his cell phone. He jutted with his chin to follow him and led her through the kitchen to a picnic table outside. He continued moving his head and tapping his fingers to the music as they sat across from each other at the wooden table, the only two people in the bougainvillea-draped, fenced backyard.

"What are you listening to?"

She repeated the question, louder.

He finally removed his earbuds and passed them to her. She listened a moment, but couldn't identify the rapper. "Who is it?" she asked.

"No wonder your record label went bust."

She laughed. "You're right. We made some bad choices, but I didn't pick the artists; I just wrote their contracts."

"I coulda schooled you," he said and proceeded to play some of the music on his playlist. Though rap was not her taste, she understood now why CASA thought they might bond. He played some mixtapes of Boosie Badazz: "They say that I'm crazy, and some time/I feel like I'm crazy/But I know I'm not crazy/My mistakes don't make me or break me." Boosie, he said, was sentenced to eight years in Louisiana State Penitentiary on drug and gun charges and released his album *Incarcerated* while serving time.

"I hope you're not planning on following his example," she said.

His sour look instantly made her regret her comment. "You're one of those church ladies, right? Looking for a way to get to heaven?"

"No, I'm not a church lady. Not at all. In fact, I'm Jewish, and Jews don't believe in heaven."

"How about hell?"

"We don't believe in that either."

"You should try three weeks in juvie."

"I don't think jails are a good place for anyone."

"Worst three weeks of my life, you feel me."

"I can only imagine," she said.

The curl of his lip suggested he didn't believe she could. He put his earbuds back in and retreated to his music.

She was quiet for a moment. Although he was intentionally ignoring her, he didn't get up and walk away. She tried again.

"Your mistakes don't make or break you." She quoted Boosie. "Whatever they detained you for, it was just one act, one moment in your life. That doesn't define who you are."

He removed one of his earbuds. "You gonna say that to the judge?"

"I will if I get a chance, but I need to know more about you. The Deshaun the judge hasn't seen."

"Like what?"

"Well, you tell me. Where were you born?"

"Here in L.A."

"Brothers? Sisters?"

"One each. Both in different foster homes."

"How old were you when you went into foster care?"

"Five . . . I was five." He looked away.

"What happened?"

He glanced at the back door of the house as if hoping someone might emerge to rescue him. "Our mom couldn't take care of us."

"That must have been difficult."

"Yeah. My little bro, he . . . " He paused again. Perspiration beaded his forehead. He wiped it away with the back of his hand. "Can we stop?" He rose abruptly. "I got homework to do. I gotta keep up my schoolwork for the judge."

His flight shamed her. Her mother had buried her face in her hands and wept whenever she asked about her past. Now she was repeating the same mistake with Deshaun. There was more pain behind his swagger than she'd imagined. They crossed the yard in silence.

Deshaun halted at the back steps of the house. "I never had no court appointed advocate before. I don't know what they're s'posed to do, but could you lend me fifty bucks to pay my phone? It's due tomorrow and I don't get paid for the chores I do here till the end of the month."

She wasn't sure if he were lying, whether he needed money for his phone or if it were for something else like pot, but she wanted to make up for questioning him so clumsily about his background. She opened her purse and gave him the three $20 bills in her wallet. He didn't promise to return them.

* * *

To find out what Deshaun found so difficult to talk about, she telephoned his social worker, who hadn't attended his delinquency hearing. They met a few days later at a coffee shop in Culver City. Mrs. Grisham was in her early forties, wearing a drab brown sweater and carrying a frayed, overstuffed briefcase that mirrored her own appearance. They exchanged pleasantries for a few minutes before the social worker reached into her briefcase and pulled out a thick folder.

"You realize this is confidential, but you deserve to know what you're taking on." She opened the file and, page-by-page, recounted Deshaun's history as if reading an obituary of someone she'd never met.

At two his father left, never to be seen again. His mother's new boyfriend beat her badly enough to go to prison, leaving his mother with Deshaun and a baby sister. The next boyfriend dealt meth, which his mother began to use as well. After the birth of a second son, her addiction worsened. Neighbors and a kindergarten teacher noticed that Deshaun and his siblings were dirty and hungry and called the Los Angeles Office of Child Protection. A social worker investigated and issued a removal order for neglect; the children were sent to three different foster families. Deshaun's mother agreed to parenting classes and drug rehab, but she never finished the classes or the treatment program. After two years, the court terminated her parental rights. Deshaun's sister and brother were both adopted by their foster families; however, Deshaun was unruly and volatile, acting out at school and at home. One family after another took him in, only to send him away again. At fifteen, after living with five different families, none longer than two years, he entered his first group home, where he lasted less than a year. At the second group home, he started a fight with another boy and broke the nose of the staff member who tried to intervene. That landed him in juvenile hall. His current placement was his third group home.

The social worker turned over the last page, straightened the papers, and closed the file. "That's it. That's his story."

"So far," Roz said, feeling a surge of anger. "Or have you given up on him too?"

Mrs. Grisham reddened; she had feelings after all. "I have twenty-three other cases, some with histories worse than Deshaun's. One of my kids saw his mother murdered by his father when he was three. Another was so badly beaten that he still walks with a limp. You can blame it on drugs, poverty, mental illness, racism—pick your poison— but all these kids have been dealt a crappy hand. A few will overcome it; most don't, no matter how hard we try. They end up homeless or in prison or having babies they can't take care of, who also have to be removed and placed in foster care. Maybe Deshaun will be one of the few who breaks the cycle. Who knows? He needs somebody to believe in him. Maybe you're the one," she said without conviction.

She stuffed the sheaf of papers into her worn briefcase and snapped it closed, leaving the bill and Deshaun's future for Roz to take care of.

* * *

Her meeting with the social worker made Roz question what she could realistically do for Deshaun. Despite his troubled childhood, he was good-looking, quick-witted, passionate about music— all qualities that suggested resilience, strength. She thought of the three-foot tall French jazz pianist, Michel Petrucciani, whose lyrical music she loved. Although he was born with brittle bone disease that fractured his bones more than a hundred times as a youth, he didn't let his disability stop him from becoming a remarkable musician.

Her parents too had managed to overcome the terrible fate of being Jews in Germany under Hitler. Her mother had been a forced laborer in a munitions factory in Fallersleben; the factory was bombed, and she'd been left to starve in a concentration camp. Her father had somehow survived two years at Bergen-Belsen. After liberation, both were interned in an American DP camp in Linz, Austria. As her mother once told her, "We didn't have in the world anybody." All their brothers, sisters, nephews, nieces had been killed. Four days after meeting, her father proposed, and in a few weeks they were married.

When they finally arrived in America, they entombed the past in silence and built a new family to replace the ones they'd lost. If her parents could survive the terror and starvation of the death camps, the murder of their families, and sustain a marriage founded on necessity rather than love, was it inconceivable that Deshaun could overcome the traumas of his childhood? Was he dealt a worse hand at birth than Petrucciani? Did he suffer more than her parents? Boosie Badazz might be Deshaun's lodestar, but she had inspirations of her own.

* * *

She waited a week, then called and invited him to lunch on Saturday. After an uncomfortably long pause—was he trying to think of an excuse to refuse?—he agreed. She picked him up in her Audi and drove to the Baldwin Hills Crenshaw mall for lunch. She'd made a reservation at the Post & Beam, but he rejected the restaurant as "too bougie" and chose Taco Bell instead. They ordered tacos and sat at a table in the crowded food court. To make up for the missteps of their last meeting, she opened her purse and gave him two Petrucciani CDs, a solo piano album and a trio with Charles Lloyd.

"This is some of the music I listen to," she said.

He looked at the CDs. "Never heard of him."

Although Deshaun knew as little about jazz as she did about hip-hop, music was a safe subject for both of them. Determined not to pry, she let him guide the conversation. He moved from the "badass" artists he admired to the people who pissed him off, the "lame" staff and "fools and fuckups" living in his group home. He brightened as he talked, and it occurred to her that he probably had few people in his life willing to listen to him. Maybe the thought struck him as well, because he suddenly grew silent. "But you don't really want to hear 'bout this shit," he said.

"I don't think it's shit."

He considered her comment, as if deciding whether to believe her. "You remind me of the lady who adopted my kid bro. When I visited, we sat at the kitchen table and she let me go on and on . . ."

"Do you still visit?" she asked.

"Nah, the family moved to Sacramento. I ain't seen my bro in three years." He shifted his gaze to a Latina custodian emptying a trash container. They both watched her a moment.

"What about you?" He changed the subject. "You got a husband? Kids?"

She delivered a quick sanitized version of her history—her brief, childless marriage, twenty-three years in the music business, unexpected early retirement, and no desire to return. Her marriage was what sparked his interest.

"How come you divorced?" he asked.

"We wanted different things." A glib explanation of a fraught relationship.

"You got a new boyfriend, I bet."

"No, no boyfriend."

"Why not?"

Now it was her turn to be embarrassed.

"So you alone too," he said.

His unexpected recognition of her loneliness touched her. She felt an urge to reach across the soiled paper plates and take his hand.

Perhaps sensing her intention, he pushed his chair back. "I'm never gonna marry," he vowed. "I didn't see one happy marriage in any home I lived."

"I grew up in a home like that too," she said.

"Then you know what I mean. No way I'm gonna have kids. If you can't get your shit together, it's cruel to have children. You just gonna mess them up."

"I guess I'm fortunate I didn't make that mistake."

"You ain't that messed up. You got it together more than the fucked-up social workers I had."

"I'll take that as a compliment." She smiled.

"Whatever." He rose. "We better be gettin' back. I got chores to do."

She had an urge to hug him, but again she held back. His faint praise was enough for the afternoon.

* * *

A week later she returned to Ladera Heights to help prep him for his coming court date. The hearing clearly worried him; he was more distracted, harder to engage than at the mall. He kept going over the reasons the judge should end his probation while they sat outside at the picnic table. His last drug test was negative; he was doing okay at school, where he was also performing his required hours of community service; and he was avoiding trouble in the group home, although he hated its rules and the "jailors" who enforced them. He didn't understand why his social worker couldn't find him a different placement. There had to be at least one foster family in L.A. who would take him. "I'm reformed, right? Ree-ha-BILL-a-tated. I learned my lesson. You'll say that in court, right?" he asked, still uncertain how much he could count on her. She promised she would speak on his behalf.

Her assurances didn't seem to ease his fears. He took out his phone and started to attach the earbuds, signaling their meeting was over.

"You know what would help?" he said as they rose from the table. "A haircut." He ran his fingers through his kinky hair. "I'm a little short this week. Could you lend me another fifty? I wanna look good for the judge."

She saw that his hair, which was styled in a low fade, was growing ragged at the edges. Maybe he was telling the truth about the haircut. When she handed him the money, his thanks seemed more genuine than last time.

"You know I listened to those CDs you gave me," he said as he pocketed the bills. "That cat could really punch those keys."

She laughed. "I'm glad you liked his music."

"I Googled him. He was a dwarf, right? His feet couldn't even reach the pedals."

"Yes, they had to build special extensions for him."

"They said he was in pain all the time," he said with surprising feeling.

She wondered if he was talking about himself as well. "It didn't keep him from becoming a great pianist," she said.

"Too bad I never lived no place where they had a piano," he said.

* * *

When Deshaun showed up at the courthouse, she was disappointed to see his hair didn't look any shorter than the week before. A haircut wouldn't have made any difference. The hearing didn't last much longer than the previous one. Although his drug test was negative, his parole officer reported that he'd skipped several days of school, which he'd failed to mention to her. Darnell, the dreadlocked staff member who'd driven him to court, testified that he was still uncooperative and failed to carry out many of his assigned duties, for which they'd docked his weekly allowance. Mrs. Grisham, who showed up this time, rifled through her briefcase to find his file. Retrieving it, she cited another complaint: he wasn't engaging in therapy in his group sessions. Hearing the evidence mount against him, Deshaun's Latina lawyer reminded the judge of his traumatic past. His alleged silence in group therapy didn't mean he wasn't benefitting. "It takes time, your honor," she appealed. The judge turned to Deshaun to explain himself.

"I know I shouldn't have ditched school or slacked off at the home. I had some black days, your honor. Mad headaches. Firecrackers goin' off every minute in my head. Like they never gonna stop. I'm tryin', but it's hard."

For the first time, the judge seemed sympathetic. Migraines he could understand. His wife also suffered from them. He ordered the social worker to make sure a doctor examined Deshaun right away and report the results at the next hearing. Meanwhile, he extended his probation for another six weeks. Deshaun's lawyer didn't even bother calling Roz. "Next time," she promised as they left the courtroom. "There was nothing you could say to change the outcome today."

Deshaun didn't look at either of them; he headed straight for the courthouse door. Roz followed him outside. "I wish you'd told me about the headaches," she said.

"You do one thing wrong, you better have a fuckin' reason for it. The fact they treat you like shit don't cut it, but if you sick, like faintin' or pukin' or can't see straight, that's a different ball game." He jabbed at his head. "Oh, it's not mental, it's physical. That's why the kid's so messed up. Send him to a real doctor, not a shrink. The doc will find the right meds for him—fancy drugs with names he can't pronounce, not cheap ones he can buy on the street. Yeah, that'll fix him."

"You mean you made all that up?"

He looked at her as if she were very slow. How could she not see that the judge and parole officer and social worker were all stacked against him? "I miss my weed," he said. "It quiets the noises in my head."

A van pulled up in front of the building and Darnell motioned Deshaun to get in. "I don't know how much more of this shit I can take," he muttered.

Roz watched, helpless, as the van pulled away.

Mrs. Grisham walked alongside her to the parking lot. The social worker's exasperation as she searched her purse for her car keys seemed aimed at Roz as much as her misplaced keys, as if she couldn't get away fast enough from all of them.

* * *

The hearing shook her, made her wonder again what she could really offer Deshaun. She wasn't a trained social worker or psychologist; she wasn't even a parent. She didn't know whether the headaches he claimed were real or imaginary, or how much he told her was true. She knew the dismal statistics for foster youth who, like Deshaun, were disproportionally Black and Hispanic: only 3% graduated from college; 40% of the men ended up homeless; 40% in prison. Had Deshaun's vitality, and the glimpses of vulnerability he revealed, deluded her about his prospects? What chances were there really for a traumatized Black youth in a racist society? She had no answers, only a refusal to regard him as a lost cause. She waited for some sign from him to decide her next step.

Two weeks later, Mrs. Grisham woke her at eight in the morning to report that Deshaun was AWOL. Did she have any idea where he might be? He'd been missing three days now and unless he showed up by tonight, the court would issue an arrest warrant. When he turned up again—and runaways always did eventually—he'd go straight to juvenile hall. "If I don't hear from him today, it's out of my hands," the social worker declared, clearly looking forward to the prospect.

Though she doubted he'd reply, Roz texted him anyway:

Are u ok? I heard u ran away. To her surprise, he answered within an hour: *Can u meet me?* She considered dialing his cell, but since he'd texted instead of calling, she thought it better to reply that way. *Where? When?* He named a McDonald's in Koreatown. *How soon can u come?* he messaged back.

She dressed quickly and drove east from Brentwood to a part of the city she rarely visited. On her way, she thought of calling the social worker; then she imagined both of them showing up at McDonald's at the same time. Deshaun would undoubtedly regard that as a betrayal, ratting him out to the authorities, who would only punish him for fleeing. Better to talk first before deciding what to do.

The McDonald's was in a tiny shopping mall of Salvadoran and Korean shops and restaurants, sandwiched between two high-rise buildings. Deshaun was sitting by himself in the back of the cramped restaurant, tapping the table in time to whatever music was playing on his phone. Fuzz darkened his cheeks and dirt spotted his T-shirt; it was the first time she'd seen him unshaven and disheveled. He removed his earbuds as she sat, his only acknowledgment that she'd rushed across L.A. to meet him. She asked if he wanted anything to eat.

He ordered a double cheeseburger and fries and a large coffee. He ate as if it were his first meal in days. "Where have you been staying?" she said.

"A friend's," he answered vaguely. "But I can't stay no more unless I pay. He wants a hundred bucks."

"That's hardly a friend." His grimy clothes and matted hair suggested he was lying and had been sleeping on the streets.

He shrugged. "There ain't a lot of people rushin' to take me in."

She told him what Mrs. Grisham had said.

"No way I'm goin' back."

"They'll arrest you, send you back to juvenile hall."

"You gonna turn me in?" he said defiantly.

"Running away doesn't solve anything. What are you going to do now?"

He gazed past her at a Korean mother and her two young daughters giggling at a nearby table. Finally, he spoke: "Maybe you could lend me a hundred so I could stay with my friend till I figure it out."

"Oh, Deshaun," she sighed. "You know I can't do that." It was what she'd feared when he texted; he was only contacting her because she was an easy mark, a gullible white lady he could con into giving him money whenever he asked.

"You don't know what that home was like," he said.

"I know you hate it. But let's talk to your social worker. Maybe she can find a better one."

"They all the same. You just bouncin' from one place to another that don't give a damn about you." He gazed again at the Korean mother smiling at her children. His expression reminded her of a child staring in a store window at an expensive toy he knows he'll never have. His eyes suddenly glistened.

She offered him a tissue from her pocket. He dismissed it with an angry wave, blinking back his tears. "You got an extra room in your house?"

The request caught her unprepared.

"You the one person I can talk to," he said. "You get me. You show me respect. The judge don't. The parole officer don't. The social worker don't. Might as well put that kid's black ass behind bars now. He never gonna amount to anything. But lockin' kids up and feedin' them bullshit all day don't change you. If I live with you, I could get my act together, make something of myself, get on a better road. You feel me. It don't have to be forever, just till I get my head straight."

She knew she should say no. She'd signed up to be an advocate, not a foster parent. Taking him home with her supported his running away. But this was an emergency, a temporary measure, she told herself, and his watery eyes and the rawness of his need made it difficult to refuse. She couldn't let him spend another night on the streets.

"Just for a few days," she said. "Until we can get this all

sorted out and find you a better placement."

"You won't be sorry," he assured her. "I can school you 'bout all the music you're missin'. There's a shitload you don't know 'bout."

* * *

Driving back to Brentwood, Deshaun begged her again not to call his social worker. "You don't know their fuckin' rules," he argued. She hadn't passed a criminal background check. She hadn't taken parent training classes or had a home inspection or filled out the proper paperwork. Unless she did all these things—which took weeks—child welfare would immediately remove him.

She told him she had no choice; it was the only way to keep him out of juvenile hall, but she agreed to delay the call until it was too late for anyone to pick him up today; at least he could have a good night's sleep.

"You think it'll be different tomorrow?" he said and lapsed into silence.

He remained quiet as they entered the modern, split-level house she'd purchased after her divorce, when she still hoped to find a compatible partner. She watched as he quietly observed the luxuries she took for granted: oil paintings and sculptures in the living room, a wine cooler in the kitchen, the 65 inch flat-screen TV and Bose stereo system in the adjacent den. Wandering into the dining room, he paused to note the silver candlesticks and antique brass menorah on the sideboard, before moving to her study. The crammed bookshelves interested him a moment; then the framed pictures atop her mahogany desk caught his eye. He fixed on the blurry photo of her mother, the one photographic remnant of her life in Germany, a fourteen-year-old girl standing between two stone pillars at the entrance to her home, a Jewish star crudely spray painted on one of the pillars, **Jude** on the other.

"Who's that?" he finally spoke.

"My mother. It was taken in Germany, just before her world collapsed."

He picked up the photograph, examined it more closely. "I got no pictures of my mom. Just the ones in my head, but they blurry like this one." He carefully replaced the picture on her desk. "I need to wash. I stink," he said.

She showed him the guest bedroom and bath and gave him an old terry cloth bathrobe to wear while she washed the clothes he'd worn for the last three days. When she checked in on him an hour later, he was sprawled on top of the covers, fast asleep, a striking, dark-skinned youth in a white bathrobe, as incongruous in her guest room as she was in his group home. She quietly closed the door and let him sleep.

As she promised, she waited until dark to call his social worker. When Mrs. Grisham didn't pick up, Roz left a message that Deshaun had contacted her. Deshaun was still asleep when Mrs. Grisham called back a few hours later, outraged to hear he was staying with Roz. What on earth was she thinking? The kid was AWOL. She was just rewarding him for running away, making it even harder for him to return to the group home. If she was serious about fostering, she should file a proper application, go through the standard procedures, get certified by the state. As Deshaun had warned, he couldn't possibly remain there.

Roz responded with the toughness she'd developed negotiating contracts. "Don't yell at me because you've failed him. It's your job to find a placement he won't run away from. Until then, he's staying here." Although she never intended to take him in for more than a night, the social worker's callousness, the system's inflexibility and bureaucracy, infuriated her.

Deshaun woke a little later, changed into the clothes she'd washed, and came downstairs hungry. She warmed up some leftover rice and chicken and sat with him while he ate. "You got more books, more CDs, more food in your fridge than any place I lived," he said.

"You're welcome to play the CDs, read whatever books interest you," she said.

"Yeah, how long? Did you call my social worker?"

"She wasn't happy I brought you here. I haven't passed the state requirements. I'm not licensed to keep you."

"You gonna be?"

Her face must have betrayed the answer.

His face hardened. "I thought Jews were s'posed to be different. They s'posed to know what it's like to be hated. Like your mother in that picture. But I guess that don't make you nicer than anyone else." He rose from the table and dumped his empty dish in the sink. Then he stomped up the stairs.

She thought of going after him, but she knew no excuse or explanation could repair the damage. Like so many others, she, too, had rejected him.

She lay awake a long time that night questioning her decision not to foster. After being alone for so many years, she'd grown comfortable living by herself. Having to be responsible for Deshaun would limit her freedom, make the travel she was planning difficult. After her cat died, she didn't go back to the animal shelter to adopt another. Why would she take in a stray youth now? Despite her growing feeling for him, did she want that burden?

She thought of the uncle she never knew, her mother's older brother who took the blurred photograph in front of their house in Hamburg, and later perished in Auschwitz because America and other countries refused to take in Jewish refugees before the war. Did she owe a debt to her mother and father because they'd survived? Or were they the reason she was so hesitant to assume responsibility for Deshaun? No one who survived the Holocaust emerged unscarred, a daughter of other survivors once told her. Everyone was broken in some way, and they passed their brokenness on to us. She knew that to be true, that the trauma her parents had tried to bury had scarred her as well.

After the death camps, her parents ceased to be observant Jews and rarely attended synagogue, but they sent her to Hebrew school anyway to learn about beliefs they no longer held and rituals they'd stopped practicing. Sunday school classes had little impact; still, she remembered the concept of *Tikkun Olam* she learned there. The world is broken and the Jewish people have a responsibility to repair it. Jews must work not only to fix the damage they see, but to build a more just world. If you see what's wrong and ugly in the world, and do nothing to fix it, then it's you yourself who needs repair.

In the morning when she rose, she was still torn. The door to the guest bedroom was partly open. She knocked softly to see if Deshaun was awake. The silence hollowed out her chest. She rushed downstairs, hoping she was wrong and he'd be sitting at the kitchen table, eating the cereal she'd left for him, listening to music on his phone. But the kitchen was empty, the cereal box unopened. Deshaun had given her less chance to change her mind than the judge had given him to reform. She thought of her withdrawn mother, who had suffered so much more than she had; her mother might have been more generous.

When Mrs. Grisham called a few hours later to arrange to pick up Deshaun, Roz was grateful that she refrained from reproaching her for being naïve, irresponsible, foolish, all charges she knew the caseworker was thinking. Still, none of those accusations was harsher than her own. She was already regretting her decision, wondering if she would ever see him again. It wasn't until later that evening that she discovered he had stolen the silver candlesticks and the menorah her mother had given her for a wedding present. It seemed fitting punishment for betraying both of them.

* * *

Only two other visitors waited with Roz to be admitted to the Riverside County Jail: a middle-aged Latina and a young Black woman with cornrow braids, a mother and a wife or girlfriend, Roz presumed. All three women avoided each other as they sat at separate metal tables outside the small sheriff's office where they'd surrendered their driver's licenses and purses. The jail stood a few yards away at the end of the road, enclosed by the usual razor wire-topped fence. A U.S. and a California state flag flapped desolately in the wind above the low prison buildings.

A uniformed guard unlocked one chain-link gate, and then another, and led Roz through metal detectors into a large room, smelling of disinfectant, which contained a warren of glass enclosed booths. Deshaun was sitting in one of them in an orange jumpsuit. He'd put on several pounds since she'd last seen him, let his frizzy hair go long, and grown a shaggy beard. The raw vitality that defined him had disappeared.

They each picked up a phone to speak across the glass barrier that separated them.

"I didn't know if you would come," he said.

"I wasn't sure either."

They gazed at each other on opposite sides of the glass, smudged by handprints of the many prisoners and families who'd been there before. The silence was as awkward as the glass between them. The lawyer had explained the multiple charges Deshaun was facing: drug dealing, burglary, resisting arrest; felonies that could keep him in prison for many years.

"I didn't think I'd ever see you again," she said at last. "I'm sorry that it's here."

"I made some bad decisions, took the wrong road. It's a hard lesson."

In a nearby booth, a man raised his voice angrily in Spanish. Roz heard, or imagined hearing, his mother sobbing in reply. Or maybe it was the pressure of her own tears threatening to leak out. "I'm sorry I didn't do more."

"You believed in me more than anyone. I shoulda believed you."

Once more she quoted Boosie's rap that he'd played for her: "We're all more than the mistakes we've made."

He shook his head. "Some mistakes you can't take back. I shoulda never stole those candlesticks and that other thing, that . . ."

"Menorah. It was my mother's. A candle holder . . ."

"Well, they didn't give me much money for it." He lowered the phone and looked away.

Roz waited for him to lift the phone again. When he did, his voice was ragged. "I thought 'bout you a lot. I wished it coulda been different."

"I wished it could have been different too," she said, but he was already laying down the phone and she wasn't sure he heard.

Suddenly he stood up and pressed his hand to the glass, adding his imprint to all the others who'd been there before him. Then he turned and signaled the guard to exit the booth. He didn't look back.

She sat there for several minutes, thinking about the times she'd held back with him. So much remained unexpressed between them. She thought of her mother's tearful flight whenever she asked about her life in Germany, her father's bitter, brooding silences as well. The rare times he spoke about Bergen-Belsen, it was with such sadness that she could only recall his grief. So many of the people she cared for had been damaged, broken by loss or indifference or cruelty. No wonder she'd been drawn to Deshaun. But she hadn't been brave or wise enough to alter his life. She'd failed him, and failed herself.

The wind rustled the chain-link fence and kicked up the desert sand as she exited the prison. A freight train rumbled in the distance, its mournful sound echoing across the barren landscape. The train, the barrack-like buildings, reminded her of photographs she'd seen of Auschwitz. She knew this jail hardly compared to the death camps her parents survived, but the fact they did survive them, and built a new life afterwards, gave her hope.

When she got home, she would look for a good lawyer to represent Deshaun. Maybe there was yet a chance to redeem both of them.

Chicken Soup

"*Cómase la comida!*"

Rose gazes at the plate of runny eggs and potatoes. Nauseated, she pushes the food away.

Amelia gently nudges the plate in front of her *patrona*. "Eat!" she repeats, this time in English. "You must eat!"

Rose ignores her plea and shoves the plate back again.

"I made the eggs just the way you like them," Amelia entreats in Spanish, although she knows that Rose probably doesn't understand. It wouldn't make any difference if she spoke in English or if Rose wore her hearing aid. She only hears what she wants. "Breakfast is important," Amelia continues in Spanish. "You know what they say: 'Eat a big breakfast, a bigger lunch, and a light dinner and you will live a long life.'"

At eighty-eight, Rose has lived long enough. "You eat!" she snaps and thrusts the plate across the kitchen table to her Salvadoran aide. Even though Amelia's already had breakfast, she picks up a fork and dutifully begins to eat what she cooked for Rose this morning. It's a sin to let food go to waste. She thinks of the many days there were only tortillas and salt in Chalatenango.

Amelia doesn't know what's provoked this sudden battle over food, but Rose hasn't eaten anything for two days now. She can't tell whether Rose is feeling sick or just rebelling against her cooking. Even if Rose understood more Spanish, or she could speak better English, there would be no point in asking. Rose isn't a *patrona* who shares her feelings with the help.

Amelia takes her time finishing the eggs and potatoes. They have another long day ahead of them and no reason to rush. While Amelia eats, Rose picks up the morning paper. She quickly turns to the obituary section to see whose passing has spared them further pain. Today she doesn't recognize anyone she knows; the fortunate are all ten, even twenty years younger.

Amelia watches her prickly, pursed-lip employer, with bald patches in her hair like the worn spots in her pink velour bathrobe, and wonders how someone who's lived so long, and with so much money, has turned out to be such a miserable *vieja*. Amelia has been attending to Rose three months now—five days a week, from eight in the morning to six at night—and finds her as hard-shelled and sharp-clawed as an armadillo.

Amelia clears the table, washes the frying pan, and puts the dishes in the washer. When she looks back at Rose, she sees the paper drooping in her hands and her head resting on her chest. With all the naps Rose takes during the day, it's not surprising that she can't sleep at night. Nights are hard for Amelia too. Alone, in the dark, it's hard to shut out memories of the past and fears for the future. Now she keeps them at bay by cleaning the stainless-steel stove and straightening the unused food in the pantry. She clatters around the kitchen noisily enough to wake Rose. Friday is their day for grocery shopping, and it's time they get started. Maybe Rose will find something at the market, an enticing pastry or a fresh piece of fruit, that will revive her appetite.

Rose takes her time getting dressed. She sees no point in hurrying. A trip to the market offers no excitement, no fresh pleasures. Still, if she's going to leave the house, she will dress properly. It's one thing for Amelia to see her without wig and makeup—she's just the help after all—but she won't go out into the world looking like a bag lady. She selects a pale-green silk blouse and seaweed-colored skirt, then searches for shoes to match. An expensive pair she bought years ago at Saks no longer fit. Even as arthritis has weakened her legs, her feet have somehow swollen. She finally settles for a cheap pair of flats that don't pinch her toes. She sits at her dressing table and puts in the hearing aid she dislikes, another reminder of her body's betrayal. When she looks in the mirror to fix her hair, she shudders at the image staring back at her. She raises her hand to block it and turns away, her wig slightly askew.

"*Tu peluca.*" Amelia points to Rose's hair as they prepare to leave, careful to protect her employer's dignity.

Rose gives Amelia an exasperated look, as if she's the problem rather than her hair, then glances in the hall mirror, and quickly adjusts the wig. They exit the house with Rose more irritable than at breakfast.

Although she no longer drives the aged Cadillac, a car with almost as much mileage as her owner, Rose still gives directions. "Left. Turn left here."

Amelia ignores the order and continues straight.

"Left! I said left. You're going the wrong way."

"No, *señora*, this fastest," Amelia replies.

"This is *not* the fastest. It is the *slowest!* I don't know how they ever gave you a license."

Amelia does not, in fact, have a driver's license, though she didn't reveal that to Rose's son who hired her, because it was clear that driving was an essential part of the job. Undocumented, with a false ID bought for $100 on Alvarado Street, Amelia avoids all government offices. She knows the danger of an accident, or any traffic violation that might involve police, so she drives carefully, and very, very slowly.

"You are a terrible driver!" Rose says, a complaint she makes every time Amelia drives the Cadillac. "I should never have given up my license."

That isn't what Arnold told Amelia. "Letting my mother drive is like being an accessory to a crime you know is going to happen. I had to take her license away before she killed someone," the *abogado* said in his halting Spanish when he flew from San Francisco to Los Angeles to find a caretaker for his mother. Rose was a *"mujer difícil,"* he explained, and age hadn't improved her disposition. He hoped that Amelia would not take her unpleasantness personally. He'd tried to convince her to move into a home for the elderly after his father died, but she refused to leave the Brentwood house she'd lived in for forty years. Now her health and mind were beginning to fail, and she needed someone to cook and clean and drive her to the grocery store and doctors. The pay was much better than work as a *doméstica* and Amelia was eager to find easier employment. Her only fear was that Rose didn't speak Spanish. Arnold assured her it wouldn't be a problem. It might even make it easier for them to get along. He seemed relieved that she was willing to take the job without even meeting his mother. Although he didn't say, Amelia guessed that Rose's aides didn't last long.

Amelia pulls into the parking lot of the 99 Cents Only store where Rose likes to shop first before they move on to the supermarket. Although the fruit and vegetables are poorer here, they're also cheaper, and despite her ample means, Rose doesn't like wasting money. Amelia parks, and then helps Rose out of the Cadillac.

As they start toward the store, a pallid old man, bent over his walker, trudges past, followed by a pretty, young Latina carrying his groceries. The girl smiles at them as if recognizing a common bond. Whether it's the sympathizing smile, or the feebleness of the old man, Rose recoils at their appearance. Like her image earlier in the mirror, this vision of infirmity appalls her. She stops abruptly. "You go," she orders Amelia. "There's nothing I want today." She turns back toward the car.

Rose's sudden reversal confuses Amelia. She understands her words, if not the reason for them, and doesn't possess enough English to press her to explain. She tries in Spanish to cajole her to change her mind. Rose pays no attention and yanks the door handle of the Cadillac. Amelia attempts once more to persuade her. There are things she needs to buy for herself in the store. Impatient, Rose snatches at the keys in her hand. Amelia pulls them away. If Rose gets the keys, she might drive home by herself. Rose swipes at her hand again. Amelia resists and Rose slaps her face. The blow is slight—unlike the hard, callused hand of the husband she fled in El Salvador—but the slap stuns her. She hasn't come all this way to *el Norte* to endure abuse like this from a mean old woman. She steps backward, closes her fist around the keys, and glares at Rose with all the dignity she can gather. "What's wrong with you, *vieja?*"

Rose's hands shake and her body trembles. She stares at the ground and waits for her breathing to slow. "Please," she says softly, "Take me home."

It's not an apology, or even an admission of guilt, but the tone is contrite enough for Amelia to soften. "You must shop. Your *refrigerador* is empty," she says.

Rose shakes her head. "I don't want anything. *Nada. Nada.* You understand? I don't want to eat."

Her vehemence alarms Amelia. This is more than just a temper tantrum. Is Rose trying to starve herself? Amelia can't let that happen. Not while she is caring for her. She will not sin against *Dios* by allowing Rose to end her life like that. Tonight, when she gets home, she will light a candle and pray for her. But before that she will have to find a way to persuade her to eat.

Rose jerks the door handle again. "*Por favor,*" she implores her.

Amelia sees the security guard in front of the market looking in their direction. She can't attract any attention that might bring trouble. She unlocks the door and helps Rose inside the car. They ride back to Brentwood in silence.

It's been a long time since Rose has struck anyone. She remembers only a few times she even raised a hand to her children, and once, in fury at her husband's stubborn silence, when she slapped his clamped mouth. But who is this ignorant woman, who can barely speak English, to defy her? She stares sullenly ahead and refrains from offering a single comment on Amelia's driving.

Amelia thinks of the several women she has worked for in Los Angeles, cleaning their toilets, changing their children's diapers. Crossing the border, she expected no less. It's an honor to work, to toil for your bread. Honest work is a blessing from God. But it isn't *la voluntad de Dios* to be treated like dirt. Nowhere is that written in the Bible. She thinks of the mother in Westwood who watched in silence as her four-year-old threw a bowl of macaroni at Amelia because he didn't like the way she made it. When the boy kicked and hit her the next day, and the mother still said nothing, Amelia didn't return. Another *patrona*, with a five-bathroom house in Beverly Hills, insisted that Amelia scrub the marble floors of her kitchen and bathrooms on hands and knees. For two weeks, Amelia complied. Then, knees sore and skinned, her back aching, she asked the woman to buy a good mop. "I'm happy to clean your floors, *señora*," she said, "but I only want to get on my knees to pray." The woman fired her on the spot, refusing to pay even for the day. Working for Rose isn't hard on her knees or back; yet Rose thinks no more of slapping her than the *muchacho malo* who kicked her.

It's past noon when they arrive home—their usual time for lunch. Rose avoids another battle over food by retreating to her bedroom and closing the door. Amelia hears the sound of the television and knows Rose is either watching or sleeping through her afternoon programs. There are three television sets in the house: one in the kitchen, another in the den, and a third in Rose's bedroom. Sometimes Amelia sits in the den and watches Rose's soap operas with her, but she prefers the *telenovelas* that Rose can't understand. Now she turns on *La Doña,* her favorite, and looks for something to eat. The bareness of the refrigerator stabs her. She knows what it's like to live on an empty stomach; it sickens her to think of Rose doing it deliberately. Arnold needs to know what his mother is intending. She has never telephoned him before, though, and worries what he might think. Will he believe his mother is really starving herself? Or will he think Amelia is exaggerating or misinterpreting Rose's behavior? She knows that prisoners sometimes go on hunger strikes to protest their treatment. Maybe Arnold will think that Rose's refusal to eat is a protest against Amelia and a way to get her fired. And maybe that is the truth and a good reason not to call.

She goes upstairs, knocks on Rose's closed door, and asks if she wants anything to eat or drink. There is only the muffled sound of the television. Rose could be asleep or simply unwilling to answer. Amelia knows better than to intrude, but fear overcomes her caution and she opens the door a crack to check. Rose is back in her pink bathrobe, sitting upright in her bed, eyes fixed on the TV. She spots Amelia before she can shut the door and shoos her away. "Go, dust, clean, do what you're paid for." Amelia quickly retreats.

She returns to the kitchen and *La usurpadora*, the current *telenovela* she's been following. She can't let a crotchety old woman who has stopped caring about life drag her into misery. The real work she's being paid for isn't cooking or cleaning but ignoring Rose's daily insults. On TV Paulina is falling in love with Carlos Daniel, another man certain to deceive and betray her, maybe even beat her badly enough to send her to the hospital, as Amelia's husband did. For many episodes to come, Amelia knows she will suffer, but in the end she'll not just endure, but triumph. Amelia hopes that one day she'll do the same.

When her program ends, Amelia goes through the house to dust the same paintings and lamps and antique furniture she dusted yesterday. The cushions on the sofa are as plumb as they were the day before. The living room is a well-kept museum, which people no longer visit. On the mantel, in a silver frame, is a photograph of Rose's late husband—a gray-haired, bespectacled man with thin lips and a meek face. Arnold said his father was a doctor who specialized in the heart. Amelia wonders if that meant he understood the mystery of Rose's heart as well. Although they were married many years, Rose hardly mentions his name. Amelia knows most men are unworthy of the women who love them, but maybe the opposite was true of Rose; maybe she was as sour and disagreeable with her husband as she is with Amelia.

Another photograph, in a plain frame, sits atop the piano no one plays. This is Rose's daughter, Lisa, posing with her two teenage sons and younger daughter. Lisa lives in Boston and Amelia has never met or spoken to her. Rose doesn't call her daughter or her grandchildren, and Lisa has never telephoned the house when Amelia is there. Occasionally, Rose will call Arnold and complain in a sharp and testy voice about things that Amelia doesn't understand. The calls are brief and Rose is usually ill-tempered afterwards. Amelia wonders if Rose treated her children as harshly when they were young and if that's why her daughter no longer speaks to her. In *telenovelas*, the heroines Amelia likes find revenge or justice in the end. Life, she knows, doesn't always reward you for your trials and suffering, but perhaps Rose's isolation, the absence of family and friends, are punishment for her mean-spiritedness.

The afternoon is long; there is little more to do, and Rose remains upstairs in her bedroom. Amelia rests in an armchair, closes her eyes, and drifts into a dreamless sleep. When she wakes with a start, the shadows in the living room have deepened. She sees by her watch that it is almost four. Distressed that she has let so much time pass, she puts away her feather duster and goes upstairs to check again on Rose. Now there's only silence on the other side of the door. Amelia knocks firmly. "Do you want anything, *señora*?"

"No, nothing, *nada*," a weary voice responds.

Amelia opens the door to see for herself. Rose is sitting in the chair by her dressing table, gazing out her bedroom window at her withering garden, as patchy as her thinning hair. She turns slowly toward Amelia. "You can go home now. I don't need you any more today."

It's moments like this, when she sees Rose's loneliness and frailty, that Amelia feels sympathy for her. "It is not time, *señora*. I stay longer."

Rose shrugs, as if it hardly matters. *"Cierra la puerta,"* she says, one of her few Spanish phrases, and turns back to the window.

Amelia returns to the kitchen, uncertain what to do. She doesn't work on weekends and worries that with no one to make Rose eat, she will continue to starve herself. Anxiously, she imagines entering the house on Monday morning and discovering Rose lying on the bathroom floor in her nightgown, unable to speak. She sees herself rushing to the phone to dial 911, then watching helplessly as the paramedics arrive, lift Rose on a stretcher, and load her into their ambulance. She must prevent this from happening.

Taped to the cupboard by the kitchen phone is a list of telephone numbers—Arnold and Lisa, Rose's doctors, the pharmacy. Arnold is the only one she's ever spoken to. Since it isn't five yet, she tries his office number first. There is some confusion with the secretary who answers; she asks Amelia to hold for a minute, but then the line goes dead. Concerned that the same thing will happen again, Amelia tries his cell phone. Her call goes directly to voice mail. Flustered, she's uncertain what to say. "It's about your mother; I fear for her," she finally stammers and hangs up. As she puts the phone back, she realizes she hasn't even left her name or number.

She considers whether to call again. What if she is wrong about Rose? What if this is just a trick to get her son to visit? She imagines Arnold being so alarmed by her call that he flies to Los Angeles in the morning only to find his mother sitting at the kitchen table happily eating breakfast. She knows Rose is capable of such deceit. Her willfulness knows no bounds. But what if she really is so sick of living that she's determined to die?

To calm herself, Amelia searches the refrigerator again for something to tempt Rose to eat. All she finds is the remains of some chicken soup she cooked on Tuesday. She is heating the soup up on the stove when the phone rings, sharper and louder than expected. She quickly answers.

"Did you just call?" Arnold asks in his awkward Spanish when he hears her voice. "Is something wrong?"

Hesitantly she describes her fight with Rose about eating, although she leaves out the slap in the parking lot, which is too humiliating to recount. "I don't know what to do," she finishes.

There is a long silence on the other end of the line and Amelia fears her account has been a jumble and that she's made a grave mistake in calling. Finally, Arnold replies. "If she doesn't want to eat, you can't make her."

"But she could die."

"Life has become a burden to her."

Amelia thinks of her own life. "That's no reason to end it."

Again there's silence. It's clear that Arnold will not be flying to Los Angeles tomorrow. "Maybe you can speak to her," she timidly suggests.

"I doubt it will do any good," he sighs. "She might listen more to her doctor."

Amelia remembers what Rose said after her last appointment with him. "I'm not going back if he won't give me what I want." Amelia didn't know then what she wanted from the doctor. Now she understands it might be pills to end her life.

"She won't listen to him," she says. "She doesn't like the doctor."

"She doesn't like anyone."

There's a click on the phone, as if someone is picking up the receiver. Arnold hears it too.

"Is that you, Mother?" he asks in English. If Rose is listening, she doesn't say. Even with her limited Spanish, she may understand what they're saying. The phone clicks again.

"My mother is a very strong-willed woman," Arnold says after a moment. "Once she's made up her mind, it's difficult to change it. I'll call her doctor and get back to you."

Amelia hangs up, saddened by the phone call. Whatever love or responsibility Arnold feels for his mother, it isn't enough to beg her to resume eating. Lisa appears to have no love for her at all. Maybe it will be a relief to both of them if she dies. Amelia is the only one now who can stop Rose's foolishness. However hard life is, only *Dios* can decide when to end it.

Amelia pours the soup into a bowl, finds some crackers to go with it, and takes them upstairs, determined to make Rose eat before she leaves tonight. Rose is still sitting by her dressing table when Amelia enters. She sees the tray and grimaces. "I told you I don't want anything."

Amelia lays the tray on the dresser. "You need to eat," she insists.

Rose looks at the soup with disgust. "I'm not hungry. Take it away."

Amelia ignores her. "I will not watch you starve yourself into the grave."

Even if Rose doesn't understand the words, she understands the tone. She dismisses Amelia as if she's an insolent child. "You can go home now," she says coldly.

But if Rose is stubborn, so is Amelia. She will not let this bitter old woman bully her anymore. If Rose fires her, she will find other work, as she always has. Losing a job is hardly the worst trouble she has overcome. Rose may have lived more years, but what does she know of hardship or suffering? Amelia sits at the foot of her bed to tell her.

She thinks of Leandro, her first born, who died at seven months with a belly swollen from hunger when her milk dried up. When she woke in the morning and went to his cradle, he looked so still, so peaceful, that she didn't realize he was no longer breathing until she picked him up and held him in her arms. With her hands, she shows Rose the size of his coffin, no bigger than a shoe box. The pain of losing a child never leaves you, even when you bear others. Now she's separated from her daughters too, who remain with her sister in the village where she was born. It's for Mia and Graciela that she's braved the dangerous journey to *el Norte,* to build a better future for them, and to escape the husband who beat her. It's her daughters who give her strength and sustain her and for whom she works so hard, sending money back to her sister, and saving to bring them to California. It's been three years now since she left them—a long time to be separated. She hopes that one day soon, when she can finally bring her daughters to America, they will forgive her for leaving them so long. She tells all this to Rose in words she knows she barely comprehends, but she wants her to know that she has heartaches of her own. And if she can bear them, so can Rose. Even if your children don't understand you, or appreciate the sacrifices you've made for them, you've brought them into the world and must do your best for them. She weeps as she says this.

Rose sees Amelia seated resolutely at the foot of her bed and knows she's not about to leave. Grudgingly, she sinks into her chair and waits. From the tears running down Amelia's cheeks, she understands that her caretaker is recounting her own sorrows. Although she cannot follow much of what Amelia is saying, she recognizes the names of her two daughters, and knows she is grieving for them. Rose thinks of her own ungrateful children who have abandoned her to the care of this stranger crying on her bed. Her children's resentments are old, the reasons for many of them forgotten or obscure. She lies awake at night reliving the years she devoted to them, wondering what injuries she could have caused that were so terrible that they can't forgive her. She thinks of the unhappy marriage she endured for their sake, the sacrifices she made for them. Do they know how many times she stopped herself from leaving? She remembers the dreams she had before she married her remote husband, recalls other men who once desired her, other choices she might have made. Life offers only heartache now, heartache and infirmity stretching till the end of her days. She thinks of what she's lost, what might have been, but will never be now. She has no purpose in the world, no reason to keep living. A sob breaks from her chest.

Seeing Rose's contorted face, Amelia rises from the bed and goes over to the dressing table. Rose turns her face away and dabs at her eyes with the fraying sleeve of her bathrobe. Amelia places a hand on her shoulder and gently rubs it.

"The soup," she says in English. "The soup will be cold. Please," she implores her.

The warm hand on her back, the unexpected kindness of Amelia's touch, moves Rose to more tears. Amelia tightens her hand around her thin shoulder. The two women look at each other through blurred eyes. Why each of them is crying, the other isn't sure, but to stop their tears, Rose lifts the spoon and tastes the soup.

A Drink with Oppie

On a Sunday evening in October 1966, while sipping a too-dry martini, Dr. Noah Aaronson noticed J. Robert Oppenheimer entering the La Fonda hotel bar. There was no question it was Oppenheimer—the spare, almost emaciated frame, the loose-limbed walk, the familiar pork pie hat. Noah's scalp prickled at his presence. Only yesterday he and Tessa were arguing about him; now here he was, almost as if he'd arrived to settle their dispute.

Noah looked around to see if anyone else recognized the physicist. If they did, they didn't appear surprised. The La Fonda bar, the biologist realized, was probably one of Oppenheimer's old haunts. He had a ranch somewhere in the Sangre de Cristo Mountains and must have been coming here to drink for years.

Oppenheimer sat down a few tables away from Noah and tossed his hat casually on a chair. His close-cropped hair was iron gray, a shade lighter than the wool suit he was wearing. He took out a pipe and tobacco pouch from his breast pocket, carefully packed the pipe, and lit it with his silver lighter. Then he sat back in his chair with the look of a man waiting for inspiration to strike. Or the waitress to bring him a drink.

Noah studied him from his darkened corner of the bar, wondering if he dare approach. He wasn't in the habit of accosting public figures to strike up a conversation. Still, Oppenheimer was different. Although they weren't in the same field, Noah felt drawn to the physicist ever since Oppenheimer was stripped of his security clearance after the government's outrageous hearings investigating the physicist's loyalty. Yet it wasn't until last night, reading Tessa's books about Los Alamos, that Noah realized just how much the two men had in common.

Noah tested an introduction: "Dr. Oppenheimer, I hope I'm not intruding, but I think you and I share a similar guilt." He could imagine Oppenheimer's response. He tried again: "May I introduce myself. I am a fellow scientist who has known sin." Would that work any better? Or would it just send Oppenheimer fleeing from the bar? He remembered the story about his meeting Truman. "Mr. President, we have blood on our hands," Oppenheimer had said. Afterwards, Truman told Acheson not to bring that gloomy fellow around again.

If Tessa were here, instead of shopping, Noah knew she wouldn't have worried what to say. She would have gone right over to the physicist's table and told him what was on her mind. "Dr. Oppenheimer, if you have a moment, there are a few questions I'd like to ask. You see yesterday we visited Trinity Site . . ." Trinity might just be the place to start. He caught the pretty waitress's eye and ordered a second martini to consider it.

Trinity had been Tessa's idea, of course. Once she discovered it was possible to visit, she was determined to go. "They only open it to the public two Saturdays a year," she said. "One is when we're in New Mexico. It's too good a chance to miss."

It was a three-hour drive each way from Albuquerque, where he'd come to lecture at the University of New Mexico. He wasn't eager to make the trip, preferring to go directly to Santa Fe instead. "What's there to see?" he asked. "There's nothing there but desert."

Tessa, a photographer whose pictures were laden with social comment, thought otherwise. Paul Strand, Ansel Adams may have come to New Mexico for the light, the space. Tessa had come for irony. There were nearly 400,000 American soldiers fighting now in Vietnam, and Tessa was looking for a way to comment on the country's continuing blindness to the insanity of war.

"Why don't you go alone?" he'd suggested.

"It's too long a drive. It'll be much less boring with you. Come on, indulge me."

It was what he often found himself doing with her, though lately more and more begrudgingly. They'd been together three and a half years now, split almost evenly before and after his divorce from Kathryn. Tessa was twenty-nine, ten years younger than he. They first met at the student union at UCLA, where she'd graduated a few years before with an MFA in Fine Arts and had returned to arrange an exhibit of recent photographs. He was taken with her dark good looks, her directness and open sexuality. When she invited him to see her photographs, he was intrigued enough to go. The photographs heightened his interest. Their irony sometimes seemed a little facile, her exposure of vulgarity and crassness a little smug. But there was a boldness to her work, a confidence—or was it reckless-ness?—that excited him. The way in which she approached her subjects revealed a willingness to risk confrontation that was reflected in the pained or startled or indignant faces she captured.

It was less clear what she saw in him: a married man struggling to raise his five-year-old daughter Caroline while Kathryn car-omed in and out of psychiatric hospitals. "Your compassion," Tessa said when he asked her that question once after a stolen afternoon in bed. "You're the kindest man I know." The answer wasn't what he expected from someone who only a few hours before had bitterly berated him for his failure to leave his wife.

What Tessa wanted, though, she went after—perhaps that was what he saw in her photographs—and her staying power was equal to the twisted tenacity with which Kathryn clung to her own illness. "I'm not going to give you up," Tessa told him one painful afternoon when he suggested that they should end their affair. "And I'm not going to settle for just part of you.

You don't have to settle either."

After a year of her prodding and encouragement, he finally decided she was right. She'd convinced him at last to damn the consequences, squeeze the shutter, and seize the moment. Unlike Tessa, however, he hadn't yet learned to live without regrets.

Regrets did not impress her. She had little use for crying over spilled milk, one of the reasons she was skeptical about Oppenheimer. In preparation for Trinity she had read several political and historical accounts of Los Alamos and, despite Oppenheimer's later public display of contrition, she judged him harshly. They'd debated the physicist's actions as they drove toward the test site through the stark New Mexico landscape.

"It was the Faustian bargain," she said. "Oppenheimer and the others sold their souls to the military in order to practice physics on a grand scale."

Tessa's politics, like her photographs, often seemed a little glib. "It was wartime," he argued. "They thought the Germans had a head start on the bomb, that if they didn't develop one first, we could lose the war."

"But how do you explain that once Germany surrendered, they kept right on working?" she countered. "Nobody at Los Alamos seems to have even raised the question of why continue."

"We were still at war with the Japanese."

"No one thought they had the bomb."

"They'd spent billions of dollars and years of work. They were on the verge of a breakthrough. I can understand their wanting to see it through."

"I'm not talking about the test," she said. "Of course they had to see if it would work, but dropping the bomb was something else. That was the real moral failure. Not even Oppenheimer opposed it. Here he was supposedly so sensitive and humane—a guy who learned Italian to read Dante and Sanskrit to study the Bhagavad Gita—yet even he didn't seem to have any hesitation about using the bomb."

He didn't like arguing politics with her. Even when she

was wrong, her certitude, her righteousness, always made him defensive. "Afterwards, he suffered great anguish for it," he said.

"So he felt guilty. So what good did that do?"

"You're being unfair. He worked for international controls, opposed the hydrogen bomb."

"I know you're looking for a reason to forgive him, but he opposed a crash program for the H-bomb, not the bomb itself," she said.

"I think you're wrong. The bomb changed him."

"I think he just wallowed in his guilt," she said.

It was late in the morning when they finally pulled up to the vast alkali plain where Oppenheimer and his colleagues had stood vigil at the birth of the atomic age. The morning was overcast and gloomy, the sky and earth as granulated as they appeared in some of Tessa's black-and-white photographs. The October wind swept the desert flats, kicking up sand devils around them as they walked. The air smelled of alkali and tasted of dust. Four hundred years before the bomb, conquistadores, on their route northwest, had named this desert *Jornada del Muerto—* the journey of Death. Oppenheimer, with his own poetic bent, had named the test site after a John Donne sonnet he had been reading:

"Batter my heart, three-personed God, for you
As yet may knock, breathe, shine, and seek to mend;
That I may rise, and stand, o'erthrow me, and bend
Your force, to break, blow, burn and make me new."

What the conquistadores found barren, atomic scientists made more barren still. Over the years since the explosion, a little sage and brittlebush had broken through the scorched earth, but the vegetation looked inhospitable even for reptiles. Despite the rare opportunity to inspect the site that the White Sands Missile Range was offering, there were only about a hundred visitors that morning. They wandered around the forlorn plain looking for remnants of sand baked into glass by the bomb's incendiary heat. Occasional shards of glass were the only traces left of the blast. To mark the event for future generations, a black basalt monument about fifteen feet high had been erected at ground zero. It was the same kind of nondescript stone marker erected along highways to commemorate Indian massacres or other historical curiosities, which Noah never stopped to look at.

Tessa stalked the sagebrush with her Leica, all business in her jeans and safari jacket, her black hair held tightly back in a rubber band in order not to impede her vision. Noah saw her shoot two young boys tossing a football back and forth near the basalt pyramid. He knew the irony would please her, although how it connected to Vietnam eluded him. He supposed it was just another representation of the world's obliviousness to the horrors of war.

She came toward him with her camera raised, stopped about ten feet away and pressed the shutter. He wondered what irony, what contradictions, his photograph captured for her.

"Are you getting what you want?" he asked.

"It's creepy, isn't it?" she said as they both surveyed the forbidding, windswept landscape.

"I don't think they really knew what they were unleashing," he said.

"Fermi supposedly was taking side bets on the chance of incinerating New Mexico."

"You really think they were so different from you and me?" he said, irritated by her unwillingness to see the world from the scientists' perspective.

"You don't think what they did was evil?"

"They believed the weapon they were building would end the war and save lives. It *did* end the war, and it certainly saved American lives."

"But did they really need to drop the bomb—two bombs— to do that?"

He didn't answer. He knew she'd already made up her mind. He thought of the community of scientists, many of them Nobel Prize winners, all working day and night to achieve their common goal. He'd met a few who were at Los Alamos and they considered their work there the most intense, the most stimulating of their lives. How could research that felt so intoxicating, that seemed so necessary, produce such tragic results?

The clicking of a Geiger counter caught Tessa's attention. She turned abruptly to photograph a middle-aged man testing rocks for residual radiation, fallout from the blast that still persisted.

"What are you thinking?" she asked on her return.

He shook his head.

She slipped her arm through his. "C'mon, I know that look. Something just struck you."

He didn't feel like explaining, but from the darkening expression on her face, he could see that she'd guessed.

"Everything makes you think of her, doesn't it?" she sighed. "Even here in Trinity . . ." She dropped his arm and broke away, scouring the desert for more trenchant photos.

* * *

Halfway through his second martini, Noah noticed Oppenheimer flicking his lighter several times, struggling to relight his pipe. It was the opportunity Noah had been looking for. He took a chance and approached the physicist. "You need a light?" he asked, offering him a matchbook from his pocket.

"Thanks." Oppenheimer reached up and took the matches.

"You're Robert Oppenheimer, aren't you?" Noah said boldly.

The physicist looked at Noah standing awkwardly by his table. "Have we met before?" he inquired.

"No." Noah introduced himself. "I'm professor of molecular biology at UCLA." He extended his hand.

Oppenheimer shook it, then recognized Noah's name. "Electron microscopy of deletion mutations, right?" He cited Noah's best-known work. Noah was flattered that he'd heard of it. Oppenheimer seemed as pleased as Noah to have identified him correctly.

"What are you drinking?" Oppenheimer asked.

"The same as you, it appears."

"Why don't you join me?"

"I'd be happy to." Noah brought over his glass. Across the table, Oppenheimer looked gaunter, frailer than he'd first appeared; even so, his presence intimidated Noah. For a moment he felt blank.

Oppenheimer helped him out. "So what brought you to Santa Fe?" he asked.

Noah told him about his lectures in Albuquerque and Oppenheimer asked a few questions about his research. Although impressed with how much the physicist knew about the field, Noah found himself becoming impatient. Science wasn't really what he wanted to discuss. Yet how to shift the conversation to more personal grounds without offending Oppie? "I was at Trinity yesterday," he finally said.

"Yes?" Oppenheimer's blue eyes seemed wary. "I'm surprised that anyone goes out of his way to see it." His voice was soft, reflective, but there was a quality to it that commanded attention.

"There weren't many people there yesterday," Noah acknowledged. "I had misgivings myself about going; still, I was more affected than I'd imagined . . . In fact, last night I started reading Jungk's book on Los Alamos . . ." He hesitated, wondering what might be the most tactful way to proceed. "I don't mean to be presumptuous, but there's something that puzzles me about the first test . . ."

Oppenheimer waited.

"Apparently there was an informal betting pool on the yield of the bomb."

Oppenheimer nodded.

"The bets ranged from 0 to 45,000 tons of TNT, if I remember right. The high estimate was Teller's of course. The official prediction, I believe, was 5,000 tons. You picked 300. I'm curious why. Is that really all you thought the bomb would yield?"

Oppie gazed past him. "It's hard to recall," he said. "None of us was even certain the damn thing would work. Perhaps I was just hedging. I don't remember."

"The yield was about 20,000 tons, wasn't it?"

"I lost the pool," Oppenheimer shrugged. "Why does that puzzle you so much? Is there something I'm missing?"

Noah could see that this wasn't going to be easy, but these were questions he needed to ask. "I've been trying to understand the thinking that led to Hiroshima." He tried to frame Tessa's charges in a less accusatory way. "As a member of the scientific advisory panel, you supported using the bomb, didn't you?"

"Yes." Oppenheimer sucked his pipe impatiently.

"You opposed a technical demonstration."

"That's right. I didn't see any that would be likely to convince the Japanese to end the war. What's your point?"

"I know this has been argued a hundred times before . . ." Noah started to defend himself.

"More like a hundred thousand," Oppenheimer said dryly. "Look, I was not in a policymaking position at Los Alamos. As I said then, I had no special competence in solving the political, social, and military problems the bomb raised."

The waitress passed by their table. "One more—straight up," Noah gestured toward Oppie's chair, hoping that another drink might hold him there a little longer. He drained his own glass. The gin braced him to go on.

"You underestimated the yield of the bomb. You also appear to have underestimated its impact on Hiroshima . . ."

"The same 'failure of imagination.' Is that what you're getting at?" Oppenheimer finished for him. What had one of his colleagues said about him? That he was so quick he gave the answer before you had time to formulate the question.

"Was it, as you say, a 'failure of imagination'?" Noah tried to keep his tone neutral. "Or was it something else?"

"Such as?" Oppenheimer struck another match to keep his sputtering pipe alive. "Why don't you just say what you mean?"

"That's what I'm trying to do," Noah said uncomfortably. He raised his glass to his lips, but it was empty. "The fact is," he blundered on, "Szilard, Franck, other scientists foresaw the consequences of dropping the bomb and spoke out against it. Their report even predicted how using it would lead to an arms race and undermine the chance for reaching international controls."

"Yes, and I didn't," Oppenheimer replied. "So what do you conclude from all this?"

Noah had to admit that things were going very badly. At any moment he expected Oppie to get up and leave. For some reason, however, he just sat there daring him to bumble on.

"I guess I've been struck by the connection," Noah continued, "or maybe it's a disconnection between intent and consequences, between thought and feeling . . ."

Oppenheimer's mouth twisted in a thin smile, or maybe it was a sneer. "You're wondering why people are human." Again, he leaped ahead of Noah, although it was not really what Noah had in mind to say. "To me, the essential question is not our initial failures of judgment, or imagination, or whatever lack you attribute them to, but whether or not we learn from them. There are many scientists for whom Hiroshima and Nagasaki changed nothing. Nothing. Many still don't see. I tried to speak about the sins we had committed as physicists, and look what happened to me. When it came to developing the destructive potential of nuclear energy, the military establishment was eager to embrace me, but when it came time to do something about that destructive potential, neither the government nor the military wanted me around anymore."

It was the same line of defense that Noah had argued the

day before with Tessa. Noah wanted to believe it. Yet wasn't Oppenheimer's eloquence a little deceiving? The bomb, after all, was not his first failure to gauge the consequences of his actions.

The waitress brought Oppie's martini, but he was too busy going on about the Atomic Energy Commission's denial of his security clearance and his banishment from government to touch it. Noah felt the conversation slipping away from him. "What about Jean Tatlock?" he finally interrupted.

"I beg your pardon," Oppenheimer said coldly.

"What about Jean Tatlock?" Noah repeated. "What did you learn from her death?"

Oppenheimer pushed his chair back from the table. "I'm afraid I misjudged your intentions, Dr. Aaronson."

"Wait . . ." Noah put his hand on Oppenheimer's arm. "Please, I need to know . . .. You see, my first wife killed herself too."

Noah was almost as surprised as Oppenheimer that he'd blurted it out.

"I'm sorry," Oppie said. "We all have our own pain to bear." He rose.

Noah refused to let him get away so easily. "But how did you live with it?" he persisted. "Just tell me that."

"Jean was not my wife."

Noah couldn't believe his callousness. "But you still had a connection with her. Even after you were married, you kept seeing her. You spent the night with her six months before she killed herself."

"You don't know anything about Jean," he said.

"But I know about my own wife. And hardly a day passes that I don't wonder whether she'd still be alive if I hadn't left her."

There was pain in Oppie's gray-blue eyes. "What is it you want from me?" he said.

"Why did you leave her? Why did you marry Kitty instead? Before you knew Jean, you were practically oblivious to what was going on outside your classroom." Noah remembered it was months before Oppenheimer knew about the stock market crash in '29. "Jean was your social conscience. Why did you give her up? Was it her depression? Did that interfere with your ambition?"

Oppenheimer peered down at him coolly from his six-foot height. "I imagine I left Jean for much the same reason you left your wife. I wanted more . . .. So I fell in love with Kitty. Falling in love is a lot like scientific research. You can never be certain how it will turn out." He turned, retrieved his pork pie hat from the chair where he'd left it, pulled the brim down over his forehead at a rakish tilt and walked out of the bar.

Noah knew that he'd blown it, that if there was any connection between them, a shared defect that had contributed to two women's suicides, or the blindness and arrogance that Tessa blamed for the horrors of Hiroshima and Nagasaki, he'd failed to find it. Or maybe it was because the real Oppenheimer was beyond Noah's capacity to imagine. Who could judge the depth of another person's sorrow and recriminations? Though he replayed the conversation many times in the years after Oppenheimer's death, the drinking companion he conjured up in the La Fonda hotel never offered more satisfactory answers.

Looking across the bar, Noah saw Tessa coming toward him with an armful of packages. "I see you started without me," she said.

"I had company."

"Who?"

"A fellow sinner."

"You're drunk," she said.

"You could join me." He raised Oppie's martini.

"You love this, don't you? Feeling sorry for yourself. You know it's not your fault Kathryn's dead."

"It's not my sins I'm grieving for." He drank from Oppie's glass. "I told you before, I had company."

Damascus

"You always read about it:
the plumber with twelve children
who wins the Irish Sweepstakes.
From toilets to riches.
That story."

Anne Sexton, "Cinderella"

Doesn't everyone, in some dark moment of despair, or burst of hopefulness, dream of radically changing his life? Bruce to Caitlyn Jenner, Richard Alpert to Ram Das, Malcolm Little to Malcolm X. Or Paul on the road to Damascus. One day you're a son of a bitch persecuting Christians; the next day you have a blinding vision that sets you on the path to sainthood. Or Gauguin—one day a stockbroker, the next a great artist. Ditch your wife and five kids, and you too can sail to Tahiti and start over again. Haven't you ever fantasized a transformation like that? Cinder maid to silver-slippered princess. Pauper to millionaire. Isn't that the magic we're all waiting for? We know the odds of hitting the jackpot in Powerball are 195 million to 1, but half the country buys a ticket anyway. Why? Because few of us are really happy with who we are. I know I wasn't. That's why I was so good at selling the lottery.

You might think lotteries hardly need advertising, that multi-million-dollar jackpots sell themselves. But it's not just riches the lottery promises; it's the illusion that winning can turn you from a frog into a prince. Money itself may not buy happiness, but it offers the chance to become who you always wanted to be. *Become your Mom's favorite* was one poster in the lottery campaign I designed. *Make your Mother-in-law like you* and *Buy the company that fired you* were others. I wasn't my mother's favorite, my girlfriend's mother disliked me, and I hated my boss—feelings which many people seemed to share. The series struck a chord.

No matter how successful a campaign you create, though, people constantly need reinforcement for their appetites, fresh justifications for their desires. My next approach was a series of photographs with the tag line: *When I Win the Lottery*. One showed a man in a director's chair, winking at the viewer, as he supervised a movie set of scantily clad women. Another pictured a Black woman in a bikini and captain's hat at the helm of a giant yacht, attended by a white waiter pouring a glass of champagne. There was also a large Chinese family standing by a Rolls Royce in front of a Tudor-style McMansion. This time the Lottery Commission was not impressed.

"These aren't the dreams of ordinary people," they said.

"I thought sex appeals to everyone," I countered.

"These posters are like tawdry ads for Vegas."

"The money you're dangling is outrageous, far more than you can win in Vegas. The dreams should match."

"These ads lack subtlety. They're sexist, racist, and crass."

We lost the account.

"I guess they didn't appreciate my efforts to diversify," I told Helen, the graphic designer I lived with, whose mother disapproved of our relationship.

"They know you're mocking them, that you loathe what you're selling. They can smell it a mile away."

"Just because I don't yearn for a yacht doesn't mean I can't relate to people who do."

"See what I mean."

Although the chief creative officer had approved the campaign, he blamed me for failing to persuade the Lottery Commission to buy it. The next week he informed me that my copywriting skills no longer matched the agency's needs. It wasn't the first time I'd been fired.

As Helen astutely noted, I never really believed in what I was employed to sell. My ambition when I graduated from college was to be a writer. Novels were passé; only movies, TV, and games mattered. I wasn't a gamer, so I set out to write the Great American Screenplay. Aim high, imagine large. Why else make the effort?

Of course, I had to pay rent and buy groceries while I was writing the brilliant script that would change my fortune. So I took a job at an ad agency. My first campaign was for a new brand of margarine. *It's not butter. It's better. Smoother, healthier, always fresh.* Margarine matched the way I felt about myself: we were both imposters. I never liked its taste and, as doctors complained when the ads appeared, it was debatable whether margarine was even healthier. Yet as successful marketers and politicians all know: *Exaggeration in promoting products is no vice and moderation in pursuit of profit is no virtue.* I could only make extravagant claims so long, though, before my imagination failed me. When I couldn't find a clever enough way to sell toothpaste that would make your mouth more kissable, the agency fired me.

Happy to stop pretending, I used my unemployment benefits to write a script I thought had mass appeal; unfortunately, no one else did. One successful Hollywood producer pithily explained the reason for his rejection: "Shit has its own integrity." Broke again, and humbled by failure, I crawled back to the world of false promises. I had a few successes, particularly my first Lotto campaign, then the disaster that got me canned again. I vowed this time would be the last.

Two months later, Helen moved out. I couldn't blame her. I found it hard to live with myself as well. Still, I had no desire to look for another job. Since my unemployment benefits and savings were enough to sustain me for a year, I decided to take one more shot at Hollywood's wheel of fortune. This time I set my sights on television and wrote a pilot for a sci-fi series set in a future where you could design your own babies, genetically engineer not just the sex or color of their eyes, but also their intelligence, musical talent, athletic prowess, whatever traits you wanted to implant. In the world I imagined, you could create the ideal person you wished to be. Unmarried, and childless, I could still dream.

The afternoon I finished the second draft of my script, I felt a rush of elation. The screenplay was clearly the best thing I'd written. I walked to the 7-Eleven a few blocks from my Carthay Circle apartment to buy a six-pack of Samuel Adams to celebrate. As I paid for the beer, I noticed the lottery tickets at the counter. I'd probably bought less than half a dozen in my life, but I had change from the beer, and was feeling uncharacteristically hopeful. So why the hell not take a chance? Bet on the sweepstakes as well as my screenplay.

If you recognize my name, you know what happened next: the $42 million jackpot. Dumb luck, of course. The odds of winning were astronomical. I think 80 million other people played the Lotto that week. I'll say this about the lottery, though; unlike Hollywood, it doesn't penalize you for talent, taste, or intelligence.

It's hard to describe the shock of discovering that overnight you've become a multimillionaire. My first reaction was disbelief. I kept reading the numbers on my ticket and matching them to the numbers in the paper. Could this really be true? The shock was followed by exhilaration. I could now fulfill every fantasy I'd envisioned in my ad campaigns. I wanted to run out into the street in my underwear and shout the news loud enough for even my dead parents to hear. I didn't of course. I called a few friends in L.A. and Helen, who hung up, thinking I was pranking her. Later that morning, I walked to the 7-Eleven to tell them they'd sold the winning ticket and bought enough beer and wine to celebrate with all the neighbors on my street.

When the press discovered that I'd written ads for the lottery, there was some temporary unpleasantness. However, a quick investigation cleared the way to award me the money: I no longer had any connection to the Lottery Commission and my winning numbers had been machine generated. I was as deserving as anyone who bought a ticket.

In the next few days, reports of my extraordinary good fortune went viral. My younger brother, my mother's favorite, whom I hadn't spoken to in over a year, called from Houston, where he worked at a sketchy right-wing radio station that promoted one conspiracy theory after another. Unmerited good fortune perfectly fit his skewed worldview. Winning the lottery could only be part of a nefarious plot to swindle the masses and enrich and empower purveyors of false truth like me. Soon I would answer for my sins. "Nothing can stop what is coming," he warned. He wasn't the only one to respond with vitriol. My prior association with the lottery confirmed for the aggrieved that the sweepstakes was corrupt. "The system's rigged, you fucking crook. How else could you win? I know where you live, you scumbag mother fucker."

The hate mail was only exceeded by the tearful pleas for hoped-for benevolence. "If God sees fit to bestow such wealth upon you, surely you must merit it in His eyes. I can only assume therefore that you are a kind and generous man who will look favorably upon my need for . . ." Fill in the blanks: a motorized wheelchair, a new car, a prosthetic leg, a new house, larger breasts "which you can be the first to caress." The emails and letters were litanies of woe, tragic tales of poverty, disability and despair, families ruined by floods and fire and illness, or torn apart by drugs or prison or death in Iraq and Afghanistan. They made me wish for a revelation like Paul's that would convince me there was redemption for all this suffering. Certainly, my millions couldn't provide it, even if I'd given it all away.

At first I read everything, the death threats and appeals for money; daily marriage proposals (accompanied by seductive selfies) from Ukraine, Russia, Kazakhstan; urgent invitations to meet from cousins three or four times removed ("I'm the grandson of your mother's first cousin Emily"); Facebook friend requests from people I'd never met or long forgotten ("Remember me, I was in Miss Godwin's kindergarten class with you"). When I didn't respond, the resourceful found my phone number and dialed. I changed my number, changed my email, cancelled my Twitter account, and stopped looking at Facebook. The desperate and insistent were undeterred. They sent letters by FedEx, UPS, the postal service; they even showed up at my apartment door. Whether appeals for aid or diatribes of hate, envy and resentment ran through all the letters and emails I received. Finally, I stopped opening them. They saddened and frightened me too much.

I abandoned my apartment, rented an over-priced new one in a high-rise building overlooking the ocean in Santa Monica, and left no forwarding address, hoping that a new residence, a beard and dark sunglasses might keep me anonymous for a while. I didn't buy a yacht or a Rolls; I splurged on a canary-yellow Ferrari 488 Pista instead. The $330,000 racing car with its twin-turbocharged 3.9-liter V-8 engines was definitely an indulgence, but I needed a distraction, or maybe consolation for feeling both reviled and guilty for my good fortune.

A few nights later, I drove the Ferrari to pick up Helen for dinner. It was the first time we'd seen each other since I'd become a multimillionaire. No longer damaged goods, I was suddenly worth a reappraisal in both Helen and her mother's eyes. She surveyed the sleek, limited-edition coupe, the beard, the Gucci Aviator sunglasses. "Wow. A new man. Do you have a tattoo to match?"

"I'll show you mine, if you show me yours," I teased, knowing that, under her skirt, daffodils were discreetly inked on her right hip.

"We'll have to see about that," she said.

At Lucques, the conversation flowed easily over bluefish wrapped in pancetta and two bottles of 2013 Domaine De Chevalier Blanc. After all, we'd lived together for nearly two years, and even in bad times, retained some affection for each other.

"So what are you going to do with all that money?" she asked the multimillion dollar question.

"I'm still thinking about it. Any suggestions?"

"A house in Bel Air," she instantly replied.

"Is that really where you want to live?"

"I wouldn't mind."

I downed the last of the too-expensive wine and called for the check.

Maybe I was angry with her, or dispirited by her Bel Air dreams, or just too tipsy, but driving back to my apartment, I failed to curb the Pista's 711 horsepower engine. When the SUV in front of me braked suddenly at a yellow light, I rear-ended it. The collision wasn't hard enough to injure anyone; the damage was to the cars.

The woman driving the Subaru seethed as she surveyed her mangled bumper; she glowered at the crumpled fenders of my Ferrari as if the car deserved even worse. "You'll be hearing from my lawyer," she said when we exchanged insurance information. Helen watched stonily from the car, clutching the shoulder strap of her seat belt. Her disgust mirrored the Subaru driver's. "Please, drive me home," she said when I returned. "I thought money might change you, but you're as self-destructive as you were before."

I interpreted the accident differently, saw it as a sign I'd bought the wrong car. Wrecking it was unconscious recognition that I didn't deserve a Ferrari. I was a poseur, an imposter donning a suit that didn't fit, driving a racecar I couldn't control. I sold it back to the dealer, at a great loss, deserved punishment for my grandiosity.

Maybe the lottery is a bipolar experience for every winner, and depression inevitably follows mania. My unexpected fortune was both a gift and a burden. You couldn't just let it sit in a bank—okay, several banks— collecting interest. I still had to figure out what to do with all that money. The only way Jeff Bezos, the world's richest man then, could think to spend his Amazon billions was to build a spaceship to travel to another planet and escape all his detractors on this one. I didn't have that much money; still, I possessed a futuristic vision of my own. I returned to pursuing it.

I found an agent who *just loved* my screenplay and immediately sent it to several highly regarded producers. One immediately saw its *potential* and set up meetings with cable networks and streaming services. So we made the rounds. The *suits*, although they rarely wore them, were all eager to talk. However, they were more eager to discuss the lottery than the pilot I'd written. The shameless letters I received from prospective brides interested them far more than the characters I'd created. What if I traveled to Ukraine or Kazakhstan to discover if the women in the photos were real? What if I actually fell in love and married one of them? Now that was a *fabulous* premise for a reality series.

We had half a dozen meetings like that. Besides the marriage proposals, the hate mail and death threats also intrigued the execs. They'd received similar mail themselves. How seriously did I take the threats? What did I do to protect myself? Finally, we'd get around to my script, which they all agreed was *a great read,* although they had various reservations. My screenplay was either *too expensive* to produce or *too similar* to a project already in development or *too cerebral for our audience.* In the end no one wanted to put up the money to make it. But you should shoot it, they encouraged. Finance it yourself. You have the resources. Prove your concept; bring it to life on the screen.

Most producers in Hollywood warn you never to mortgage your house or put up your own money to make a film. The producer who'd shopped my screenplay urged me to take the plunge anyway. "Why not spend your money on something you believe in? You do believe in yourself, don't you?" Put that way, it was difficult to say no. I'd always hoped to direct some-day, and since I was paying for it, why not helm the project too? Aim high, imagine large. Only now the actresses would be wearing space suits instead of bikinis.

For a hefty salary, I hired the producer to guide me through the process; in turn, he hired a professional crew to make up for my inexperience. Though never able to cast the A-list actors we first discussed, he had no problem finding replacements. Everyone was eager to work for a man blessed by luck; they hoped it would rub off on them and turn them into stars. Un-fortunately, I quickly discovered that it's easier to bed actresses than direct their screen performances. Maybe I was blinded by lust, but I couldn't tell whether they were faking it in bed or on the set. Or both.

Although I was smart enough to follow the lead of my crew, in the end, the final decisions are the director's. Even when I wasn't sure if what I was capturing was true or false, credible or laughable, I was the one who had to determine if the take was good enough to move on to the next setup. Much of the time I couldn't tell. Sometimes I stalled for time and asked the actors to repeat the shot; other times, at a loss how to improve the scene, I just moved on and hoped we could fix it in the edit room. Each day was more excruciating than the last. I woke with the taste of dread and nausea and returned home at night with my temples throbbing, too drained to do anything but pour myself some scotch and crash. It was a relief when the shooting ended.

Watching the film the editor finally stitched together, I felt as heartsick as I did when I smashed up my Ferrari. My money had purchased an even more expensive suit that didn't fit. I was no Orson Welles, no Spielberg, no wunderkind. No Gauguin either. The reception to the film confirmed my own reaction. It was stillborn, lifeless. The Syfy channel bought it for less than the auto dealer paid for my ruined Pista and aired it late at night when few people were watching. Humiliated by my failure, I remembered the famous adage of Saint Teresa, who spurned wealth to become a nun: "There are more tears shed over answered prayers than over unanswered prayers."

Instead of enabling me to realize my dreams, my wealth had further exposed my limitations. Miserable as I was, I still had no desire to follow Saint Teresa and give my millions away. To quote another revered woman, not a saint: "I've been rich and I've been poor. And, believe me, rich is better," Mae West declared. I agreed. Yet if you can't become the person you dreamed, who are you? I looked at myself in the mirror. Maybe I was as bad at reading faces as I was judging performances, but I couldn't tell if the haggard face staring back at me was a perpetual imposter or something more I couldn't see. To discover that, I decided to retreat, recalibrate, so I bought a small, split-level house at the end of a dirt road, high in the hills of Topanga Canyon. My neighbors were coyotes and rattlesnakes, lizards and gophers, scorned creatures whom I found fitting company. I knew my distress paled in comparison to the pain suffered by the hundreds of people who'd entreated me for help; yet I couldn't shake my gloom.

Alone and isolated, I had time to read books I'd had no time to explore before. I started with memoirs of self-transformation, Caitlyn Jenner's *The Secrets of My Life* and Ram Das's *Be Here Now*. I moved on to *The Moon and Sixpence,* Maugham's novel about Gauguin, then to books about the life of Paul. It was encouraging to see that none of their transformations had occurred overnight. Like Bruce/Caitlyn Jenner, they'd all struggled with the terrifying question, "What the hell am I going to do with my life?" Paul was tormented by a constant feeling that he wasn't accomplishing what he wanted and that he fell agonizingly short of perfection. Nietzsche called him a morbid crank, repellent both to himself and others. Though I heard no voice of God calling to me, I understood Paul's feelings of inadequacy.

Most days I slept late, read a little, or simply sat on my deck smoking pot and watching hawks soaring high above the ridges and lizards sunning themselves on the rocks. The hawks scanning for prey, and the lizards waiting to snatch insects from the air, all had intention, purpose, biological imperatives to stay alive. I had nothing comparable to drive me. Whatever ambition I once had seemed meaningless now. Perhaps I was clinically depressed, but I saw no future for myself, no reason to leave the canyon or engage with other people. Rarely did I even turn on the news to check what was happening in the world outside my hideaway. The outbreak of COVID-19 in China and its rampage through Europe confirmed my decision to remain on the mountaintop. Who knew how soon the contagion would reach the U.S.?

One afternoon, while sitting on my deck, mildly stoned, I heard a car slowly working its way up the incline. Through the haze of pot and dust, I finally glimpsed the intruder, a FedEx van, which stopped at the parking area, about fifty yards below the house. The driver emerged from the van and started up the gravel path. I rose to meet him, the first person I'd seen in weeks.

"This is a helluva place to get to," he said, handing me a standard FedEx envelope.

"But you found me anyway." I opened the envelope with trepidation, worrying who'd managed to track me down. Inside was a neatly handwritten letter from a woman I'd never met who lived in the same apartment complex as my brother:

I hope this reaches you. I couldn't find your phone number or email and am unsure if this is even the correct address. I write because I worry your brother is very sick and has no one to take care of him. He doesn't know I'm writing you and would be very angry if he did. He says it's just a bad case of the flu. I worry it could be this new virus. He speaks of you often, his rich and lucky brother. Can you bring that luck to Houston to help him? Please come, come as soon as you can. I fear for him.

My estranged brother and I hadn't spoken since he called to castigate me for my unearned and undeserved wealth. Harry was born with a congenitally dislocated hip that no one detected until he was two and started walking with a limp. The hip required major surgery, which the surgeon botched and crippled Harry. My mother blamed herself, and her doctor, for not noticing the deformity earlier. To absolve her guilt, she focused her love and attention on my frail, hobbled brother. Since I was three years older and had all my limbs intact, I was entrusted to look after him every place we went—school, playground, social gatherings—a responsibility I resented and often shirked, especially when I was in high school. When he was bullied or ridiculed, I often failed to protect him. Despite my mother's love, he saw himself as an outcast, irremediably damaged, unfairly treated by God and doctors and me. He grew up waiting for the Day of Reckoning, the Great Awakening, when justice would be restored, the mighty would be brought low, and the lowly become king.

"Nothing can stop what is coming," my brother had predicted. I doubted that COVID-19 was what he'd imagined. Though I knew he wouldn't be happy to see me, how could I not go?

I didn't know much about the coronavirus—it was just beginning to reach America—but on the way to the airport I stopped at a CVS and bought some packs of medical masks in case my brother was contagious. Only Asians seemed to be wearing them at LAX. Although I was conscious of the coughs and sneezes I heard on our flight to Houston, none of the nearby passengers appeared concerned.

Harry lived in Garden Grove, a village of two-story, wooden apartments in the northwest section of the city. Brick pillars that dotted the buildings at regular intervals were the only feature that distinguished the complex from a cheap motel. I parked my rental car, put on a precautionary mask, and found my brother's apartment. Harry opened the door wearing a loosely tied, garishly colored cotton bathrobe over an undershirt and boxer shorts. He hadn't shaved in days and there were dark patches under his hollowed eyes. He stared at me as if I were an alien from another planet or a character from some comic book. "The Lone Ranger and Green Hornet wore masks over their eyes," he said. "Isn't yours in the wrong place?"

"Your neighbor wrote to tell me you were sick. She's worried about you."

"I told her it was just the flu," he said, still clinging to the half-opened door as if he needed it for ballast. "This virus shit is just a hoax, another plot by Gates and his fellow globalists to take away our freedoms."

"Are you going to let me in? Or are you just going to stand there haranguing me?"

Begrudgingly, he opened the door. I followed him as he limped into his cluttered apartment and sank onto the rumpled couch. Newspapers, magazines, and unopened mail were piled on two mismatched armchairs and a glass coffee table. I cleared a chair and sat. "Have you spoken to your doctor?" I asked.

"You know I hate doctors. You know what they did to me." He started to cough, a harsh, unnerving rattle that reddened his face. I quickly went into the kitchen and poured a glass of water. The counters and sink were filled with dirty dishes. The odor of stale grease permeated the room.

"Maybe it's more than just the flu. Maybe you should get tested," I suggested when I handed him the water.

"Are you a doctor now? Did you use your lottery money to buy yourself a medical degree?"

"I don't know any more than you. That's why it would be a good idea to find out."

"I'm taking Tylenol, Vitamin C, drinking lots of liquids. I'm getting better. I'm not going to any damned hospital." Harry rose unsteadily. "Go back to California. I don't need your help. I never did." He stumbled, grabbed for the nearest armchair for support and missed, face planting on the dirty carpet. He tried to rise and sank to the floor again. I immediately dialed 911. By then, he'd managed to turn over on his back; his face was bloody and his breathing labored. I insisted he lie there until the paramedics arrived. He glared at me while they carried him on a stretcher to the ambulance as if I'd betrayed him once again. I followed him to the hospital in my rental car, and watched them rush him into the E.R. in his hideous bathrobe. That left me to fill out the paperwork. I was ashamed how little I could answer; I had no idea of my brother's current health condition, or medical insurance, or whether he was even employed now or where.

After returning the forms with their many blanks, I joined other anxious strangers in the waiting room. The crowded room was like a United Nations of the sick and ailing, people of all races, speaking in different languages, coughing in different registers, united by a common fear and helplessness. It reminded me of all the desperate letters I'd received and failed to answer. Now here I was among the desperate.

It took four hours before a doctor called me into the E.R. "We won't get the test results back for a few days, but your brother probably has Covid," a man in green scrubs, about my age, said from behind a mask and helmet-like plastic shield. "His chest X-ray shows no pneumonia and his oxygen level is still high, so I'm sending him home." He told me to buy an oximeter at a drug store to monitor Harry's blood oxygen level and pulse rate and watch them closely. "This virus is unpredictable. He could crash at any time."

"That's it?"

"Look, we're just learning about this beast. We only have so many beds and we need them for people who're in worse shape than your brother. He doesn't want to be here anyway. He thinks he just has a bad case of the flu."

"Well, he's no doctor."

"I am," he said, "and I don't have any better answers." Then he was gone.

Harry was triumphant about his release. Even the treacherous doctors had vindicated his self-diagnosis. He berated me all the way back to Garden Grove as he wiped perspiration from his feverish forehead. What right had I to call the paramedics? I'd freaked out, panicked over an unfortunate tumble, and rushed him to the hospital in his bathrobe and underwear. For what? A bad case of the flu. What made me think I knew what was best for him? Why my sudden interest in his life anyway? I'd never given a damn before.

I half-listened to his grievances. Even if the test confirmed he had Covid, I knew he wouldn't accept the diagnosis. My goal wasn't to change my brother's beliefs, just to insure he survived. He wasn't about to don a mask, so whatever precautions I took were up to me. The nurse at the hospital told me the virus was most contagious two to three days before symptoms began, less after the illness hit; maybe I hadn't been infected yet. En route to the apartment, I stopped at a CVS, bought an oximeter, a thermometer, rubber gloves, bottles of sanitizer, and cleaning supplies.

"What's all this for?" Harry asked.

"If I'm going to stay with you, I'm going to make sure your place is at least clean."

"What's the matter?" he scoffed. "No rooms at the Ritz?"

When we reached his apartment, he wobbled into his bedroom and, exhausted, careened onto his bed. I spent the rest of the day washing the dirty dishes, vacuuming the apartment, and disinfecting the kitchen, bathroom, every surface where the invisible virus might be lurking.

Two days later, the hospital called while Harry was sleeping to report that he'd indeed tested positive for COVID-19. I knew telling him would only provoke another argument. It was difficult enough to get him to use the oximeter to test his oxygen level and heart rate. The hospital had warned that it could take two to three weeks for the virus to run its course, that Harry could appear worse one day, improve the next.

He only grew weaker. He lost his appetite, could barely keep down the soup or eggs I cooked for him. His phlegmy cough grew harsher, his breathing shallower. He wore the same pajama bottoms for days because it was too hard to put on a new pair. Most of the time he huddled under the blankets in his "Make America Great" hoodie to ward off the chills from his fever. I waited for his fever to spike too high or his oxygen level to plummet too low to justify returning to the E.R. Every day I called the hospital, I spoke to a different doctor. They prescribed antibiotics, which I hurried to CVS to get, and which Harry took along with his Tylenol and Vitamin C. Despite his rattling cough and soaking sweats, he insisted that this would pass. I anxiously monitored his oximeter levels, worried that I might miscalculate, wait too long to take him back to the hospital.

Nights were the worst. I slept fitfully on the lumpy living room couch, listening to my brother toss and turn and cough in his bed. As children we shared a bedroom, and I remembered him moaning in his sleep after his failed surgery. Our mother would rush into the bedroom to comfort him, while I covered my ears with my pillow to shut out his groans and sobs.

The fourth night after our return from the E.R., I heard a loud crash in his bedroom. I turned on the light to find him sprawled on the floor. He waved me off, but was too weak to stand. I struggled to lift him and help him to the bathroom, then led him back to bed. The tissues I saw beside his pillow were spotted with blood.

"I think tomorrow we should go back to the hospital for another X-ray," I said.

He leaned back against the headboard and pulled the blankets up around his shoulders, shivering. "How come you got all the good luck? Health. A winning lottery ticket. Why you instead of me?"

"I know it isn't fair."

"No, it's cruel."

I took a deep breath. "You mean I've been."

He didn't answer.

"When this is over, when you get on your feet again, I'll be happy to share my winnings with you." It was all I could think to offer.

He began to laugh, which turned into a fit of coughing. When he stopped, he wiped blood from his lips. "I don't want to be you," he said.

"But if you could be anything you wanted, what would it be?"

"I'd like to walk right," he said instantly. "But it's too late for that now, isn't it?" He slid down into the bed and pulled the covers over his head.

The next morning, at the first light of dawn, I helped him dress—a clean set of underwear, loose-fitting pants, and a T-shirt he selected that said "Deplorable Lives Matter"—and drove him to the hospital. This time he was too exhausted, too depleted from his struggle with the virus to protest. Because of the virus's contagion, the hospital was now closed to everyone except patients. I had to leave Harry at the door to the emergency room. "Maybe this is the beginning of the Apocalypse," he said as a masked attendant put him in a wheelchair to take him inside. "If it is, you know your lottery winnings won't save you."

"I didn't expect they would," I said.

For the first time since I'd arrived in Houston, he smiled, as if the admission of my vulnerability, my precarity on this planet, confirmed a bond between us. I watched his wheelchair disappear into the hospital, wondering if we would ever see each other again.

There was nothing I could do now but wait. I found a diner a few blocks from the hospital and ordered a breakfast I could hardly eat. Suspended between hope and fear, I couldn't think. I just sat there, drinking one cup of coffee after another until the hospital finally called. New X-rays revealed diffuse pneumonia in Harry's lungs and they'd immediately placed him in intensive care. I'd brought him to the hospital just in time, the doctor said.

I walked slowly back to the hospital parking lot where I'd left my rental car.

Three people were standing by the front entrance. A heavy-set, middle-aged Black woman leaned against a tall, dark-skinned man in an Astros baseball cap, who I took to be her husband. A pigtailed girl around seven clung to her mother's waist. Tears ran down both the woman's and her daughter's cheeks as the man alternately stroked the woman's back and the little girl's head, murmuring words I couldn't hear. I watched them a moment, unabashedly, feeling a rush of compassion for them, for Harry, for all the sick and dying in the hospital. The man noticed me staring, and I nodded in sympathy for whatever loss they were grieving. He returned my gaze with a slight dip of his head as if acknowledging my gesture. Then a late model Ford pulled up and a young Latino with a bandana over his mouth jumped out and opened the doors for the family. The father took the wheel and steered the car into the late morning traffic.

I handed my parking ticket to an older Latino attendant who was using a red kerchief to cover his face. Suddenly I realized I was no longer wearing my own mask. But it wasn't just the medical mask in my pocket that I'd forgotten. It was all the others I'd worn for so long. The arrogant copywriter, the failed filmmaker, the guilty brother. The pandemic had erased all those past identities, including the extravagantly lucky lottery winner. All obscured what I shared with Harry, and everyone else who struggled to find purpose and meaning in our lives. The thought lifted me for a moment. I felt lighter than I'd been in a long time, curiously liberated and alive. I put my face mask on again to affirm my connection to everyone I'd scorned before.

Acknowledgments

These stories were originally published in slightly different form in the following:

"Land Mines" – *Rock and a Hard Place Magazine 8*

"Mute" – *Spoonie Magazine*

"Trail's End" – *Riddlebird*

"Misfits" – *Kairos*

"Layover" – *The Creative Café*

"The Mink Coat" – *Arcturus*

"The Cactus" – *Book XI: A Journal of Literary Philosophy*

"Doubles" – *Mystery Tribune 17*

"Tikkun Olam" – *After Dinner Conversation Magazine*

"Chicken Soup" – *Passager 70*

"A Drink with Oppie" – *New Mexico Humanities Review*

"Damascus" – *Literati Magazine.*

* * *

Epigraph for "Damascus" from "Cinderella," from *Transformations* by Anne Sexton. Copyright ©1971 by Anne Sexton, renewed 1999 by Linda G. Sexton. Used by permission of HarperCollins Publishers.

About Atmosphere Press

Founded in 2015, Atmosphere Press was built on the principles of Honesty, Transparency, Professionalism, Kindness, and Making Your Book Awesome. As an ethical and author-friendly hybrid press, we stay true to that founding mission today.

If you're a reader, enter our giveaway for a free book here:

SCAN TO ENTER
BOOK GIVEAWAY

If you're a writer, submit your manuscript for consideration here:

SCAN TO SUBMIT
MANUSCRIPT

And always feel free to visit Atmosphere Press and our authors online at atmospherepress.com. See you there soon!

About the Author

Mark Jonathan Harris is a Los Angeles writer/filmmaker who has published essays, award-winning children's novels, and non-fiction books. He's also written, directed, and produced numerous documentary films, including three which won Oscars. *Into the Arms of Strangers: Stories of the Kindertransport*, a feature documentary which he wrote and directed, won an Academy Award in 2000 and was selected by the U.S. Library of Congress for permanent preservation in the National Film Registry. For many years, he headed the documentary program at the School of Cinematic Arts at the University of Southern California, where he was a Distinguished Professor.